STONES FOR IBARRA

STONES FOR IBARRA

HARRIET DOERR

THE VIKING PRESS NEW YORK

First published in 1984 by The Viking Press
40 West 23rd Street, New York, N.Y. 10010

Published simultaneously in Canada by
Penguin Books Canada Limited

The author gratefully acknowledges the support
of the Wallace Stegner Fellowship, the Henfield Foundation,
and the National Endowment for the Arts
that made possible the writing of this book.

LIBRARY OF CONGRESS CATALOGING IN PUBLICATION DATA

Doerr, Harriet.
Stones for Ibarra.
I. Title.
PS3554.O36S8 1984 813'.54 83-47861
ISBN 0-670-19203-1

"The Evertons Out of Their Minds," "A Clear Understanding," "The Inheritance," "The Red Taxi," "Christmas Messages," and "The Doctor of the Moon" appeared originally in *The Ark River Review*; "The Night of September Fifteenth" in *The Southern Review*; and "The Life Sentence of José Reyes" (under the title "The Retreat and Final Surrender of José Reyes") in *Quarterly West.*

Printed in the United States of America
Set in Meridien

Fifth printing May 1984

For
A. E. D.

Por el cariño que el mismo sentía al lugar

CONTENTS

STONES FOR IBARRA

1

The Evertons Out of Their Minds

Here they are, two North Americans, a man and a woman just over and just under forty, come to spend their lives in Mexico and already lost as they travel cross-country over the central plateau. The driver of the station wagon is Richard Everton, a blue-eyed, black-haired stubborn man who will die thirty years sooner than he now imagines. On the seat beside him is his wife, Sara, who imagines neither his death nor her own, imminent or remote as they may be. Instead she sees, in one of its previous incarnations, the adobe house where they intend to sleep tonight. It is a mile and a half high on the outskirts of Ibarra, a declining village of one thousand souls. Tunneled into the mountain whose shadow falls on the house an hour before sunset is the copper mine Richard's grandfather abandoned fifty years ago during the Revolution of 1910.

Dark is coming on among the high hills and, unless they find a road, night will trap at this desolate spot both the future operator of the Malagueña mine and the fair-haired, unsuspecting future mistress of the adobe house. Sara Everton is anticipating their arrival at a place curtained and warm, though she knows the house has neither electricity nor furniture and, least of all, kindling beside the hearth. There is some doubt about running water in the pipes. The Malagueña mine, on the other hand, is flooded up to the second level.

Richard and Sara Everton will be the only foreigners in the village and they will depart in order, first Richard, then his wife. When Sara drives away for the last time, taking a studded leather chest, a painted religious figure, and a few flower pots, there will be no North American left in Ibarra.

For an hour the Evertons have followed footpaths and wagon trails that begin with no purpose and end with no destination. Although they can see their goal, a steep range of mountains lifting abruptly from the plain, they have found no direct way to approach it. The distant slopes rise first on their right, then on their left, and occasionally behind them.

"Let's stop and ask the way," says Sara, "while there is still daylight." And, as they take a diagonal course across a cleared space of land, she and her husband notice how the flat, pale rays from the west have lengthened the shadows of a row of tattered cornstalks, stunned survivors of the autumn harvest.

But the owner of this field, the crooked fig tree, and the bent plowshare dulled by weeds and weather is nowhere in sight.

Richard points to a drifting haze. "There's some smoke from a cooking fire." But it turns out to be only a spiral of dust whirling behind an empty dam.

"We won't get to Ibarra before dark," says Sara. "Do you think we'll recognize the house?"

"Yes," he says, and without speaking they separately recall a faded photograph of a wide, low structure with a long veranda in front. On the veranda is a hammock woven of white string, and in the hammock is Richard's grandmother, dressed in eyelet embroidery and holding a fluted fan. Beyond is a tennis court and a rose garden.

Five days ago the Evertons left San Francisco and their house with a narrow view of the bay in order to extend the family's

Mexican history and patch the present onto the past. To find out if there was still copper underground and how much of the rest of it was true, the width of sky, the depth of stars, the air like new wine, the harsh noons and long, slow dusks. To weave chance and hope into a fabric that would clothe them as long as they lived.

Even their closest friends have failed to understand. "Call us when you get there," they said. "Send a telegram." But Ibarra lacks these services. "How close is the airport?" and to avoid having to answer, the Evertons promised to send maps. "What will you do for light?" they were asked. And, "How long since someone lived in the house?" But this question collapsed of its own weight before a reply could be composed.

Every day for a month Richard has reminded Sara, "We mustn't expect too much." And each time his wife has answered, "No." But the Evertons expect too much. They have experienced the terrible persuasion of a great-aunt's recollections and adopted them as their own. They have not considered that memories are like corks left out of bottles. They swell. They no longer fit.

Now here, lost in the Mexican interior under a January sun withering toward the horizon, Richard and Sara remember the photographs that turned first yellow, then sepia, in family albums. They remember the packets of letters marked *Mexico* and divided into years by dry rubber bands. They remember the rock pick Richard's grandfather gave him when he was six. His grandfather had used the pick himself to chip away copper ore from extrusions that coursed like exposed arteries down the slope of one mountain and webbed out into smaller veins up the slope of the next.

Richard, without stopping the car, gropes under the seat for the rock pick, touches it, then heads across a field of stubble toward a few stripped trees in the west.

Halfway to the trees, behind a clump of mesquite, a posted sign confronts the Evertons. According to the federal power commission, the community of El Portal is about to be electrified. A moment later, beyond a broken arch, they come to El Portal, a cluster of nine adobe houses and a colonial chapel so small, perfectly proportioned, and vividly domed that it might have been designed to be attached to the nursery of a princess in Córdoba or Seville.

"Only a very short priest could enter to say mass and only children worship there," says Sara. As if summoned, a boy and a girl with the half-formed bones and oversized front teeth of seven-year-olds materialize, staring, in a doorway.

Richard lowers the window. "Which is the way to Ibarra?" he asks, and the children, unable to reconcile the Spanish words with the aspect of the stranger, turn rigid as stone.

"Ibarra," the American says again. "In those mountains." And he points in the direction of three peaks, skirted all around by a somber border of foothills. "Where the mines are," he says.

"What does he know about mining?" Richard's friends have asked one another. "What does she know about gasoline stoves and charcoal irons? In case of burns, where will they find a doctor?" The friends learn that the Evertons are taking a first aid manual, antibiotics for dysentery, and a snakebite kit. There are other questions, relating to symphony season tickets, Christmas, golf, sailing. To these, the answers are evasive.

Heedless of criticism and disbelief, the Evertons have gone ahead, mortgaged their house, borrowed on their insurance, applied for bank loans against dwindling collateral, and invested the total proceeds in rusty machinery apparently racked beyond repair.

"It's supposed to be a concentrating mill," one of the friends told the others. "Who's going to assemble it?"

But the Evertons neither notice the rust nor seem concerned about finding mechanical engineers in a village where only the youngest generation has graduated from the fifth grade. They indeed propose to operate the family mine and occupy the family house, and they see no reason why their project should not succeed.

The two seven-year-olds in the doorway, as if they had never heard of mines, remain fixed and speechless in their places. Suddenly a farmer, leading a lame burro, approaches the car from behind.

He regards the two Americans. "You are not on the road to Ibarra," he says. "Permit me a moment." And he gazes first at his feet, then at the mountains, then at their luggage. "You must drive north on that dry arroyo for two kilometers and turn left when you reach a road. You will recognize it by the tire tracks of the morning bus unless there have been too many goats. Or unless rain has fallen. But this is the dry season."

He does not ask why the Americans are going to Ibarra, where they are sure to be conspicuous because of their car, their textbook Spanish, and their four suitcases, which he imagines to be full of woolens, silks, and lace.

He merely points and says, "The arroyo is beyond that tree." Together they look at the six remaining top branches of a leafless cottonwood whose destiny it has become to cook the beans and toast the tortillas of the nine families of El Portal until it is reduced to a stump. Then that other cottonwood, farther down the arroyo, will in its turn perish gradually by the ax.

Before going on, the Evertons look around them at El Portal.

"You have a beautiful chapel," they say.

At these words, the man and the burro and the two children in the doorway turn their heads to regard the miniature structure with its carved stone lintel and filigree cross as if it had been built today, Saturday the twenty-seventh of January, between noon and four o'clock. But they don't reply. They cannot decide so quickly if the chapel is beautiful.

The Evertons drive toward the last of the houses, where a rooster stalks the flat roof, pecking angrily at crumbs of plaster.

"Probably, in a high wind, cornhusks fly up there, or acorns, or wild berries," says Sara, imagining a meal for the rooster, who now leans in the attitude of a vulture from the roof's edge and assesses them through hooded eyes. But there is not a gust of wind to carry husk or seed aloft.

"Without a tail wind we won't be bothered by the dust," says Richard, and turns north.

He is mistaken. The arroyo is smooth and soft with dust that, even in still air, spins from the car's wheels and sifts through sealed surfaces, the flooring, the dashboard, the factory-tested weather stripping. It etches black lines on their palms, sands their skin, powders their lashes, and deposits a bitter taste on their tongues.

"This must be the wrong way," says Sara, from under the sweater she has pulled over her head.

Richard says nothing. He knows it is the right way, as right as a way to Ibarra can be, as right as his decision to reopen an idle mine and bring his wife to a house built half of nostalgia and half of clay.

When they have gone two kilometers, they stop and look for the road to Ibarra. But it is as the man in El Portal half suspected. There have been too many goats. While the Evertons search the trampled ground, they notice that all around them the winter afternoon is folding in on itself. Toward the west, in the direction they must turn, are only random boulders, nopal cactus, and the shadows strung out behind.

But from the east, where a moment ago there was nothing, runs a boy, and, for the first time, the Evertons witness a recurring Mexican phenomenon: the abrupt appearance of human life in an empty landscape. Later it would become a commonplace experience. They had only to turn their backs momentarily on a deserted plain and a man on a mule would have ridden up behind them or a woman with a child settled on a nearby rock.

Now, out of a vast unpopulated panorama, here, close at hand, is a boy with a satchel. He observes the two North Americans without astonishment through quick eyes that are wide apart and expectant. The Evertons realize immediately that he is a person wholly committed to what is going to happen next. Within a minute he has offered to show them the way to Ibarra. It is the village where he lives.

"Then ride with us and be our guide," says Richard, and the boy climbs into the rear and accommodates himself between the suitcases and cartons.

"What is your name?" Sara asks in careful Spanish.

"Domingo García," says the boy. "At your orders." He smiles with white, even teeth.

"To the left of that big rock," he tells Richard. "Between those two huisache trees. Across that bridge."

The bridge is two parallel planks set about five feet apart over a canyon, and Richard has trouble aligning his wheels with the boards. He walks to the bridge and notices the depth of the gorge.

Domingo joins him and steps on a plank to try it. "You drive," he says, "and I will show you." Balanced on the brink, his back to the abyss, he extends his hands, palms facing. They move an inch to the right and half an inch to the left. When he is satisfied that the wheels are aimed at the boards, he runs back to insert himself again among the luggage.

"Straight ahead," says Domingo, and the Evertons are introduced to a second national peculiarity, one they will soon recognize on the streets of Ibarra and in towns and cities beyond. It is something they will see everywhere—a disregard for danger, a companionship with death. By the end of a year they will know it well: the antic bravado, the fatal games, the coffin shop beside the cantina, the sugar skulls on the frosted cake.

There are two more bridges, but Richard refuses further help. Sara shuts her eyes and sits still as a stone image while they cross. When it is over, she turns to the passenger behind.

"Did you walk far today?"

Domingo says he missed the bus this morning, so he had to walk all the way from La Gloria. La Gloria is where he has been enrolled in preparatory school by his older brother, Basilio, who does not permit him to miss even one class. But, thanks to this ride, he will arrive in Ibarra in time for the fiesta tomorrow, on the saint's day of the town. He asks if it is the annual visit of the bishop of the state or the carnival itself that is bringing the Americans to Ibarra. There is no hotel, he tells them, only Chayo Durán's *mesón*, and the four rooms may already be occupied.

"We are not visiting Ibarra. We are going to live there," says Richard. "In the house my grandfather built."

Domingo, now in possession of a clue, falls silent.

In the last century Richard Everton's grandfather built an adobe house in Ibarra for his wife. He took a stick and drew the shape of the house in the dirt while his mason observed the plan. First he drew a square around a patio, then one wing and then another, and then a veranda around it all.

The Evertons follow the invisible track pointed out by Domingo for half an hour until it abruptly mounts an embankment and they find themselves on a scraped dirt road.

They have traveled smoothly along it for ten minutes and are already in the foothills when a careening carnival truck overtakes them. Behind the cab, the wooden legs and tails of horses and the wooden necks of swans protrude from the splitting canvas that secures them.

"Did that truck have to cross the plank bridges?" asks Richard.

"No," says Domingo. "It came by this road which has been cleared as far as Ibarra. If you had remained on the highway from the capital, from Concepción, instead of turning toward El Portal, you would have seen the sign and the arrow. But the way you chose is five kilometers shorter."

Sara, reminded, lowers her window to shake dust from her sweater. Richard makes no comment.

They are climbing into the mountains now and negotiating a series of sharp blind curves. Ahead of them the truck shifts in and out of low gear, each time threatening to roll back and bury them under a carousel.

Now Domingo resumes the conversation he left off earlier. "Then you will live in the big white house and work the Malagueña mine," he says. "Like your grandfather."

Richard glances back at his passenger. "How do you know about my grandfather?"

"From the old men of Ibarra." And Domingo takes this opportunity to apply for a job. He says he is fifteen and strong, and has completed the ninth grade.

"Listen to your brother Basilio and stay in school." In the mirror Richard's clouded blue eyes meet Domingo's unshadowed black ones. "Later on you can start your career as a miner."

"Where is it?" the Evertons' friends had asked, and were shown Richard's map. On a blank space north of Concepción he had printed the name, Ibarra.

"It's on the outside edge of nowhere," said the friends. "You can't mean to spend the rest of your lives down there."

But it is indeed the Evertons' intention to spend the rest of their lives down here. They will not know until July that in Richard's case this will amount to six years.

"Count on at least six active years," they will be told by the doctor who diagnoses an irregularity or, put more clearly, a malignancy, in Richard's blood the summer after their arrival in Ibarra.

But by then they are already whitewashing the old house and pumping water from the third level of the Malagueña mine; the concentrating mill has already been installed and blessed. By then they will have planted the bougainvillea and the rose. By then the noon whistle at La Malagueña, silent for fifty years, will divide the day again, and in the plaza of Ibarra the sacristan, hurrying back to the church with a new broom, will notice that the clock in the tower is eleven minutes slow.

But they will not meet this doctor, a hematologist, until July.

"You have plenty of time," Richard says to Domingo. As the incline becomes steeper, he allows his car to drop farther behind the listing truck.

Now Domingo starts to identify the roofless sheds and rotting headframes that slant against the hillsides. He begins to pronounce in sequence the rich names of abandoned mines. "El Indio Gordo, El Paradiso," he tells the Evertons. "La Bonanza, La Purísima, La Lulu."

"I wonder," Sara suddenly says, but she does not disclose what it is she wonders. Looking at Richard's profile, she sees the thin scar on his cheek turn white and knows he has preoccupations of his own.

Halfway up this mountain, in the increasing chill and gloom of the winter evening, he has assumed, as he might assume a yoke that could break him, the awful responsibility of apportioning jobs. As though he were a seer, he envisions a group of men who will already have been standing at his gate for an hour when he opens it tomorrow. They will squat on their heels or lean against the wall or sit on rocks until he comes. Then each man will stand to introduce himself and shake hands. Their grandfathers knew his grandfather. Their fathers caught rabbits and killed snakes with his father when they were boys. They have survived by the thinnest margin since the mines shut down, one by one, after the Revolution.

When the truck and the car have passed the summit, descended a hundred meters on the other side, and started to accelerate along the level approach to the village, Richard is still composing what he will have to say.

"This will be a small operation. At first I can only employ a few. Everything depends on the grade of ore. We must install the machinery and find out how things go." He foresees the men looking at his face and then at the ground. They will not believe him. They have already heard about the car and the suitcases and the ham-and-cheese sandwiches the Americans divided with Domingo.

Then the Evertons, still caught in the wake of the truck, turn abruptly to the right, find themselves on a cobbled street dropping down to a plaza, and here it is, Ibarra.

An immense stillness fills the square. Somewhere in it sound and motion lie suspended. Eyes, under the brims of hats or over the folds of shawls, follow them from park benches, deep-set doorways, and the lighted interiors of the grocer's shop and the pool hall. Even the driver of the carnival truck, already entering the cantina, stands fixed at the swinging door.

We have come to live among specters, Sara tells herself. They are not people, but silhouettes sketched on a backdrop to deceive us into thinking that the stage is crowded. She searches for an expression, any expression, in their eyes—the eyes of that man on the corner whose raised hand holds a cigarette he is allowing to burn to his fingers; the eyes of that woman who has lifted a dripping jar of water halfway to her head. They will never speak to me, she thinks. I will never know their names.

On the far side of town the Evertons leave Domingo at his house. Even in the dark it seems to sag. In front of it a fat woman sits on an overturned pail.

"My mother," says Domingo, and gives them final instructions. "Follow those pepper trees up the hill to the high stone wall and push open the gate," he says. "You will see your house in front of you."

So it is night when they arrive and too dark to examine the interior. They eat bananas in an empty room that smells of mice and weathered wood and, by the beam of a flashlight, set up camp cots on the veranda which, after tonight, they will call the porch. Rolled in blankets that still exude dust, they find they can see each other's faces by the stars. They are asleep almost at once, too tired to hear the quick, light feet of possums and raccoons as they approach and then retreat. Nor does a coyote, crying the night apart beyond the town, disturb them.

But at two o'clock in the morning, when the brittle leaves of the ash tree at the corner of the house cease to stir, Sara sits up in her cot. "I think I hear frost," she says to her sleeping husband.

Four hours later they awake shivering to a sudden dawn that floods up behind the eastern mesa and stains half the sky coral.

Now the house is revealed, and the garden.

But where is it all, the splendid past? The roof of imported cedar shingles, the wallpaper from France? The chandelier that held three dozen tapers? The floors that took so high a polish they seemed designed for dancing? Where is the clay tennis court that was rolled and chalked twice a week by the coachman, while the gardener, an expert with roses, tied back the profusion that threatened to overwhelm it? Where is the fountain, the gazebo, the hedge?

They might as well ask, where are the people in the photographs? Where the gentlemen in white flannels who lobbed slow balls to ladies running in shoes with French heels and silk laces to lob them back? Were they really here, the girls who rode sidesaddle from one parched hillside to another, the young men who came to house parties and said, "May I?"

"May I carry your camera?" they said. "May I fetch your watercolors?" Or at night, "May I show you Orion from the orchard?"

Now, in the uncompromising light of a new day, the Evertons, avoiding a column of red ants, stand on the cracked tile of their doorstep and stare across the expanse of naked earth that extends before them. On the balustrade of the porch three lizards, touched by the first rays of the sun, begin to puff out their throats. Hornets swarm in and out of a mud nest in the eaves.

"I wonder," says Sara, completing her unstated thought of last evening, "if we have gone out of our minds."

At this moment, which is six-thirty, Domingo García walks up the driveway whistling to himself. He has come to ask how they slept and to report that eighteen men are waiting at the gate.

"Is this a convenient hour?"

"I will talk to them now," says Richard, and, as if to celebrate these words, the jukebox on the plaza inaugurates the day with a mariachi song. A fanfare of trumpets spears the sky. Then a church bell rings, and dogs, burros, and cows confuse the thin morning air with their complaints.

Domingo, to let in this outburst all at once, pulls the gate wide. Sara watches her husband walk through, watches the small crowd rise and wait. Then she sees the men come forward, one by one, to shake his hand.

2

A Clear Understanding

In Ibarra half a year is no more than a shard chipped from the rock face of eternity and too short a time for newcomers to become known and understood.

So it was that, as late as July and in spite of their thick adobe walls, the Evertons, even when they believed themselves to be alone, were much observed. Only the bathroom of their house had curtains. Sometimes Remedios Acosta and her daughter Paz came quietly up the driveway after dusk and put their faces against the kitchen window. At first the two shawled heads, appearing so abruptly out of the night and at such close quarters, caused Sara a cold contraction of the heart. Then she learned to nod and smile as she heated canned stew or canned hash over the unstable flame of the Coleman stove.

The Acostas reported back to the village. "The señora cooks food from cans over a gasoline fire. It must be very expensive. While she stirs the pot, the señor is in the kitchen. A man in the kitchen and not to eat. He is pouring from a whiskey bottle into glasses. He adds a thimble of Tehuacán water and gives one glass to the señora. They lift their glasses and laugh. We saw it ourselves," said Remedios. "The señora wearing her shirt inside her ranchero pants instead of loose outside, decently covering that part of her. And drinking alcohol as she cooks, while the señor, whose father was born in that house, sits on the table and lets his long legs swing."

The kitchen table was the Evertons' first piece of furniture, not counting the bed with the protesting iron springs. The carpenter constructed it from the materials at hand, six dynamite boxes. The surface was unmarked but underneath were the stenciled words: PELIGRO! EXPLOSIVOS!

Sara believed that she was being observed not only by the townspeople but by the ghosts of her husband's ancestors, his grandfather, grandmother, and a great-aunt. Also the shade of the family *nana* who, when Richard's father was small, slept on the floor beside his crib. She imagined that they gathered in the kitchen to look at the table, the plastic plates, and the Boy Scout frying pan, and in the bedroom to listen to the creaking springs and to notice the condition of the ceiling and the wallpaper.

The ancestors lived here with a coach and coachman quartered behind, and a windmill that drew water. They walked on waxed floors through papered bedrooms under a roof of cedar shingles. They could not foresee that when the house was untenanted during the Revolution of 1910 their friend and neighbor, don Elizondo, compelled by necessity as he was, would bring his mules and wagon and carry off the roof in sections to fuel the power plant he owned. Nor that half a century of summer rains would cause the cloth and plaster of the ceilings to sag and split, and leave brown stains, like maps of hemispheres, on the walls. Here and there the torn strips still revealed bleached poppies and loops of milky morning glories.

Sara has held in her hands the ancestral legacy that was left behind: two books, *Ben Hur* and *Kidnapped;* an oil lamp with a base of amethyst glass; and a single clay garden tile bearing the raised outlines of a flower.

"Only the purple lamp lights their way at night," said Remedios Acosta. "They cannot afford a transformer of their own because of their extravagances. Because the mason had to construct and tear down the stone pool in their patio twice before they agreed it was the right size. Because more than once they have driven a hundred kilometers to buy a bougainvillea or a honeysuckle. In their wanderings through the tuna cactus behind the stable they found an old tile from the first garden. Now they will have a thousand copies made to pave their paths. The carpenter has already spent six hours carving a wooden mold. Every day they heat water for their baths. They buy special food for three dogs and a cat that are not theirs. Will those animals remember how to hunt mice and hares if they are fed on plates at the door? The señor and señora are preparing them to starve."

Luis Fuentes, who spent weekends in the cantina and weekdays helping Sara in the garden, said the pepper trees that lined the drive were being stripped of dry branches for firewood, so that at least one room of the house could be kept warm through the winter. Every day he piled kindling in the room where the two North Americans ate.

Each evening the Evertons were revealed sitting close to the hearth. At one side of them, over a long bench, half a wall of small-paned windows faced the outer gates. During the day anyone approaching the house could be noticed through these windows. At night the Evertons themselves, lit up by the lamp and fire as though by footlights, were visible to all who entered unseen. Some of these visitors pondered the Americans from under a twisted olive tree just inside the wall. Others advanced immediately to tap on the windowpanes. They kept their eyes close to the glass until Richard put down his fork and went to meet them at the door.

They shook hands. If it was a woman, she might say, "My husband is out of jail. The child he struck with his bicycle has recovered after all. And the accident would never have occurred if he had not been drunk at the time. Will you employ him again at the Malagueña mine?"

If it was a man, he might request a job for his wife's father, who lived with them as a guest but was still strong enough to work an underground shift, or money for the smuggler who could get him across the Texas border, or a bus ticket to the city for a chest X ray because he was coughing a little blood.

Here was Goyo, a miner, spitting into the potted jade tree on the porch. Transportation in the mine van to the doctor's office eighty kilometers away was arranged for tomorrow.

At seven in the morning, the mine driver knocked on the Everton's bedroom door for his instructions.

"Goyo's wife is to be examined, too," said Richard.

"Which one?"

"How many are there?"

"Two," said the driver. "The one Goyo married in the church a long time ago and her sister, fifteen years younger, who lives with them and sleeps in Goyo's bed."

"Take both," said Richard, "and all the children."

The night visitors confirmed everything Remedios Acosta had described. As well as kindling a fire they did not cook on, the Americans lit candles at their evening meal and let them burn down while they talked. Occasionally they both talked at once, and loudly. At these times the señor jumped up and walked around the table, and the señora forgot to bring the hard rolls from the oven. They had been seen and heard by the postmaster's son, who lived for a winter with his cousin in Chicago and learned some English words.

"The señor and the señora do not agree about the next president of the United States. He will vote for one candidate, she another. In that case, why do they vote at all?"

Sara asked this question, in reverse, of the village women she had met. Knowing women's suffrage had lately become Mexican law, she asked, "Did you vote in the last election?" But the grocer's wife and the priest's aunt and Remedios simply shrugged and offered the señora cuttings from their begonia or their mint.

One day she spoke to Lupe, the master mechanic at the mine. "Did your wife vote independently?"

"Everyone in Ibarra over the age of eighteen voted to avoid paying a fine," said Lupe, "and, except for a few socialists and one communist, all voted for the Party of Institutional Revolution which has governed Mexico for thirty years. It is this party that brought electricity to the plaza of Ibarra. Now they have promised us a clinic and new drains."

"So you voted for yourself and for your wife."

Lupe regarded Sara, who stood hatless under the October sun on the packed earth in front of her house. Currents of dust from the road blew over the wall to stir the leaves of trees and lift strands of her light hair.

"Yes," he said. "In favor of the clinic and the drains." She said nothing, and he added, "You are forgetting, señora, that when we voted we already knew the name of the next president of the republic." He pointed to the hill of the Santa Cruz behind them. Halfway down the barren slope, below the cement cross on the summit, letters ten feet high made of white-painted stones had, long before the election, made all Ibarra familiar with the name of the candidate who would be elected. Sara noticed goats picking their way through the letters and the goatherd stretched out on the *Z*.

That afternoon she waited at the gate for the delivery of an enameled kitchen sink from the state capital. Sitting on a boulder at the edge of the road she considered the recent election. They are good wives, she thought, not like me. They have handed over their suffrage to their husbands without argument, as they might hand over a plate of food or an ironed shirt. She looked up at the letters on the hill. The goats were cropping thistles and spines farther on. An old woman with a cane had stopped on her way to the cross to rest on the *M*. A girl in a cerise shawl was nursing her baby on the *T*.

In the evening Luis, the gardener, told his friend Victor, the potter, that there was no need for the señora to spend an afternoon at the roadside in order to point out the house. Because on its way to the plaza the pink afternoon bus, seeming to know these gates, came up the drive and delivered the purchase to the kitchen door. Passengers occupied all the seats except the one next to the driver where the sink rested at his arm. Luis and the señor unloaded it while the señora spoke through the open windows to people she recognized. The bill was paid, the bus made a wide turn, chipping off an edge of the adobe house, and everyone waved.

During this first year the Evertons traveled to California and brought back special plant food, sacks of wild-bird seed, powdered milk, and three bottles of pills for Richard.

Remedios explained the medicine to her friends. "The señor keeps pills next to his wine glass and swallows them with his meat and squash. These pills are for his heart," said Remedios. "He is too thin for a man so tall. And he often walks the uphill kilometer to the mine with his wife running after him, telling him to drive instead. He has an illness of the heart."

Remedios, unaware that the scar on Richard's face was old evidence of a splintered windshield, explained the mark to her friends. "The señor was injured in a knife fight," she said. "It is the scar of a knife."

By the end of a year the Americans had planted all the parched space at one side of their drive with rows of maguey cactus carried one by one from the mountainside in a basket on Luis's back. The project attracted passersby from the road. They came up the drive and leaned on the low stone wall to watch.

"You are raising these plants for pulque and mescal," they said.

"No. For their shape and color," said Richard. "And because they don't need water."

"If you decide to make mescal, I can help you," said Victor, the potter, reeking of it as he spoke.

Behind him Manuela Reyes paused. Balanced on her head and supported by the reed of her neck was the Evertons' laundry. Manuela lived in the only house between the Americans and the mine. She was a fourteen-year-old who wore a child's size-eight dress.

"How is your mother?" asked Sara, and thought of the bucket where the clothes would soak, the mesquite bush where they would dry, and the charcoal iron that would press them. She did not inquire about Manuela's father, who had been convicted last year of murder and sentenced to the penitentiary for life.

Manuela said, "She is well," and stared at the cactus.

Even the parish priest came to look. "Very curious," was all he said of the new garden, but Sara imagined he had blessed it.

One morning, while Sara wandered between the strewn magueys, measuring lines and distances with string, a woman separated herself from the onlookers and approached. From under straight black brows she directed a straight black gaze toward Sara. Two red-ribboned braids hung to her waist. It turned out that this woman, who walked as proud as Montezuma's daughter, wanted to work for the Evertons, to cook and to clean. Her name was María de Lourdes.

"Perhaps later on," said Sara, reluctant to surrender hours better spent alone with Richard. "But your day would be only from ten to five," she told the woman. "Never too early and never at night."

Domingo García, who had shown the Evertons the way to Ibarra, also came to observe the new project. "If you want the work to go more quickly," he said, "I can be here all day Sunday and a friend of mine, Paco Acosta, for half a day. He is nineteen and has to go to his army drill, but he can get away before noon."

That evening, as Sara put out the gasoline lamp over their bed, she asked Richard about the army drill. He pulled the blanket higher over them and said, "Military service is obligatory for nineteen-year-old men, all day Sunday for a year."

"Paco Acosta can be here by noon," she told him, but Richard showed no interest in this circumstance.

For the next two Sundays Paco streaked through the gate on his bicycle at eleven o'clock to join Sara and Domingo, and the three bent together over the magueys until an hour before sunset when Domingo caught the last bus back to La Gloria and his school.

"How far away is Paco's drill?" Sara asked Domingo the following Sunday on his arrival from his mother's house, which was the first to the left down the road.

"It is in Bombiletes, fifteen kilometers from here."

At the sound of this word, Bombiletes, Sara was distracted from her investigation of Paco's schedule. "Bombiletes," she repeated. "Is that a saint's name?"

"No, it is not the name of a saint," said Domingo, "and not the name of a Mexican general, or of a town on the map of Spain. It is the name of that place, Bombiletes. Six houses, six cornfields, and a corral."

"How can Paco leave his army drill in the middle of the morning?"

"He gives the sergeant one-fourth of what he earns from you."

Sara straightened with her spade in her hand. Half of the magueys were planted and the flat dust was spiked with green.

"After he has drilled for two hours, Paco pays the sergeant ten pesos," said Domingo. "At that moment he is dismissed."

"The Americans are rich and foolish," said Remedios. "They have employed Domingo García and my son Paco to do work that Luis, their gardener, would in time have done himself. Lourdes is going to be their cook and will be paid a full day's salary for only seven hours spent in rooms that are more commodious than her own. The señora has taken up the flowers that Luis planted in oil cans and chamber pots he found behind the coach house. She has divided them into fifty clay pots that line the *corredor* from the kitchen past the *sala* and the bedrooms. Sometimes the señor and the señora eat out there in the middle of the day and watch the wild birds flock to the imported bird seed. They look for a small red bird in the fresno tree as though it were the eagle on the cactus of the national emblem. Then the señor returns to the mine while the señora remains on the *corredor,* scattering imported fertilizer on her fifty flower pots."

By the end of the first year, the number of men on the payroll at the mine had grown from eighteen to forty-five. The concentrating mill had been installed. Once a month a truck carried the muddy concentrate away to be refined at the San Luis smelter. But there was still water below the third level and another pump must be bought, as well as an air compressor. And the price of copper was unstable.

Even as these threats to prosperity became known and feared in the village, Remedios uncovered a further extravagance at the Evertons' house.

"They are scraping off the green paint in the kitchen, hall, and *sala* so that they can whitewash the walls. They have employed Miguel Velásquez to chip away at the paint which is still in excellent condition."

Miguel Velásquez had lived for sixty years and was thin as a tule stem. He stooped as though he had the north wind at his back, and the Evertons never saw him smile. Miguel repeated the last word of every sentence spoken to him.

"We want to remove the green paint," explained Richard. *"La pintura verde."*

"Verde," said Miguel.

"And later, with water paint, make the walls white. *Blancas."*

"Blancas," said Miguel.

When the interior work had been completed and the entire exterior also whitewashed, Miguel asked the Evertons if there was anything further he could do. He said he had made a purchase that would require installments of one-third of his monthly income over a period of four years.

It took the Evertons two weeks to find out what the purchase was.

"Es una moto," said Miguel, and repeated *"moto."*

"A motorcycle," said Richard. "My God."

Miguel explained that, as part of the contract, the salesman was teaching him to ride. The painter had a lesson every Saturday but there was still much to learn.

"Return it before your kill yourself," said Richard.

And Miguel said, *"Matarme."*

There followed a series of minor falls and finally a major one in which the painter suffered internal injuries. He allowed the motorcycle to be repossessed.

"You are lucky," said Richard, "that you are not in your grave."

"En mi tumba," said Miguel.

Remedios Acosta remarked of the Americans, "They are kind and friendly, but they are strangers to the exigencies of life. They do not go to church, neither to theirs, nor to ours. The señor says the mine will be responsible for the medical expenses of its workers, but he will not pay the *brujo* for his cures."

"We must have a clear understanding," Richard kept saying. "There is no money for witch doctors."

Remedios said her brother-in-law went to three medical doctors for his ulcer and they all told him, "Stop smoking, stop drinking. No coffee, no *chile,* no fried beans." Then he went to the *brujo,* who gave him an emulsion of roots and pods, and instructed him to wear a snakeskin around his waist and by no means to speak to his wife for two weeks. When the brother-in-law went back, the *brujo* said, "You are cured. Have a good time."

"But the señor would not pay the *brujo*'s bill for only two hundred pesos," Remedios said, "which is the more surprising since the señora herself is thought to be a *bruja.* She can bring back dying trees by means of spells. When her fruit tree started to dry up she poured an imported liquid around the trunk. Then she lifted her hand and said, 'Grow!' in English and in Spanish, and the tree grew.

"When she is with children the señora reduces herself to their age. But an hour later she will tell their mothers not to have any more and explain how not to. In conflict with the pope. In conflict with God."

At last the village found a word that applied to the North Americans. It was a long word, *mediodesorientado,* meaning half disoriented. Like the child with the bandana over his eyes who is turned ten times in a circle before being handed the long stick to break the *piñata* hanging high above his head. As he flails at his elusive prize, a paper rooster stuffed with candy, he strikes the empty air in all directions. Everyone about him laughs. The blindfolded child laughs.

3

The Life Sentence of José Reyes

When Sara walked from her house to Ibarra to buy bread or mail letters, she nodded to everyone she met along the road or in the square. Within a few months their profiles and voices, their quick steps or shuffling hobble had become known to her. But of their raptures and their furies she understood almost nothing until she learned enough Spanish, first to grasp phrases, and then whole sentences of the individual histories related to her by Remedios, Lourdes, and Luis. But there still remained words she failed to translate, and the problem of local idiom, and the occasional sudden silences of the narrator. Sara had to fill in. When complete these were accounts half heard and half invented.

One of them was the tale of José Reyes.

Even after the state prosecutor won his case against José Reyes and sentenced him to life imprisonment in the penitentiary, José's wife, Luz, and his two children, Manuela and Pancho, continued to exist in a tight cage of fear. Within this cage it still seemed possible that José might suddenly intrude to beat and cuff them, though they and indeed all the village knew that his right hand, the one that killed two men, had been crippled beyond use.

Fear suited their way of living as did cold and hunger; the thin borderline of existence, no wider than a ray of late sun penetrating a slit in the shutter, was their whole terrain. So that even with his father behind bars Pancho continued to hide in secure places the occasional coins he earned and Manuela, half expecting to be intercepted on her way home from delivering the clothes her mother had washed, still left part of the money with the woman who paid her, saying, "I will come back for it in an hour, or tonight, or tomorrow."

After José's conviction, Luz visited him every other Sunday in private quarters provided by the prison authorities for copulation. On the day José saw that she was pregnant, he said, "Why should this one live longer than the three before it? The infants you bear are crowding the graveyard."

Luz did not visit the state penitentiary again. The child, a girl named María del Rosario, was born a month early and lived five days.

That was the family of José Reyes, who had been sentenced to life imprisonment but who once was a man of worth in this town of Ibarra, a man whose field was plowed and seeded in good time for the summer rains, whose cows were led every day to water and to grass, a man who kept a few tiles on hand to mend his roof and an extra sack of corn to feed his children.

Then came two years of drought, one after the other, when such showers as there were only dampened the treetops and spotted the dust. José watched his land parch and crack. As each cloudless evening forecast the unwinking glare of tomorrow's sun he became more and more of a fixture at the cantina. Here he took his place not only on Saturday nights to have beer with his friends, the potter and the stonemason, but often during the week to drink tequila or mescal alone. It was at this time that José gave up farming and started to depend for livelihood on a variety of odd jobs.

When he was short of funds, José Reyes stole or pocketed what he felt was justly his from his wife and children to subsidize his visits to the Copa de Oro. Once there, he stood at the bar behind the swinging doors with his feet visible to passersby and in the rich interior gloom isolated himself from the turbulence outside. He did not seek to buy happiness or peace or fulfillment but their substitute, a sharpened image of himself, José Reyes, as a man still to be reckoned with. Each time he looked in the mirror behind the shelf of bottles he was newly revealed as a formidable figure, long-boned, weathered, and quick. He dropped three pesos on the counter as if there were a hundred more in his pocket and, to prove who was master here, held the glass in his hand for a full minute before he drained it. Then, as he had expected, the splendor was upon him. Like God, the mescal created a man.

There was a midsummer full moon on the night José Reyes was hurt at the cantina, and when Luz awakened to shouts and cries and came to the besieged door of her house, she saw with no other light than the luminous dark that blood was wetting half of her husband's face, as well as the hair on his head. His inert body drooped in the arms of four friends who strove to keep it upright. From among them the two Palacio brothers spoke first to reassure her. Tomás said, "It is nothing. He is not seriously injured." And Julián Palacio added, "Look for yourself. A few scratches."

At first it seemed they were right. Once the dirt was washed away and the bleeding stopped, the wounds appeared to be bruises that had scraped off hair and skin, rather than cuts that slice into the flesh and must be stitched together like a torn glove or a split shoe.

José did not refer to the incident and without shame exposed his battered countenance for all to see. Only from Antonio, the storekeeper, who spoke a few words one day and a few the next, could Luz pry out the full account.

Antonio, measuring rice and sugar into newspaper twists, said that on the night in question José Reyes was so drunk that, at least at the outset of the foolishness, he may have assumed he was cooperating in some game. In any case, he was carried away from his habitual place at the cantina bar and through the double doors by the Palacio brothers, who laid him, face up, on the buckling sidewalk. Then Tomás Palacio took José's feet and Julián his hands, and they started to swing him back and forth as though they were children and he a rope. José rose to increasing heights on right and left until it seemed he must complete his own circle and the two brothers revolve to bring him back. At last, with a final joining of force and momentum, the Palacios lifted him high overhead on the one hand, then down in a rush, and high up again on the other. Here they let go, allowing José to soar toward the plaza, where he hung in the air for a moment before falling headfirst to the cobblestoned street below.

When Luz asked why, the storekeeper said, "Who can tell? Perhaps they were drunk also. Perhaps José owed them money."

Before the accident José Reyes had no regular employment, though he could be observed from time to time on the shoulder of the highway, scything weeds for the secretariat of public works. If not there, he could sometimes be seen with pick and shovel, digging a ditch from the cura's house, where the first toilet in town was to be installed, to the arroyo, where it would drain. On his frequent idle days he systematically reduced the balance of his wages at the bar of the Copa de Oro. But after the accident, this same José reversed the downward spiral of his course and, with black scabs lifting from his scalp, worked continuously for five months, cutting and selling the firewood he brought down on his uncle's burro from the top of the mountain, Altamira.

Then, at the end of November, as he crossed the plaza between rows of cement benches inscribed with the donors' names, Coca-Cola, Pan Bimbo, Exide, where his fellow townspeople rested in the calm of dusk, José Reyes reached for something in the air, uttered a groan drawn from an inner abyss, and fell to the brick walk. Here he writhed on his back with eyes starting from their sockets and a trickle of blood from the right corner of his mouth. For more than a minute he lay convulsed at the feet of old Pablo, the beggar, not far from two little girls who stared, transfixed with terror, and only later on at home wept for no reason in their mother's apron.

"*Es un ataque*," said the cura, brushing past in his black habit ahead of three nuns, who might have paused to offer aid or at least to phrase a prayer had they not been beckoned on by the priest. "Call the doctor," he instructed those on the nearest benches, and he waved his hand in the direction of the new government clinic.

The doctor, an intern and recent graduate of the medical school in Guadalajara, was performing his six months' government service in the town of Ibarra. On the occasion of José's attack he had gone to Concepción, the state capital, for the night, to present his report to his chief, or make love to his girl, or take a hot shower. As soon as he returned, however, he sent José Reyes to the hospital in the city for tests. When the doctor had the results, he said, "It is not inherited. Your accident induced it. The lesion is pressing right here," and he tapped José's head. "Without medicine the seizures will come more often and be more severe. With medicine they will cease. Never drink alcohol. Take one of these tablets every day." And the doctor handed him a prescription. When José learned that each pill cost a peso, he discarded the coded formula on the linoleum floor of the Farmacia La Piedad.

The accumulated earnings of the firewood negotiation lasted almost a month at the Copa de Oro. During this time José Reyes had three attacks, one on his own doorstep and two under the tables and chairs of the cantina.

He no longer found employment, even by the hour, and when he sometimes awoke at noon from suffocating sleep at the edge of the cura's drainage ditch, he spat into it and invoked the spirit of the Revolution. Taking no pains to lower his voice, he would deliver imprecations against the church, exclaim, "Frocked vultures!" and spit again.

On the second Saturday in January, at four in the afternoon, José Reyes took money from his children and entered the cantina for the last time. An hour later he was drunk, out of funds, and ignored by those who had been his friends. The first smoke of his erupting fury might have been detected then by any man who cared to see.

It was now that the Palacio brothers entered the Copa de Oro and walked up to the bar. They worked in the concentrating mill of the Malagueña mine and carried with them like an aura the bitter smell of cyanide. José Reyes first approached Tomás, then Julián. He asked for a small loan of money to be repaid tomorrow and was refused. When the Palacio brothers tried to turn away, he held them back and said, "I am not as rich as you are with a week's salary in your pockets." When they refused a second time, José pulled from the wide belt under his denim jacket the machete he had used to strip twigs from the firewood and, as if they had attacked him, cut Tomás in the neck and Julián in the stomach. Then José Reyes was outside in the street, running faster than one so besotted should run, with thirty meters between him and those who came after. There were five who followed him, and two were Palacio cousins and one a Palacio son.

José Reyes, grasping the machete that was his advance guard, his deployable force and his entire reserve, displayed in headlong flight the same shrewdness that had served him well in petty thievery. He hid behind half-open doors and doubled back, he scaled a wall and stood with three cows in their dung until he heard his pursuers pass, he rolled under a cart of alfalfa until his long legs betrayed him. Whatever his maneuvers, the unarmed five came on.

Beneath the fading light, children still spun tops on trodden dirt, and in the plaza a flock of starlings settled first in one tree, then another. Lunging past what was left of the Spanish bullring on the outskirts of town, José Reyes made for the hill directly ahead, the Cerro de la Cruz, which rose a steep two hundred meters above the road.

Given darkness, even though a second band of five had waited in ambush for him on the hill, a man like José, familiar with this ground since he first walked, might have crept past them unsuspected. Given darkness, such a man, who had learned from the coyote, the snake, and the hare, might have climbed unnoticed the front slope and accomplished undiscovered the twisting descent behind.

Thin sunlight shone on the white cement cross at the summit, but the advancing shadow had already obscured the whitewashed rocks that spelled the name of the president of the republic. To the left, where the overgrown path rounded the hill to start its winding drop to the valley beyond, loomed the limestone columns known as Los Púlpitos. Indeed, they appeared much like an accumulation of giant pulpits, massively perpendicular and flat enough to support a prophet's lectern.

José Reyes made for these sheer rocks, for the shallow cave he knew was behind them, for the narrow track that led away. Although he had widened the distance between hunters and quarry, they had gained crossing flat ground while he struggled up the rough hillside. The five overtook him close to the pulpits in a twilight bright enough for him to recognize each of them.

It may have been Tomás Palacio's son who picked up the first stone. It hit José Reyes behind one ear, and, when he wheeled to see who threw it, another tore the skin of his shoulder, and another struck the back of his neck. So he circled with his sharp blade under a bombardment of stones, stones round and pointed, stones gray as granite and white as crystal, stones with traces of copper and traces of lead; circled like the minute hand of a clock, circled until he was brought to his knees, and then still circled, blood flowing from his nose and chin and ear and ribs, until Jesús Palacio, one of the cousins, taking time to calculate his aim, hurled the ordinary common stone that knocked the machete out of José's broken hand.

José Reyes, surrounded by his captors, lay on the ground and closed his eyes. Long before the arrival of the fat captain of the *cárcel,* who had trailed the others at his own pace, José heard the snapping of dry brush, the grinding of gravel and cascading of pebbles that marked the government official's ascent. By these sounds he knew when the captain was near, but only when he smelled sweat and garlic did he open his eyes to regard the bulging cheeks under the visored cap, the paunch swelling over the cartridge belt and revolver.

José Reyes observed the appearance of three stars near the zenith and was aware of a cold wind from a new direction. At this instant the day surrendered, as obedient as a woman, to the night.

4

KID MUÑOZ

For more than a year the Evertons unwatered their mine, level by level, and room by room they rebuilt their house, digging away adobe until every view had a window to contain it. The first April new beds arrived, and a pair of heavy Spanish gates for the driveway; that fall two Spanish cupboards, and by the next spring there were six colonial paintings of apostles in the hall, and in a corner of the porch a stone Saint Francis that had the square mouth and bulging eyes of the rain god, Tláloc.

These things were discovered in various remote places. But in Concepción, only an hour's drive away, were shops and warehouses that sold lumber, sheets of glass, nails and sandpaper, and, on occasion, blocks of ice to carry back to the kitchen in Ibarra. From Concepción Sara brought back curtain rings and watering cans; Richard, pipe fittings and a drawing board, and, not long after arriving in Mexico, regular reports from the medical laboratory.

From the beginning, at least once a week, Richard and Sara had traveled the eighty kilometers to Concepción and the eighty kilometers back to Ibarra. Sometimes, when the only water in the Evertons' pipes was mine water pumped from the fourth level and still smelling of explosives and ore, Sara went to a hairdresser in the capital. It was a ground-floor *salón* and open to the street. Buses raced their motors a few feet from the dryers, and a procession of vendors came in from the sidewalk to offer the patrons straw toys or lace or molded yellow gelatin on trays. Small scabbed boys competed to sell gum, and a beggar girl would often pluck at Sara's sleeve and ask her to notice a deformity. Then Sara would look down at a sandaled foot much like the other, except that this foot pointed backward.

On the Evertons' days in Concepción they separated at the plaza in the morning and met later for lunch in the narrow, high-ceilinged dining room of the Hotel París.

It was on one such trip to the capital that Sara encountered a blind man standing between her and the double glass doors that had PARIS etched in Gothic letters on one side and HOTEL on the other. She had seen him somewhere before, perhaps at the *salón,* or in front of a market stall.

"Win one thousand pesos on tomorrow's drawing," he said, and through his shaded glasses fixed an opaque stare on her. There was a sheaf of lottery tickets in his right hand. He carried a cane and wore a bruised hat set at an angle that, on another man, might have been jaunty.

"Señorita," he said, addressing her as though she were still a girl, "I have these particularly fine numbers." And Sara realized he had recognized her sex, and perhaps her age and nationality, by her footsteps. She glanced at his wide flat cheeks and wide flat nose. His face had a pounded look. One front tooth was capped with gold.

"Perhaps later, when my husband comes," she said, and circled him to enter the hotel lobby, where a pair of bellboys in rust-green jackets were mopping the black tiled floor. Six times a day they mopped it, to erase the footprints of guests coming in from the street, the wheel tracks of a bicycle that twice a day delivered fresh rolls, the trail left by the cook's loose slippers when she carried in a wire basket of eggs.

The nearest bellboy took Sara's packages from her and carried them to an alcove behind the reception desk. Sara paused here in the small dark space to fold her sweater on the trowel, the linseed oil, the teapot she had bought that morning. Beside her were three empty armchairs in front of the television set where last September don Nacho, the hotel's proprietor, sat with his cousin and a nephew through all seven days of the World Series. Don Nacho was a lifelong St. Louis fan and throughout the season spoke with confidence of Cardinals present and nostalgia of Cardinals past.

"Bob Gibson," don Nacho reminded Richard. "Lou Brock, Curt Flood."

In the dining room, where the light was dim for the middle of a cloudless day, Sara took a table set for two. Here, facing a vase of wax roses, she waited for her husband's return from the laboratory. She stared in its direction as if there were not two hotel walls, a cathedral, and fifty houses between her and the one-room, ground-floor establishment that had a sign, ANÁLISIS DE SANGRE, over the door.

Fifteen minutes later, don Nacho discovered her gazing in another direction, toward the square, through tall windows that produced an undulating image. The jacarandas that lined the plaza were in flower, and a man with trousers rolled to his knees was scrubbing a tiled pool with Fab. Beyond, in the shadow of the governor's palace, the blind ticket vendor held out his fine numbers to passersby hurrying home to eat.

Sara looked up at don Nacho. Everything about him was distinguished, his domelike forehead, his jutting brows, his mellow voice. He greeted her in almost perfect English.

"And don Ricardo, where is he?"

"He is at the light and power department." She lied easily, without compunction, perhaps believing she could force falsehood into fact. In any case, the Evertons allowed only the American doctor and the local technician to know of Richard's illness. No others were told. There would have been no room for them inside the fortifications.

Don Nacho suspected nothing. "I bring you the morning

paper to read while you wait. Please to notice the day of the month."

Sara saw it was June fifth and rummaged through the miscellany in her mind. "Exactly one month after the Cinco de Mayo," she said. "The victory of Mexican recruits over a French regiment at Puebla."

"No, no. That is not what I meant," said don Nacho. "One year ago today your husband inaugurated the concentrating mill at the Malagueña mine."

"How can I have forgotten?" she said, without explaining that the events in a doctor's office last July had eclipsed the festivities of June.

There was a torpor in the air of the dining room in spite of the draft created by a ceiling fan that stirred the pages of the newspaper as she turned them.

According to the *Heraldo,* citizens were protesting the price of corn, the backfiring of motorcycles, and the presence on the streets of rabid dogs. An editorial condemned the situation of a brothel between two schools. The governor once again appealed to employers to comply with the minimum-wage laws, and the bishop urged responsibility to God.

Now Feliciana, the waitress, approached with the measured tread of a somnambulist and placed in front of Sara a basket of rolls, a glass of water, and a menu. Then she started to gather the silver and the napkin from the setting at Sara's left.

"No," said Sara. "Leave them," and in the time it took to speak three words foresaw a whole future of this clearing away of the second place at tables, saw it in Arizona and New Mexico motels, in an El Paso coffee shop and a Chihuahua restaurant.

"No," she said again. "My husband is coming."

"Will you eat now?" said Feliciana. "Meatball soup is the soup of the day."

"No, I will wait for him." In her mind, Sara counted the blocks between the hotel and the laboratory. Only six, and they were short. She met Feliciana's placid gaze. "What is the name of the blind man who sells lottery tickets outside the door?"

"Kid Muñoz," said the waitress, but she pronounced it Keed. "He used to be a boxer. He was blinded fighting in your country."

Sara added this tragedy to the accumulating burden of guilt that with each passing month in Mexico weighed more intolerably upon her. Now, to the guilt of having too much food, too many dresses, she added the guilt of seeing.

She turned the *Heraldo*'s pages and found the weather forecast for June fifth. A warm day was promised, and a mild evening.

On this day a year ago the paper had predicted the continuation of an early rainstorm but, as it turned out, the skies over Ibarra cleared by afternoon and the inauguration of the mill took place in thin sunlight among puddles of water that reflected a faint blue. One hundred men who hoped to be miners were there, as well as two priests, six nuns, a governor, and a mayor. Besides these, a dozen of the Evertons' friends and relatives had come, skeptics drawn from great distances to touch the ore and the machinery, to be on hand when the pulling of a switch transformed Richard's unrealistic vision into an orderly process of crushing, sorting, grinding, and floating. And finally to dip a finger in the sandy foam, rub it on their palms, and thirty seconds later see copper glisten in their hands.

On the day of the inauguration a tasseled silk Mexican flag flew from the hoist tower of the Malagueña mine, and children in the costumes of Jalisco and Veracruz danced on the drenched ground. Honor students recited odes and there were speeches. One of these was delivered by a tall, big-boned priest who wore a miner's yellow helmet with his conventional black habit. He had come from a neighboring parish and drew so much applause that the mother superior Yolanda left her band of sisters and came to Sara.

"Padre Arenas is at the microphone and in the center of

attention while our own cura stands unnoticed in the background."

Sara found the cura of Ibarra on the fringes of the crowd and spoke to him in her formal, beginner's Spanish. "Please take your place among the guests of honor."

"My time will come," said the cura.

And now, a year later, Sara waited for Richard in the becalmed dining room of the Hotel París, which was gradually filling with vineyard owners and salesmen traveling for IBM or Datsun. Also finding tables were a few families who would stop here overnight on their way to other destinations, towns that had nightly concerts in the plaza and hotels with swimming pools. Everyone in the room was Mexican except Sara, who had left off reading the paper, left off playing piano scales on the tablecloth, and presently stood at the high narrow windows that faced the square. The cathedral clock struck two, confirming that Richard was half an hour late, that there had been a problem at the medical laboratory, that the technician in his dark-stained white coat had been unable to interpret the results and was drawing out vial after vial of blood.

Sara looked across the street, past the shoeshine stands where business was always slow this time of day, through the heliotrope blue of the jacarandas, past benches where old men and babies slept, to a stone-wreathed column commemorating the Constitution of 1917. She waited there for fifteen minutes, watching pedestrians as they appeared, picking out men who were almost as tall as Richard, almost as thin.

Seated again at her table, Sara broke a roll into four pieces. She turned to the back page of the *Heraldo* and found that the governor had left the city with the secretary of hydraulics to inaugurate a dam. Since it was a federal project, Sara knew this dam would have to operate with its gates and sluices eternally unblessed.

At the Malagueña mine, however, things had gotten off to a more auspicious start. The Evertons' ore traveled over a system of belts and pulleys to be sorted by machinery that had received the benediction of the church. For on the day of the inauguration of the mill the cura's time came as he had predicted it would. Wearing a surplice and stole over his cassock, accompanied by the bright chiming of a bell and the slanting flames of candles, he proceeded from the jaw crusher to the cone crusher, from the classifier to the ball mill, and finally to the flotation cells, speaking in Latin to each machine and sprinkling on it, as though on an innocent child's head, drops of holy water.

That was on the afternoon of June fifth, one year ago this moment to the day and hour. After the blessing, Sara went to a dance in the superintendent's house at the mine. She remembered a crowd of men, music reverberating from an old phonograph, the smell of crushed ore, beer, and Delicados.

She was dancing with the superintendent when a miner stepped out from a corner, nodded, and cut in. He wore his work clothes, thick-soled boots and a cap that advertised tires, with the words GENERAL POPO stenciled over the visor. This was how she met Basilio García when, in a circle of clapping hands, she danced the polka with him, danced with the man who had gone to work at the Socorro mine when he was twelve, the same man who now insisted that his brother, Domingo, prepare for the university.

In the hotel dining room Sara heard the clock chime the half hour. She ate a crust of the quartered roll and searched the paper for other news. The dateline at the top of each page reminded her that eleven months of the projected span had already passed. Last July was the month of the diagnosis. Six years, six active years.

And already they had scattered eleven months behind them as if days were nothing more than the feathered seeds of a thistle. Since July Sara had found that, of these days, even the flaws were indispensable. And she imagined all around her a sharpening of outline, as when sand is washed from a shell.

Feliciana materialized again at her side. "Will you have iced tea or lemonade?" She placed a glass of toothpicks next to the three wax roses.

"No, I will wait," and for the second time Sara left her chair to stand at the window. She saw the rippled image of the bank and Kid Muñoz in front of it. He stood on the curb in the middle of the block, his right hand holding the tickets, his left on the shoulder of a small tattered boy. Armed with the vendor's extended cane, they stepped into the traffic and were halfway across to the park benches when brakes shrieked, voices cried, and a panel truck passing a bus almost ran them down. The child pulled Muñoz back and the cane went flying.

Chance is everything, Sara concluded. By chance the man and boy had just been saved. By chance the gloved fist landed a blow with the precise aim and force to blind Muñoz. And now it was chance alone that paid for his food and blanket, and for the rent of his room which needed no mirror and no lamp.

Sara sat at her table, closed her eyes, and listened. She heard a spoon in a cup, a bottle against a glass, the rubber-tired wheels of the serving cart, the slow revolutions of the fan, a male voice laughing. With her eyes still shut, she stretched out her hand to feel the wax flowers, scraped her finger on the toothpicks, touched the spoons and forks in front of her and then the ones at Richard's place.

It was almost three when he came up behind her, reached over her shoulder, and spread all twenty sections of a lottery ticket across the napkin still folded on her plate.

"What do you think of that number?" he said, having relegated the clinical laboratory as soon as he left it to a place among lesser concerns. Sara was forced to ask the results of the test.

"No change so far," said Richard, as though he were reporting the barometric pressure, and he pushed the ticket toward her.

Instead of relief, Sara felt resentment. She distrusted the technician who should have handed Richard revised findings. Who should have told him there had been a mistake in the original diagnosis, that his ailment was minor and had passed. A brief rage surged in her against her husband for having contracted this disease.

The number of the ticket was 1441.

"We could use some good luck at the mine," Richard said. He had already forgotten the laboratory.

Feliciana approached at calm and even pace to take their order. Already, in midafternoon, the light in the dining room was diminishing. It was hard to read the menu. Was the vegetable string beans or corn? Was the pasta cooked with cream or cheese?

"I can hardly see," said Sara.

Richard held up his menu toward the window. In the end, they both ordered enchiladas París.

"The same as last time," said Feliciana. Her voice implied a failure of imagination, a reluctance to take risks.

Lassitude had invaded the room and subdued the diners. At the next table a family of five drank through straws from bottles of Squirt. The youngest child knelt on his mother's lap. All five sucked slowly and at once.

The lottery ticket lay spread out between the Evertons.

"How was Muñoz blinded?" Sara asked.

"Fighting in the preliminaries at the old Olympic." Richard had heard about the boxer from don Nacho. "He was outmatched for six rounds. The punches he took detached both retinas."

"Can he see at all? Light and shadow?"

But Richard told her the ex-fighter was totally blind.

"There he is now," Sara said. "Under that jacaranda."

Through the window they saw Kid Muñoz, his cane in his hand again, leaning against one of the elevated shoeshine stands. The owner of the stall leaned there too, a grizzled wiry man who flicked his polishing rag at the two footrests as if they were attracting flies. Muñoz was staring in the direction of the cathedral, where he could not see the bald beggar on the steps or the mourners and celebrants entering the nave. The vendor pulled his hat lower and turned to the Hotel París. He exchanged a few words with the shoeshine man and pointed in the direction of the dining room. Gathered there to eat were a number of potential clients. All rich, as far as he knew. All gamblers.

"I remember the old Olympic," Sara said, and sat again beside Richard in the galleried arena, smelled the air thick and sluggish with cigar smoke, pomade, and old sweat, heard again the tide of voices out of which rose an occasional cry that flashed as deadly as a shark's fin in a wave. The fighters climbed into the ring and the tide swelled. They touched gloves and it lifted to a roar. It broke when a series of jabs brought blood. "Hit him again!" yelled the men. "Kill him!" called the women.

The walls of the dining room of the Hotel París were painted moss green and the plaster ceiling, molded into urns and garlands, was white. The aqueous half-light, sifted first through the jacarandas and then through the imperfect glass of the windows, drifted into the room like fog. Out of it Feliciana emerged to set before the Evertons dishes of *flan* they had not ordered.

At the next table, the youngest of the family, who had made his lunch of the soft drink and two saucers of ice cream, was napping. Drugged by sugar and the quiet ebb of afternoon, he slept with his head sunk deep in his mother's breast. Sara believed there was no one in the room who wouldn't like to change places, at least for a moment, with this child.

The cathedral clock struck four and the Evertons had waved twice to Feliciana for their bill, when don Nacho came toward them. He shook hands with Richard and noticed the lottery ticket on the table.

"So you're a gambler," the proprietor said, and he picked

up the ticket. "You have a good number. 1441. Pairs. Add them up and the total ends in zero."

"Zero," Sara repeated. She recognized it at once as the sum of Richard and herself five or six years from now and reached toward him so quickly that water, spilling from her glass, spread over the striped cotton cloth.

"Watch it," said Richard, and touched her hand.

Feliciana had cleared the table and wheeled away their plates. Richard and Sara were about to leave when Kid Muñoz entered the dining room from the lobby. His small guide was no longer with him. He stood alone at the threshold and listened, but the diners had nothing to say. Using his cane, Muñoz tapped his way to an empty table. He located the legs of a chair and offered his tickets to the customer who might have been sitting there.

"For tomorrow's drawing," he said. "One hundred thousand pesos." He fanned the tickets out like playing cards and exhibited them first to the right and then to the left.

"Please take a look at these excellent numbers," said Muñoz.

When there was no response, he circled the table and discovered it to be unoccupied. He advanced into the room and listened again. Then Muñoz became as silent as the rest who sat there wordless, those with their forks halfway to their mouths and those others with their bills already paid and their chairs pushed back.

5

THE INHERITANCE

In August of their second summer in Ibarra, the Evertons brought electricity to their house. They installed the transformer they had needed and, soon after, a toaster and a record player. On the last day of September, evening visitors to the Americans' windows heard for the first time the andantes and vivaces of Schumann and Liszt. Also on this day, Pablo, the cobbler's nine-year-old grandson, drowned in the tailings dump at the Malagueña mine.

"But why was he out there on the dam?" Sara Everton asked Lourdes. "A boy who . . ." and she paused, distracted, to search for the Spanish words. "A boy who could only partly comprehend," she finally said.

The people of Ibarra were more matter-of-fact. They called Pablo "the idiot" as easily as they might label another child tall, short, left-handed, right-handed.

Sara, though she had often seen the boy alone, making his crooked way across the square or along the dry arroyo, said, "Someone should have been with him."

"Someone was with him," Lourdes told her. "His cousin Juan."

When old Mateo, the cobbler, died of fevers, chills, and the sum of his eighty years, he left his house in equal shares to his grandson Juan and his grandson Pablo. After Mateo's funeral mass and burial the cura of Ibarra read the will to the two heirs in the *sala* of his residence adjoining the church. Under the high ceiling of this room, where the air was heavy with the smell of damp plaster and the lengths of old cloth hanging at the windows, Juan stood next to the priest and Pablo stumbled, lopsided, from the desk to the ladder-back chair to the splitting red satin of the sofa. The boy laid his face against these things and tried to speak to them.

The will occupied a single paragraph, and before the cura could read it aloud for the second time Juan understood that Mateo had given him half a house and all of his cousin Pablo.

After allowing a pause for reflection the cura asked Juan if he had a job. And Juan said, "I have worked at La Malagueña since my eighteenth birthday."

Meanwhile Pablo, discovering a cushion covered with the fur of an animal, touched it with his finger and licked it with his tongue.

"Remember your grandfather," said the cura, and Juan nodded for himself and for Pablo.

Juan's inheritance was so familiar to him that there was no need to examine it, but after the reading of the will he took an inventory of all that now belonged to him and Pablo. Inside the house, behind Mateo's workbench, were two cots, a cupboard, a straw mat, and a trunk. Without looking Juan knew that in this trunk were two rosaries, two rings, and two white lace veils. These had belonged to the mother of Juan and the mother of Pablo, the cobbler's two daughters who were dead.

Their wedding photographs stood on the trunk. The sisters had been twins and for a long time after he came here as a child Juan was unable to tell them apart. But as soon as he learned to read he would turn the photographs around to see which name was written on the back.

Pablo had come later, when he was three and his cousin twelve, and from the beginning had refused to share Juan's bed. Instead, he slept rolled up in a blanket on the mat as close as possible to where his grandfather lay on his back and made the night safe and ordinary with his snoring.

After three years, when Pablo was six, his grandfather had taken him to the mother superior Yolanda, who directed the nuns' school. "Madre," he said. "I know there is intelligence in this boy's head. Look at his eyes."

But later that morning the mother superior herself brought Pablo back to the cobbler. Mateo glanced up from the bench where he was cutting leather for new soles and saw the two standing in the doorway with the sun behind them. The nun held Pablo by the hand.

"He has the special intelligence God gave him," she said. "But it is not the intelligence that masters words and numbers." She started to go and then turned back. "To God, this makes no difference," she said.

During Pablo's first years with his grandfather he was sometimes mocked by older boys and Juan more than once had to fight his own friends to protect his cousin's dignity. But even as Juan drove his fist into the eye of the offender, an inner voice reminded him, "No one else in Ibarra has a cousin like Pablo. The cousins of the rest can knot a halter and kick a ball."

When Mateo died in early summer, Juan had already worked at La Malagueña for a year. From one June to the next he had swept and washed down the floor of the concentrating mill and the patio outside it. Then, on the first anniversary of his job, he was promoted to the tailings dam.

Juan walked its length as surefooted as any goat balanced on the steep slope behind him. Distinguished by his energy and his red shirt, he could be picked out from the other workers as he pushed a wheelbarrow full of ore tailings across the rim and spilled it out for men with shovels to shape, as it stiffened, into an endless series of rising tiers.

Juan could stand at the center of the dam and look up the canyon over the lake of sludge to its source, the mill of the Malagueña mine. It was Juan's intention to become foreman of the mill someday, and he imagined himself standing in front of it and gazing down across the tailings that turned from thin mud at his feet to wet silt farther down and finally, at the dam itself, to a substance hard as lava. In his vision Juan saw his two selves, the future one who stood at the mill and the present one on the dam. The future Juan from his vantage point stared across the expanse of waste and recognized the Juan of today, a man of nineteen who wore a red shirt, was cousin to an idiot, and had recently fallen in love.

On the day Juan's salary was raised he bought a bottle of perfume and gave it to Otilia, the storekeeper's daughter, when he found her alone on the alameda. She pushed back two long strands of hair and touched the stopper to her skin, behind her ears, on her forehead, at the base of her throat, and farther down, at the edge of her low-cut blouse.

"You have guessed my favorite flower, the carnation," she said, and stood in Juan's arms for a long time, stood there until she felt a tugging at her skirt, looked down, and saw Pablo.

The boy now trailed Juan about the house and through the streets of Ibarra as he used to trail his grandfather, not far enough from his heels to let light separate their shadows. As for Juan, only when he had purposely eluded his cousin or was away at work could he consider his hours his own. During these times Pablo roamed free, visiting the fruit stand and the church, the fountain and, occasionally, the school. Here he would pause in the classroom doorways and listen to the nuns explaining fractions and the verbs.

One Sunday morning the North American woman, wife of don Ricardo who had personally chosen Juan for his job, approached the two cousins in the plaza. Doña Sara, carrying cans of evaporated milk in a straw bag, had already crossed the square between two rows of newly planted jacarandas when she turned around and came back to speak to Juan.

"Your cousin . . ." she said. "Is there anything . . .?" And Juan, hearing the broken sentences, understood that the señora was introducing a subject for which she had neither the vocabulary nor a settled opinion.

She glanced at Pablo, who seemed to be listening with his eyes and his open mouth. "Alone in the fields . . ." she said. "On the hills . . ." Then she said, as if it were not a question, "He has never followed you to the mine," and Juan shook his head.

"I am buying Domingo García's old bicycle," he told her. "It's too fast for my cousin to follow."

"I've been thinking," doña Sara said. "Perhaps the doctor in the clinic . . ." And when there was no answer she started home for the second time in ten minutes with her bag of canned milk.

This conversation surprised Juan, who had thought until now that the Americans did not believe in miracles. A few weeks later he took Pablo to the clinic.

The doctor examined the boy and gave his report. "You are giving him food, shelter, and protection," he said to Juan. "No one could do more."

To this Juan made no response. The doctor, on his part, stared through the open door of his office into the waiting room where three mothers with babies and a man with his arm in a sling sat on a bench. At last he said, "No one has yet discovered the medicine that will cure your cousin." There followed another long silence. Then the doctor spoke again. "Such children seldom live to maturity."

But he did not say why, whether it was a deficiency in the muscles or nerves, in the heart or the lungs, that might sweep Pablo off the face of the earth.

From the moment of the doctor's remark Juan, though he continued to wash and dress his cousin, feed him twice a day and cover him at night, began to look for signs of Pablo's failing health. A cough, a fever, a refusal to eat.

In September of that year, three months after his grandfather's death, Juan went to Otilia's father and asked permission to marry her. The girl's mother sat in the same room, poking a needle into her embroidery, but neither parent spoke.

"Where would you live?" the storekeeper finally asked.

"I have my house."

"What of your cousin? Would the three eat and sleep in one room?"

"I have thought of building Pablo a small bedroom of his own," said Juan, but even as he spoke he knew that such a room would accomplish nothing. It would be as easy to keep Pablo in this room as a fish in a torn net or a sparrow in a cage with half the bars rusted away.

There was something else he could have told Otilia's family. That Pablo would die soon. For the doctor was not alone in predicting this. The cura also had spoken to Juan. Only a week ago the priest had observed the cousins from the church steps and, perhaps wishing to prepare Juan, had told him, "With children like Pablo nothing is sure. When you least expect it, God may take him."

And as soon as he heard these words Juan, though he continued to pull Pablo back from the bridge and out of the path of the bus, entered into complicity with God.

Otilia now walked about Ibarra crowned and garlanded with invisible flowers. She invented reasons to pass Juan's house, and on the Sunday after his visit to her parents she found him alone at home.

"Where is Pablo?" she asked.

"In the plaza," said Juan, without explaining how he had managed to separate himself from his cousin.

"Then we are alone," and, with this, Otilia pushed past him.

She was no sooner inside the house than she made plans to redecorate it from the corrugated iron roof to the smooth dirt floor. She spoke of plaster and tiles, of curtains and a square of flowered carpet. Out of her fantasy she produced a matrimonial bed and piled it with cushions.

"What is in that trunk?" she asked, and Juan showed her the two mantillas, the rosaries and the rings. He explained which had belonged to his mother and which to his aunt.

"So these were your mother's," said Otilia, and she tried on the triangle of white lace and the ring. She circled the room in search of a mirror. "What will Pablo do with his?" she said. "Can he find a girl like him?"

And Juan saw against his will the image of Pablo and a girl like him reeling the whole length of the church from the glass-encased statue of the Virgin to the splintered carved oak doors.

Otilia felt in her pocket, and took out a radio. A second later a woman's amplified contralto, accompanied by guitars, erupted into the room.

"Do I look like a bride?" and with her foot Otilia pushed the street door closed behind her.

In the sudden dimness Juan and the girl, tangled in each other's arms, drifted to the nearest cot, which was old Mateo's, and fell upon it. But Juan had barely got his hand inside Otilia's blouse when the door burst open and Pablo threw himself across the threshold. Light flooded in, together with the boy's wordless protestations and his irrational tears.

To mirror Juan's despair the summer skies clouded over and for three days no single ray of sun touched the bust of Juárez in the square, the wet stone under the village pump, or the church's tiled dome. On Wednesday night a thin persistent rain began to fall and continued for two days and two more nights. It soaked little by little to the roots of scrub oaks and mountain ferns; the leaves of the nopal cactus, shrunken by drought, began to swell.

"As long as there isn't a runoff, we have nothing to worry about," said the men at the dam on Saturday morning. They looked in the direction of Ibarra over the broad steps they had molded with their shovels as they turned the rising wall of the dam into the profile of a Mayan pyramid. They contemplated an overflow, imagined the pouring down of waste from the mill into the arroyo that bordered Ibarra and on from there into the valley to wither new corn and blacken alfalfa.

Then one of the men said, "Look. It is over," and pointed up to a strip of blue between the clouds. An hour later Juan waited in line at the paymaster's window under a sun that drew steam from the ground. But as he bicycled home there was a bank of clouds piling up behind him in the west.

At his house he washed himself and then washed Pablo, who by an instinct that kept time always found his way home at the moment of his cousin's return. Juan was setting two plates on the cobbler's bench when he heard the first rumble of thunder. He handed Pablo his food and said, "Eat. The noise can't hurt you." But through the window the boy could see that fork lightning had begun to drill into the mountain tops.

Juan stood up. "You stay here," he said to his cousin. "There's going to be a cloudburst." He closed the door hard behind him and ripped off the branch of a mesquite bush to serve as a barricade.

He had gone only a dozen steps from the house when he stopped and returned to shout through the door. "Pablo," he called. "I'll be back again soon." And into the silence he repeated the word "soon."

The downpour began with a great clap of thunder at the same moment that Juan found Otilia in the square. Simultaneously the lights went out and everyone who had been strolling on the walks or resting on the benches crossed the street and crowded under the arcade.

Juan and Otilia took refuge in a corner. She stood with her back to the café and he faced her, leaning toward her with his palms against the wall. Then he leaned closer in the dark and pressed himself, from his knees to his mouth, against her.

"Tomorrow at three," he said at last. "At my house. I will take Pablo to the nuns and say it is an emergency."

Then he became aware that a chorus of voices was calling his name. "Juan! Juan! Here is the boy, weeping and soaked to the skin."

When they arrived home and Juan lit a candle, he saw that Pablo was not only wet and crying but had fallen on the road and broken a tooth. Blood bubbled in the corner of his mouth. Juan cleaned and dried his cousin, wrapped him in his blanket, and blew out the light.

Then, before he could close his mind to it, a thought occurred to Juan. Pablo will have an infected mouth, he told himself, and a case of grippe he may not be able to overcome. It is as the doctor said, such children are weaker. It is as the cura said, God is reaching for him.

Rain fell all that night and at noon on Sunday was still blowing in barely transparent curtains between the houses and over the roofs of Ibarra. Juan listened to torrents racing in the drainage ditches outside his walls and, inside, where he and Pablo sat, to a measured dripping from new leaks in the ceiling.

At one o'clock there was a pounding on the door. Two of the men who worked on the dam stood outside. "Come on," they said. "There's an overflow."

As Juan left the house to go with them, Pablo tried to follow and had to be pushed back in. Holding the door ajar, Juan reached through and pulled Mateo's bench against it. Then he slammed the door.

"Stay here," he shouted to Pablo, and heard the dark wet hill behind him echo, "here."

The three men took a shortcut to the canyon and, with the brims of their straw hats slanted down against the storm, made their way along its bank. Arrived at the dam, they walked out on its slippery surface with their shovels. At the ends where the dam met the canyon walls the tailings lay gray and half congealed a hand's breadth below the rim. But by the time the men reached the center their feet were covered over by a stream of waste and water that had eaten into the dam and was spilling down the steps of the pyramid behind it. Under a new onslaught of rain the men started to shovel gray sludge.

By two o'clock the stream had become a tide. "We need help," said one of the men, and he dropped his shovel and started away. When he was still not back in half an hour, the second man said, "Only God knows what's delaying him." And he, too, ran off in the direction of the mine, calling to Juan over his shoulder, "Wait for me here at the side."

This man had no sooner disappeared than the rain stopped as suddenly as it had begun the night before. In the stillness it left behind, Juan heard all around him the rushing of the runoff through a hundred new channels in the hills.

He picked up his shovel and, testing each step, walked out on the dam. Standing at the center he pounded a few shovelfuls of thick tailings into the erosion but his work accomplished nothing. He looked up the canyon to see if help was coming and then down the canyon, over Ibarra, to the wide valley that had turned green overnight. It was when he started back to the hillside that he saw Pablo, drenched and barefoot, lurching across the dam.

"Go back!" shouted Juan. But his cousin continued toward him and even seemed to be singing and dancing as he came. Juan raised his palm in the gesture of "Stop!" but the boy came on, careening from one side of the rim to the other as his feet slid under him. The older cousin called "Go back!" until suddenly Pablo was within his reach and Juan stretched out his hand.

At this, Pablo lost his balance entirely and toppled into the great pool of tailings behind the dam. A few seconds later his head, plastered gray, and one flailing arm emerged above the surface.

Juan went to his knees and stretched his hand toward Pablo, but the space between them was too great. Then he remembered his shovel, took it by the blade, and started to extend the handle toward Pablo's wild, circling arm.

But at this moment Juan seemed to lose the power to act. For, though the implement was long enough and at first there was time, he allowed three seconds to pass, then five, then seven, while he crouched there and withheld the shovel from Pablo's grasp. Much can be considered in seven seconds. Perhaps Juan, as he watched the tailings rise to his cousin's mouth, remembered the doctor's prophecy. Or he may have observed, through the subsiding clouds above him, the hand of God.

In any case, he recovered himself too late, and it was too late when he leaned out to thrust the handle into Pablo's groping hand. By then the mud had climbed to the boy's ears and all Juan saw of him were his eyes and this hand. Pablo, impelled by some instinct or a reflex at the moment of dying, took the handle in a grip so tight that even after Juan raised his body, and carried it along the rim of the dam to the hillside, and laid it down, Pablo's fingers had to be pried from the wood.

Pablo was buried in the stony ground of the cemetery the following morning. After the litany had been recited and the blessing spoken, the cura put his hand on Juan's shoulder. "Now he is in the company of saints and angels," said the priest.

But Juan would speak to no one that day. He remained all afternoon in his house with the door nailed shut. When Otilia called to him from outside, and came back to call again, he made no answer. He lay on his cot and wished he were a boy again, just come to his grandfather's house to live. Then he wished he were in school and could fight a friend again, and win.

But by the time night fell he had only one wish. He wished last Saturday back, when he had buttoned his week's salary in his pocket and, trailing the miners who were leaving their shift, pushed his bicycle out to the road. He had pedaled hard, waved as he passed the others, and with his wheels spinning to a blur coasted down the grade ahead of them all. So it had almost seemed this was a racing bike, and new, and paid for.

6

PRAY FOR US, FATHERS

The Evertons met the cura as soon as they arrived in Ibarra and by the time two years were up had come to expect him to visit them weekly with a message or an invitation, or simply to have an hour's talk over a glass of rum. After Lourdes had met him at the door and kissed his hand, he would sit in the *sala* in a high-backed chair with his worn black shoes flat on the floor. Then he would give Sara a lily bulb his aunt had sent and inform Richard of the latest wind damage at the deserted monastery, or invite them to a kermess in the plaza for the benefit of the nuns' school.

But the cura was too busy to loiter through the dusk at the Evertons' window, with its view over Ibarra as far as the mesas that climbed in steps toward the east. One afternoon he said, "In my parish I have six ranchos that lie in six directions. Every day except Sunday I must drive my pickup along wagon tracks and through gullies to offer the sacraments in one or another of them."

"The town needs a second priest," said Richard, and Sara nodded as if both of them had been baptized and confirmed in the Church of Rome.

"An assistant," she told the cura.

The priest stood up to leave. "The bishop has promised me one." And within a month, as if his words had brought them, the assistants started to come and to go.

The first one came in March, at the end of an unusually mild winter. The Evertons' plum trees had already flowered and the old ash tree was in leaf.

Richard and the cura passed on the road between Ibarra and the mine.

"I will bring my assistant to meet you and your señora next Saturday afternoon," said the cura. But Richard forgot to tell Sara and she was in the village instead of at her door when the priests arrived.

Walking up the stony lane that bounded her garden wall, she was startled by a fusillade of gunfire. Shots rang out. She stopped at the gate and watched a series of round white disks sail over the roof, two at a time. Near the stone pool in the patio stood a robed priest pointing a shotgun. Out of twelve attempts the priest hit every target. Fragments of clay pelted on the roof, the path, and into the pool.

When the firing ceased she advanced.

"You're a good shot," she said to the father.

"Sports were a former vocation." And the priest reloaded his weapon from a pocket sagging with shells. He introduced himself. "I am Padre Raúl. Your husband has kindly lent me his gun. He and the señor cura are discharging the targets from an apparatus behind the house." Without further waste of time he aimed into the sky and shouted *"Listo!"* to indicate he was ready.

From behind the house the parish priest and Richard shouted back *"Ya!"* and two small plates soared in separate arcs over the roof. Ten times Padre Raúl signaled *"Listo!"* and ten times the other two called *"Ya!"* until nasturtiums and geraniums and a border of dwarf pomegranates were crusted over with white splinters.

Padre Raúl, surrounded by the aura of a perfect score, stood in the middle of it all, holding the wood of the gunstock as if it had grown to his hand.

Sara noticed how tall he was and how lean, and presumed that his habit swathed an elegantly muscular frame. His vocations are reversed, she told herself. If he could discard clerical dress he would probably win the World Soccer Cup for Mexico.

"What were your other sports?" she asked, and Padre Raúl said, "Soccer. Baseball. Jai alai. But I have not participated in them for a number of years."

A week later the new priest appeared again at the house of the North Americans, this time to ask for a contribution toward a basketball court. "To defray the cost of cement," he explained.

There was a silence while the Evertons considered the justice of supporting this project which promised enjoyment for its own sake when only yesterday they had refused to make a gift to the campaign for Catholic Action.

"The purpose of the basketball court is to provide healthy pleasure for the youth of Ibarra," said Padre Raúl, as if he could read their minds. And he went on to say that the court would be built in the open space in front of the nuns' school near the well, now full of rubble, that had once been fed by a spring.

Three months later the court was completed. The inauguration ceremonies took place on a glittering Sunday afternoon in June under a sky of blue so intense that what could be seen of man and all his works appeared to blanch beneath it. School benches had been set up at each side of the court. On the east sat the visiting team and its supporters. On the west the local team and a crowd of townspeople overflowed the seats and formed in ranks behind. The visiting players wore matching sweaters and regulation shoes. The members of the Ibarra team had on the familiar pants and shirts they were seen in every day. Two wore the stiff black shoes that were usually saved for mass.

"This isn't going to be fair," Sara said to her husband. "The others are bigger and have brought a coach."

"We have Padre Raúl," said Richard.

The cura and his assistant stood in their cassocks under one of the new baskets. The backboard was red and had COCA-COLA inscribed across it in white letters. Throughout the conference between the two priests Padre Raúl kept the basketball in motion between his hand and the cement paving, thus reproducing the ominous beat of a war drum.

Then the cura welcomed the guests and offered thanks to God for his bounty, to the Evertons for the cement, to the Coca-Cola Company for the baskets and backboards, and to El Mundo Deportivo of Concepción, the store that had given the ball and might soon become the donor of uniforms.

"Now Padre Raúl of the parish of Ibarra will bless this court," said the cura, and started to withdraw.

But no one had thought to bring holy water, not the cura, nor his assistant, nor the sacristan, and the cobalt afternoon was slipping away.

"We will have a symbolic blessing," said the cura, and the spectators clapped.

Padre Raúl stood in the center of the court with the basketball tucked under his left arm. Raising his right, he drew down great handfuls of air so pure that, unlike water, it could not be seen or heard. This air he sprinkled in the four corners of the court and along its boundaries.

After this the cura rose from his seat to announce that the visitors' coach would act as referee during the first half of the game and Padre Raúl during the second. Then he said a brief prayer and crossed himself, as did all the players and both referees.

The teams took their places, the whistle blew, the sky remained the color of azurite in raw copper ore, and the audience on one side exulted and cheered while the audience on the other lapsed quiet. At the half the visitors led 18 to 9.

"Our team should have been allowed a handicap," said Sara.

But Richard was hopeful. "Padre Raúl may have a few ideas," he said.

The second half of the game was less monotonous than the

first. The assistant priest was everywhere. "Out of bounds!" he kept calling. "Violation! Foul!"

His whistle blew so often and with such authority that arguments went unheard. Six times the visitors' coach advanced to appeal decisions, but the towering presence of Padre Raúl, vested in the garments and the prestige of the church, one powerful hand fingering his crucifix, the other incessantly drumming the ball to the ground—all these things served to stifle protest. The two small boys in black hard-soled shoes completed nine free throws between them.

To the accompaniment of shrill and constant whistling the sun sank to the west, the radiant air turned cold, all traces of blue evaporated from the sky, and evening came on. By the time the game ended, the shadow of the spire on the nuns' chapel stretched across the court and the old dry well and all the empty space beyond. The cura announced that Ibarra had won 33 to 28 and shook hands with the visitors' coach.

The crowd dispersed in all directions, toward the main square, the bus, the kitchens of their houses. But the Americans stayed on in the dusk, and lingered not far from the benches. They seemed to be waiting for the first star, or for moonrise, or perhaps to congratulate the assistant priest, who stood in the center of the court with his hands at his sides and his eyes fixed on nothing.

The church bells had begun to ring for vespers by the time Padre Raúl picked up the ball. He bounced it down hard and on its third rebound lobbed it over his shoulder into the basket behind. It dropped through without touching the rim. The net shivered.

As a farmer resigned to the even-handedness of God will accept the seasons as they come, so the cura of Ibarra accommodated himself to the succession of priests who were delegated by the bishop to assist him. After two years Padre Raúl was succeeded by Padre Ignacio.

"What is His Excellency thinking of?" the cura said to his

aunt and housekeeper, Paulita, as she set a third place for midday dinner. "He has sent us a man who would ransom his soul for a pullet cooked in cream and butter."

"A servant of the church who satisfies his appetites in good conscience," said Paulita, and neither she nor her nephew spoke of Padre Ignacio's overnight stops at the rancho of La Emancipación. The assistant priest traveled to this spot once a week to celebrate mass in a lavender-domed chapel that stood intact among the outbuildings of a gutted hacienda and cast its shadow over the adobe huts crowding the broken walls.

To reach La Emancipación where it lay prostrate on the bank of a dry stream bed, Padre Ignacio borrowed the cura's Dodge pickup truck. But he seldom returned to Ibarra the same night, and the cura and his aunt and their neighbors would hear the old Dodge at sunrise, bouncing over the ruts and hitting loose stones on the washed-out street that led down to the church.

The cura and Paulita did not remark on this to each other, but if they had they would have said, "It is all for the best that Padre Ignacio has discovered a girl in La Emancipación rather than in this town. Rather than Paz Acosta, for instance." And they would have conjured up in their minds the image of Paz, who had burst into beauty at twelve, borne an infant at thirteen, and now at fourteen, still single and radiant, sat in the front row at mass.

Soon after Padre Ignacio's arrival the cura took him to meet the Americans.

"The señor Everton is the operator of the Malagueña mine," he explained to the other priest, "and a contributor to the restoration of the old monastery, ransacked by revolutionaries during the war of 1910."

But Padre Ignacio was already inspecting the North Americans' house. He discovered six portraits of holy apostles and a dozen representations of saints and martyrs painted on tin that was already rusting through. In addition to these things he noticed on a red leather chest a wooden religious figure, ravaged irreversibly by time and the infestations of termites.

"So you are North American Catholics," said Padre Ignacio, "come to live in a Catholic country."

"No, we are not," said Richard.

"We are nothing," said his wife, and Padre Ignacio turned the two black buttons of his eyes upon this woman so quick to deny the fact of her own existence, the existence of her husband, and of that deity through whose grace they lived and breathed in spite of themselves.

Beyond the window of the *sala* where they took their refreshments was a rock wall and in this wall a stone plaque, carved in low relief, of the Virgin and Child.

"My favorite," said Sara, her eyes following Padre Ignacio's glance.

There is much to be explained here, the new assistant said to himself, and he held out his glass for more rum.

That evening at supper the cura said to the new priest, "These two Americans are confirmed in their agnosticism. To them purgatory and hell hold no threats and paradise no promise." Then he said, "But think of this. Better heretics than Baptists."

Padre Ignacio served Ibarra from one spring to the next, although toward the end of his mission it seemed that he spent more time in La Emancipación, on the outer margin of the parish, than he did in its center. Frequently he would be off and away in the pickup truck for days and nights at a time. Then the cura had to make his rounds alone from the church to the nuns' school to the monastery chapel, and sometimes to the graveyard, with the uneven hem of his habit dragging in the dust and collecting weeds.

When Padre Ignacio's single year in Ibarra was almost up, a scandal occurred. Occurred and became known, though no one in Ibarra could have made clear to an outsider how news could travel in less than an hour over twenty kilometers of harsh countryside where the road was lost to cactus and mesquite more often than not.

At eleven o'clock in the morning Padre Ignacio was seen to alight from a bus in the plaza. By twelve o'clock there was nothing left to hide.

It turned out that the padre, whose ruddy face and stout form had been absent from Ibarra for half a week, had suffered an accident in the cura's Dodge. At some time during the previous night the assistant priest had attempted to drive without lights across the dry arroyo that bordered La Emancipación, spun his wheels in the sand, and impaled the truck on a pointed rock that immediately pierced the oil pan. There was no remedy but for Padre Ignacio to seek help in the darkened settlement. After knocking on a dozen doors he found two mules, one belonging to a maguey farmer, the other to the blacksmith. By the time the two owners had assembled this team and led it to the truck, the milky light of dawn had begun to reveal the outlines of everything—hilltops, cornstalks, and the animals' morose faces. This light made it easy to hitch the mules to the Dodge. Also to see its occupant, María de la Luz, who was the farmer's niece and the blacksmith's goddaughter.

"Why did not this Marilú run away to hide?" asked the people of Ibarra as soon as they heard the news. "And thus protect the reputation of the padre."

"He surely must have told her where to hide," they said. "Or led her to the hiding place himself. But this Marilú, in her arrogance, chose to defy the very man who might have saved her soul."

It took one month to complete the repairs to the pickup truck and during all that time the cura wore out his shoes trudging the rough lanes of Ibarra. As for Padre Ignacio, he was granted a vacation and at the end of this vacation was called to the parish of Todos Santos, one hundred kilometers away. To the people of Ibarra this place might as well have been situated on the map of another country.

Within a month, the bishop sent the cura an assistant priest so old and frail that he seemed to be standing at the very threshold of heaven.

When the cura first brought him to visit, Padre Javier had

sat silently on the Evertons' porch no more than five minutes when a hound, separated by two or three pounds from being a skeleton, trotted up to him, sniffed the skirt of his habit, and dropped at his feet. At first it appeared that the dog had come to this spot to die. He lay on one side with a single fang protruding from his mouth, his legs still bent in pairs as if he had been struck down in the middle of a race.

"Whose dog is that?" said Sara. "It needs a bath, for mange."

But none of them, the new padre, the cura, or Richard, could identify the hound.

Padre Javier was so old that it seemed he might decide at any moment to carry his body about with him no longer and discard it wherever he happened to be. On his cot at night perhaps, or at noon on the stones in front of the altar. Or here this afternoon on the chair where he sat, gazing at who-knows-what horizons beyond the actual horizon of mesas, hills, and mountains that was visible to the rest of them. Padre Javier had white hair which strayed in wisps and eyes so pale that the original color could only be guessed at. Had they once been hazel, brown, or gray? Now they were the color of wood smoke seen from so far away that no one could tell whether laurel was burning, or oak, or pine.

When it was time to go and Padre Javier stood up, the hound stood up, too, and walked close to the old man's heels down the drive. Halfway to the gate the two priests were intercepted by another dog, as tall as a mastiff, as gaunt as a coyote.

"That's the tax collector's Duque," said Richard. "We're about to see a fight."

But El Duque merely fell in next to the hound, and the two animals followed Padre Javier side by side like two cardinals behind the pope.

"His Excellency the Bishop has sent us another mouth to feed," said the cura's aunt, "and two hands so frail that they cannot drive your truck nor toll the bells for mass. And tell me if you can why the padre carries his plate of food with him from the table to his room."

Then the people of Ibarra began to notice that, in addition

to the street mongrels, more and more of the dogs that had masters were chewing through ropes and clawing footholds in adobe walls to be with Padre Javier. First they saw El Coronel, the grocer's watchdog, escape through the storeroom window to run after the old priest, then La Mariposa, the baker's bitch, then El Bandido, who lived under the counter of the post office, and then five others all named Lobo because they looked like wolves.

The Evertons, awake at six to meet the morning train in Concepción, caught sight of Padre Javier striding toward the abandoned monastery of Tepozán as if he were a much younger man. Eleven dogs accompanied him in a dignified manner.

"Why does he spend so much time at the monastery?" the Evertons asked each other. "Masses are said there no more than once a month."

The cura, posing the same question to himself, drove up one day to find out. Six enormous ash trees shaded the courtyard that was bordered on one side by a stone balustrade, on another by the ruined and roofless monastic cells, and on the third by the chapel that had survived the Revolution. On the steps outside lay a dozen dogs of variously mixed breeds. A few lifted their heads to watch the parish priest open the door a crack, look in from the threshold, close the door again, and drive away.

"He goes to El Tepozán to pray," the cura told his aunt. "The animals are left outside."

But some old women started to pray there too, perhaps because they remembered all over again how Christ, soon after the Conquest, had appeared in a tree at that spot and said, "Build a chapel for me here." Or perhaps they were curious to know if Padre Javier prayed out loud and, if so, to discover the subject of his prayer.

These old women came through the heavy door one by one and each gave it a push behind her. But their arms were like dry sticks and their fingers like brittle twigs, and by the time three or four had entered the door would be standing ajar.

So the animals who had waited outside until now began to

enter the chapel and, after they had examined the place, made themselves at home there. They lay under the pews near the altar where the padre knelt or sometimes stretched themselves out on the closest benches or curled up against the wall under the statue of María la Dolorosa or the statue of María la Purísima. When the old priest left the sanctuary they paced respectfully behind him without slashing with their teeth at one another or balancing on three legs to scratch at fleas.

Only a month had passed since the government veterinarian last visited Ibarra to inoculate the village dogs against rabies. "Now there's nothing to worry about," Sara said to her husband.

"Unless he missed a few," said Richard, and they remembered the scene on the baseball field, the doctor with his needle, the animals struggling against pieces of rope, lengths of wire, and an occasional leather belt.

"I must have the name of the dog," said the doctor, whose superb courage, like a suit of chain mail, protected him from mortal wounds.

And many dogs, nameless until this moment, were christened on the spot. El Capitán became their name, or El Conejo, or La Paloma. In those cases where nothing else came to mind they were pronounced to be El Lobo or La Loba.

On that day eighty-four dogs were immunized against rabies. And for every animal the owner was given a metal tag to attach to the collar he did not intend to buy.

One summer day after a rainstorm Sara Everton walked up the road, under the washed leaves of the ash trees, past the row of weather-streaked cells, and into the chapel of Tepozán. Through a window shaped like a rose and paned with clear glass, a column of sunlight slanted down on Padre Javier. Except for the dogs he was alone, without the usual congregation of midwives and crones. Although he spoke audibly, the American woman could not separate one word from another.

That evening she questioned Lourdes. "For whom is Father Javier praying?"

"For the souls of all Catholics living and the repose of all Catholics dead."

"There were twelve dogs in the chapel, occupying the seats closest to the altar. Remedios Acosta's Tigre was in the front row."

Lourdes was slicing an onion in the palm of her hand. "Padre Javier has looked so long in the direction of God that he has ceased to notice what is around him."

But the cura found out that even the Americans, who attached no importance to the customs of the church, were talking about the motley company that padded everywhere after the old priest and realized that the matter must be put before the bishop in Concepción.

"I will try to see His Excellency next Monday morning," the cura told his aunt.

"I believe those animals are eating the food I cook," said Paulita.

The events of that weekend, however, made it unnecessary for the parish priest to call upon the bishop. A few days earlier the potter's cousin had moved his family to Ibarra. Besides his wife he brought five children, a few chickens, a goat, and a listless dog with yellow teeth and one tattered ear. This dog was already sick but on Friday he went mad; and before he could be cornered and caught he bit two of the inoculated dogs and one who had not been present on the baseball field, a liver-spotted mongrel who was one of Padre Javier's Lobos.

This Lobo was not among the animals that trailed after the old padre to Tepozán on Sunday. But Padre Javier had not been long on his knees or the dogs settled down on the pews before the frenzied animal burst through the door of the chapel with half the men of Ibarra after him waving axes and clubs. Here at the altar, under the unfocused stares of the two Marys, this Lobo sank his teeth into the bowed shoulder of the priest.

To everyone's astonishment, Padre Javier did not die of the savage attack. The cura, without wasting a second, drove the old man to the city hospital of La Merced, where Padre Javier, in spite of his age, survived not only the shock of the assault but the agony of the treatment that followed.

After the violence in the monastery all the people of Ibarra prayed for Padre Javier. But the old priest was never seen to pray again, neither in the hospital of La Merced, nor later on in the hospice where he lived out the short span of the rest of his days.

"On whose behalf was the padre's last prayer in the chapel of Tepozán?" the people of Ibarra asked one another.

But it was impossible to know whether Padre Javier had prayed on that day for believers or heretics, blasphemers or saints. Or whether he prayed then, or had ever prayed, for those creatures who run across the latitudes and down the longitudes of earth, bent on errands of their own, unsuspecting of God.

7
The Red Taxi

Ibarra was a town of a hundred burros, half as many bicycles, one daily bus, and two automobiles. One of these cars belonged to the Evertons, the other to a former mayor. But the mayor set his Studebaker up on blocks outside his door after the tires and some engine parts were stolen.

The cura made the rounds of his parish in a Dodge pickup and the Malagueña mine had a pickup, too, as well as the ore truck that jolted down the mountain once a week with its load of dripping concentrates and climbed back empty a day later.

Except for the drivers and passengers of these vehicles, everyone here traveled from one place to another on the bus, or on a bicycle or burro, or on foot. And until Chuy Santos conceived his plan, no one in Ibarra understood that what the village had lacked was a taxi.

Chuy Santos was not the sort of man who would kill his two best friends in order to own a car. The part in his hair was too straight, his glance was too direct, and his voice was the voice of an archangel.

On Christmas, Ash Wednesday, Good Friday, and his saint's

day Chuy attended mass in the parish church of Ibarra, having confessed the previous day to his transgressions of the intervening months. The cura, on his side of the curtained screen, listened absentmindedly to Chuy's accounts of lust and avarice and said to himself, This man is Jesús Santos Larín, who should have been singled out as a boy and guided to the seminary. Such a voice should properly be an instrument of God. At the end of the confession the priest recovered himself and told Chuy to sin no more.

When the idea first came to Jesús Santos that he might establish a taxi service between the village of Ibarra and Concepción, he was the proprietor of a side-street café of four tables and twelve chairs. Here his wife knelt every morning to scrub the floor with a fiber brush while her hair fell over her shoulders into the greasy suds. Then she would cook tripe on a stove in the corner and set out twelve earthenware plates as if they might attract twelve diners.

Chuy did not confide to his wife his ambition to own a taxi. He only said, "This café might as well be situated at the entrance to the graveyard." Or occasionally, "I should have married a beautiful woman or a good cook, one or the other."

But when Chuy made these complaints he had already been to Concepción to visit a certain weedy piece of ground that was partly a used-car lot and partly a junkyard. He had only to walk two minutes along the ruts, stepping around rusty axles and inserting himself between crushed fenders, before he discovered the car that was to be his. It was a twelve-year-old Volkswagen with patched tires and a windshield so splintered that through it the sky and two huisache trees in full yellow flower and all the accumulated wreckage surrounding it appeared as fragments of precious gems. Chuy pulled open a door that hung loose from its hinges, sat behind the steering wheel between two coiling springs, and leaned from left to right. This motion caused the appearance and disappearance before his eyes of emeralds, amethysts, rubies, and a mosaic arch of sapphires over it all.

Chuy put his hands on the wheel and listened to his own arresting voice talking to itself.

"This glass will have to be replaced as a condition of purchase," Chuy heard himself say. "And the engine, of course, must be inspected. Another thing, what about the lights?" As though commanded by his own words he pulled out a knob and a single headlight lit up, as well as a weak bulb over his head.

"I will insist on a review of the entire electrical system," said Chuy, and as it indeed came about, the faulty headlight and one taillight were in time adequately repaired. But the left taillight, through an eccentricity of the wiring, never stopped blinking from the moment it was put in order. Because of the confusion caused by this unintended signaling, the Volkswagen later on became involved in a number of accidents, but none of these resulted in fatalities.

Nor could the bulb in the ceiling be turned off except by unscrewing it. Most of the time Chuy considered this to be more trouble than it was worth, so the light generally shone night and day. Those of Chuy's passengers who traveled after dark became accustomed to the continuous glow in which they sat faintly visible to all the world, like actors on a stage lit by fireflies.

Chuy discussed the purchase of his car with the two men in Ibarra who had been his best friends since childhood. Together they shared these things: the ability to keep a secret, the desire to become rich, and the same godfather. But this godfather had already died in an accident involving foolhardiness, pulque, and knives.

Like Chuy, whom the cura addressed as Jesús Santos Larín, these friends had three names. The first name their parents gave them at birth, then their father's last name, then their mother's family name, which would not succeed them, and, once carved on their gravestones, would be abandoned there. But there was no need to know the names of Chuy's friends. They had never been called anything but El Gallo and El Golondrino, the Rooster and the Swallow. These nicknames suited each man as neatly as a sheath fits a blade.

El Gallo had a big chest, chips of flint for eyes, and a habit of kicking at the ground wherever he stood, whether there were pebbles and clods underfoot or not. Had he actually been a rooster in a barnyard he could have claimed six hens. These were his wife, his second cousin Lili, the two Benítez girls, a woman in Loreto, and a woman in Lagos.

El Golondrino was small-boned and light as a tissue-paper kite on a gusty March morning. He could cross the plaza from one arcade to another and never be seen in passage. The Swallow lived alone in a mud house furnished with packing crates for tables and nail kegs for chairs.

Within three hours of his visit to the used-car lot Chuy Santos outlined his plan to El Gallo and El Golondrino. They met where they could have privacy, in the middle of an old stone bridge on the outskirts of the village. This bridge crossed the arroyo between two mining properties that, once gutted of pure silver, had been abandoned to cave-ins and rising water.

At first Chuy's friends listened in silence. Then they said, "What is the price of this car?"

Chuy looked up the arroyo past the low white house of the North Americans, past the old monastery, to the hoist tower of La Malagueña, the copper mine where El Gallo and El Golondrino worked underground.

"Twenty thousand pesos," said Chuy, "and three years to pay at 40 percent annual interest. Remember this. While we are buying the car we will be living on its profits." Then Chuy looked the other way, toward the bend of the arroyo and the nuns' school where the three men now on this bridge had sat at one desk in the first grade. "The down payment is a third of the total cost."

El Gallo scuffed at a stone block with his right foot.

Chuy went on as if he had studied law at the autonomous

national university. "As driver, the car will be registered in my name. As equal investors in the down payment, you will have your money back in one year and double it in the next. But first I will try to borrow the entire amount from don Ricardo, the American. He is a man who acts on impulse." Chuy smoothed his hair with both hands. "An example of this is his presence here in Ibarra. And the presence of the wife he brought with him."

The men leaned silently on the ancient balustrade of the bridge.

"What color is it?" asked Chuy's friends, and first Chuy said, "Like a tomato." Then, "More like fresh *vino tinto.*" He thought again. "Exactly the color of a cardinal's cape," and the other two nodded as if the Cardinal of Mexico had celebrated mass in the parochial church of Ibarra yesterday and emerged later on into the sun to prove to the mongrels on the steps the eternal verity of red.

On a cold starry evening Jesús Santos went to the house of the North Americans and stood outside the window of the dining room. Don Ricardo Everton and his wife, doña Sara, were inside, eating *chiles rellenos* and dividing a single bottle of beer between them. This economy seemed odd to Chuy, who knew that in the regular size Dos Equis cost only three pesos and was even less by the case. Wall lamps lit up the room and two unnecessary candles burned in green glass chimneys on the table.

There is no way to understand this señor Everton and his señora, said Chuy to himself. So rich and yet so poor. He tapped on the window and saw don Ricardo stop eating and cross the hall to open the front door.

From her place at the table Sara heard Chuy's voice and sat transfixed, listening, her beer glass raised in her hand. When the door closed behind the visitor she said, "Who is that man with the beautiful voice?"

"Chuy Santos," said Richard. He looked at his wife, who

was gazing abstractedly through the window into the dark. "But I have no idea if he can sing." For he had detected behind her eyes an image, a gathering of people in the walled patio under an April moon. There would be paper lanterns strung from trees, and roses and grapes on the vines. Notes of a guitar would scatter like a broken necklace on the tiles. Then the voice of Jesús Santos would pour into the night to astound the gentlemen in hand-tooled boots and the ladies in thin silk slippers.

Richard noticed all this unfolding in his wife's eyes and said, "Chuy wants to borrow twenty thousand pesos. For a taxi. Who knows if he can sing?"

Jesús Santos met again with his two friends on the bridge. "The American will not cooperate," he said.

El Gallo clapped his arms against his side as if he felt a chill. "Then we must acquire the money some other way," he said. He looked down into the arroyo where a few plastic bags and rusty cans had been cast away for the first heavy rains to float off to the valley. "I have an idea in connection with a tunnel at the mine," he said, and met the eyes of El Golondrino.

The Swallow said nothing. He picked up a rock from the bridge and with a single wide swing of his arm let it fly at an Orange Crush bottle twelve meters away, causing the glass to explode into tawny fragments that burned like coals on the sandy bottom.

"What do you propose?" said Chuy to El Gallo.

"I must discuss this matter first with the Swallow here," said the Rooster, and tapped his small friend on the shoulder. "But before we execute my plan, which is dangerous, we must try two other things."

"What things?" said Chuy.

"First you must go to the owner of the car and persuade him to lower the price. Then you must go again to the American and prove to him that the vehicle is now a bargain."

"I may or may not do these things," said Chuy.

The next morning he was waiting at the iron gate of the used-car lot when the owner pulled it open. The Volkswagen, looking brighter and more powerful than ever, was still there.

"I would like to try it out," said Chuy.

"Come back in one month," said the owner. "But leave a deposit."

Chuy pulled out a wad of money and from the top peeled off the two five-hundred-peso bills he had borrowed the day before from his father-in-law. These he held casually, as he would have held a losing lottery ticket or a burned-out cigarette. Now the dealer, all at once turned cordial, invited him to enter the detached cab of a truck which he used as an office. Here the two men bargained and at the end of an hour, half of talk and half of silence, the price of the car had dropped from twenty thousand to fifteen thousand pesos, the down payment to only five thousand.

They returned to the red Volkswagen, where Chuy stood a moment in reflection, his hand resting on the hood through which he felt the echoes of the engine's long career. He gave the dealer one of the bills.

"My restaurant business permits me very little time away," said Chuy. "I cannot return here for two months." And he gave the proprietor a second bill. "That is your deposit, to be applied against the down payment. But I must drive this car before I buy it." His palm still lay on the blistered paint. "And it must be in the finest condition." With this, Chuy lifted his hand and walked away.

He returned to the North Americans' house that afternoon and asked to speak to don Ricardo. He made his request of the señora who, bareheaded and wearing workman's pants, was standing on a stone wall three meters high to thin out the olive tree that stretched over it.

Soon she will be climbing the branches, thought Chuy, which, thin as she is, may fail to support her.

"*Buenas tardes,* señora," he said out loud.

Sara, halfway into the tree, her head sprinkled with silver leaves and her face with powdery dust, heard his voice and was struck motionless, holding a branch in her left hand, a pair of clippers in her right. She waited for him to speak again, and when he did not she disengaged herself from the tree and looked down. A web, with the spider curled tight at the center, hung from her shoulder.

"You are Jesús Santos," she said. From the wall she stared at the part in Chuy's hair, so exact it might have been plotted by instruments. "Do you sing?" she asked.

Chuy ignored this question. "Look, señora," he said. "I must speak to your husband."

"What about?" said the woman, making no move to descend from the wall, though a ladder was propped against it.

"A matter that can only be discussed with don Ricardo himself."

"He is working on the drawings of a new head frame for the mine and has asked not to be disturbed."

She is lying, thought Chuy. She wants no one to know that don Ricardo is ill again.

"*Otra vez la gripa?*" he said out loud in tones that seemed to have healing powers of their own. Above him the American señora denied this and set off a small rain of leaves which fell from her head down to his.

Leaves still dotted her hair as she descended the ladder and pulled the cobweb from her sleeve. "Is it about your taxi?" she asked.

"About my taxi, yes," said Chuy. "But the entire situation has changed as of this morning."

"Tell me," she said, and they sat down under an olive tree on a carved wooden bench with a cracked back.

"This car," began Chuy, and went on to describe it as he might describe a racing stallion, the ex-president's yacht, or the

Emperor Maximilian's festooned and gilded carriage, three things he had never seen. He noticed that don Ricardo's wife listened attentively to every word he spoke. When he paused briefly in his recital she said nothing and seemed only to be waiting for him to go on.

At last she spoke. "But who will your passengers be? To travel by bicycle or bus is much less costly."

"Señora, you have forgotten those to whom time is a matter of life or death. Those who, if they hope to survive, must travel by car whether they can afford it or not. Those with lungs that bleed and wounds that fester. You are not considering the damage inflicted by knives and guns, and by the maniacs at the wheels of trucks."

Sara remained silent.

"Think of this, señora," Chuy went on. "While the mine's van is delivering an accident victim to the hospital in Concepción, at the same time I, in my taxi, can deposit at the specialist's door the grandmother with the abscessed tooth, the infant with the club foot, the young wife who has been in labor for two days."

"Come back tomorrow afternoon," said doña Sara. "I will speak to my husband before then. But don't count on his support."

It is hard to move the hearts of these Americans, Chuy thought to himself.

Later the same day Chuy met his friends on the arch of the bridge. When they heard his report El Gallo looked toward the hills with eyes the color of lead and El Golondrino produced a slingshot, loaded it with a pebble, and killed a sparrow perched on the branch of a cottonwood.

To stiffen their resolve Chuy said, "Remember. The price is down and the American may yet support us in some way. Unless it is true that he is losing money on the mine."

El Gallo fixed the shards of his slaty glance upon his friend. "He is certain to be losing money. The *conquistadores* themselves could have found no profit in this ore." He kicked at a milkweed that had sprouted from a crack. "But all that is about to change. Eh, Golondrino?" and he poked the little man's ribs.

"Next week we will enter an unwatered tunnel where no one has set foot since the War of the Independence. This tunnel might as well have been excavated by an earthworm making a path through the roots of a cedar tree." El Gallo let forth a strident laugh. "It is so crooked that not a man working there will see the neighbor to his right or to his left." And El Gallo thumped his fellow miner hard upon the back.

"What is there to gain from that?" asked Jesús Santos, the restaurant proprietor.

"Precisely this," said El Gallo. "This tunnel intersects an unexplored deposit of silver. Not mere traces of silver but enough to be separated and weighed."

At these words Chuy heard a motor start up eighty kilometers away. He watched a car that was out of sight, beyond the mountains, split the countryside in two, dividing the landscape as a line of red ink would divide a map. He saw himself at the wheel of this car.

The next afternoon Chuy presented himself at the Evertons' door. To his regret it was doña Sara who opened it.

"Forgive me, Jesús," she said, as if she had committed an infraction of federal law. "There were so many . . . I had so much . . ." At this point her voice wandered off and was lost.

Chuy stared at her and said to himself, It is becoming increasingly difficult to communicate.

Finding a few words at last, she asked him to wait inside. Then she disappeared, closing two doors behind her.

He stood in the hall next to a scarred leather chest which in his opinion would have been better strapped to the back of a tinsmith's mule. On the chest was the señora's handbag. Also a wooden religious figure in poor condition, its painted robe scattered over with chipped roses.

"Who is this personage?" Chuy asked himself, speaking aloud since there was no one to hear. He gazed for a moment at doña Sara's bag, then back into the sunken eyes of the figure. "It is not San Juan, San Antonio, or San Francisco. It might be San Pedro without his keys." Again he considered the señora's handbag. "She is a reckless woman," he said, "to leave her valuables in open view, next to the unlocked door." Listening, and hearing two voices at a great distance, Chuy opened the bag. Then he turned his back to the figure on the chest, took from the wallet two five-hundred-peso bills, and folded them into his pocket.

Now footsteps approached from behind the closed doors. Chuy was disappointed for the second time to see the señora appear instead of the señor.

She brought the answer he anticipated. Don Ricardo refused to finance the Volkswagen and would promise only this, that if neither the mine pickup nor his own car were available he would depend on Chuy's taxi in the event of an emergency at the mine.

Then doña Sara said, "With all the warnings to miners and the posting of signs there should be no accidents. Even the dynamiting of tunnels is under the supervision of a cautious foreman. Therefore," she went on, "it is hard to believe an accident could occur." And Chuy saw that she had deposited her faith, all at one time, not in God but in the common sense, good nature, and predictable behavior of man.

"I imagine you can borrow the money to cover the down payment from any bank," said the señora.

What an imagination, thought Chuy. This woman probably notices faces in clouds, spirits in water, and words in the wind.

On the following Saturday Chuy, making an unscheduled visit to the church, sat across from the cura in the confessional booth. He had no sooner said, "Pray for me, father, for I have sinned," than the priest recognized him as Jesús Santos Larín and began to wonder if he might be taught to sing aves and alleluias.

First Chuy confessed to the ordinary vices, then he allowed a silence to fall, and finally said, "I came across two five-hundred-peso bills and kept them."

The cura concentrated with an effort. "Did you ask those around you if the money was theirs?" And when he was told there was no one in sight, the priest said, "In that case the two bills were yours to claim since the next passerby would have picked them up if you had not." Chuy was silent again and in order to listen a little longer the cura asked him how he would spend this money.

At that, Chuy entered into a complicated response, beginning with an analysis of the Volkswagen and ending with an account of the proposed taxi service, but the cura heard only the rich tones that conveyed this torrent of information.

The priest, who had a collection of old Victor records, identified Chuy's voice as tenor and soon found himself becoming fretful once again as to why he had been passed over for elevation to monseñor and eventually to bishop. For the present occupant of the episcopal throne had been a country boy like himself and they had entered the seminary on the same day. There was no more difference between them than between two pinto beans. A simple matter of politics, thought the parish priest as he listened to Chuy's resonant appraisals of pistons and valves.

Had I had the good fortune to be appointed bishop, the priest told himself, I might have attended the ecumenical council in Rome and from there traveled the length of Italy from Naples to Milan. And while Jesús Santos Larín explained one by one the rehabilitations his car would undergo, the cura removed himself from Ibarra, first to a tier of boxes at San Carlo *(Tosca)* and then to a red velvet seat at La Scala *(Bohème)*. When Chuy stopped talking the priest restored himself in a single second to his parish, absolved the penitent, and said, "It would be appropriate for you to make a donation to the church out of your new prosperity." Chuy accordingly, as he approached the warped and massive outer door, pushed ten pesos into the slot of a box marked FOR THE PROPAGATION OF THE FAITH.

From now on events that had merely crept began to surge ahead. El Gallo and El Golondrino put their plan into effect. Every morning after the daily dynamite blast they stationed themselves ahead of the others at the entrance of the tunnel under a sign that read: FOR YOUR SAFETY—LOOK, LISTEN, AND THINK BEFORE YOU ACT. As soon as the foreman gave his signal El Golondrino, guided by the lantern in his helmet, raced in faster than his Chichimeca ancestors could run at the height of their dynasty, located the most promising site, and claimed it until his friend arrived gasping a few paces behind.

Crouched against the dripping walls, their mouths bitter with the taste of explosives and metal, they ate their lunches of rice and *chiles*, drank Pepsi-Cola, and into the henequen bags that had held these things they stuffed all the ore they could take away without suspicion. At the end of eight hours they carried the vividly striped sacks out of the tunnel, into the hoist elevator, and off down the road as if they weighed nothing and it was only pots and bottles that made them bulge.

Each evening they met at the house of El Golondrino and here behind the shuttered window and bolted door transferred the day's accumulation of ore to a thick paper sack labeled CEMENTO AZTECA, S. A. Twice a week Chuy lifted these sacks to the top of the bus, where they traveled among baskets of pottery and trussed pairs of live turkeys to the town of Caballo Muerto. Chuy had a friend in Caballo Muerto who collected the sacks and delivered them to San Luis, where an associate was connected with the smelter. Payment for the silver came back at the end of every week by the same route the ore had taken.

After a month Chuy said to his friends, "We will need twice as much ore, or twice as rich ore, if we are to meet our obligation in thirty days."

El Gallo eyed him from profile. "There is only one way to get more," he said, and El Golondrino nodded.

After that Chuy's friends no longer waited for the signal to enter the tunnel. While the foreman held back the rest of the shift, the Rooster and the Swallow edged behind his back into the choking dust and drifts of rock until they saw silver.

Within three weeks the profits from the smelter doubled. When only seven days remained until the down payment was due, Chuy said, "We are still two thousand pesos short." But in this calculation he did not include the money he had taken from the American woman's purse. "You will have to get into the tunnel sooner in order to have more time to work the vein alone."

"Are you trying to blow us up?" said Chuy's friends.

On the morning of the accident Richard was alone in his office between the carpenter shop and storeroom of the mine. He heard the explosion and felt it under his feet, but the shuddering reverberation of a dynamite blast was as commonplace to him as the striking of a clock or the purring of a cat. When the hoist operator burst in, the owner of the mine looked up from a sheet of drawing paper with a compass still in his hand. The hoist operator might as well have spoken two words instead of a thousand. All Richard heard was, "Both dead."

Standing outside in a crowd of men he issued the necessary orders: "Notify the priest." And someone went. "Advise the state coroner." And another turned to go. "Let the families know and bring them here." But no one moved. "El Golondrino lived alone and the wife of El Gallo is visiting relatives in the state of Veracruz," said the men watching Richard.

These exchanges were only the monotonous accompaniment, as of muffled drums, to the hollow tolling of bells. "Both dead," rang the bells.

"Let me speak to the foreman."

"*Sí, señor,*" answered the crowd.

Tears had streaked the grime on the foreman's face. "But there is no way to explain it," he said. "Two experienced miners."

"You are blameless," said Richard Everton.

Before he left the mine he said, "Who were the closest friends of these men?"

"Chuy Santos," said the chorus around him. The closest friend of El Gallo and the closest friend of El Golondrino."

"Then ask Chuy Santos to come to my house this evening."

"*Sí, señor,*" replied the chorus.

The foreman spoke as Richard turned away. "Both dead," said the foreman.

The following morning Jesús Santos crossed the market square of Concepción and approached the coffin shop. When he entered La Urna del Oro still humming, the salesman came forward soberly and said, "If you have suffered a bereavement, may I extend my sympathy?"

But Chuy was already walking up and down the row of coffins designed to accommodate adults. Behind him, on the opposite wall, the small white ones intended for infants were stacked to the ceiling with a lid propped open here and there to expose a stitched pink or blue lining.

"Is it for a gentleman or a lady?" said the salesman.

"For a gentleman. That is to say, for two gentlemen," said Chuy.

"You are buying two caskets?"

"Yes, two. Identical in style and price. And in size, too, for that matter, although in one instance it will mean wasted space."

"To what extent will your finances allow you to honor these deceased?" asked the salesman, who had noticed Chuy's frayed cuffs and turned collar the moment he entered.

"It is not my money that will pay for these coffins," said Chuy. "It is the money of the mining company."

At these words the manager of the shop came out of the back room where he had been listening and said, "What mining company?" When Chuy said, "I represent the owner of the Malagueña mine in Ibarra," and showed a note to prove it, the manager sent the salesman on an errand to the upholsterer six blocks beyond the plaza.

"Are the caskets for the victims of yesterday's disaster?" asked the manager, who had read a full report in the morning *Heraldo.*

"Yes, for those two miners," said Chuy, "who might have been buried in the plain pine boxes made by the company carpenter and provided gratis. But in the cases of these men no families were at hand to choose between the pine there and the oak here."

"So the decision has been left to you, to choose and spend as you please."

"Yes, and this is why. The American owner, don Ricardo Everton, has taken the entire responsibility for the accident upon his own conscience, as though he himself had purposely lit a fuse to destroy two men."

"Here is our finest casket," said the manager. "Lined in tufted satin with a cushion for the head. Included is a satin quilt to pull up as you please and a full-length mirror inside the lid."

"A mirror," said Chuy, and he stood silent for a moment, considering the suitability of mirrors for El Gallo and El Golondrino.

"What is the price?" he asked.

"Four thousand pesos each."

"That is a great deal of money to sink into the ground," said Chuy. "And the Malagueña is not Anaconda."

The manager fell silent to meditate. He leaned back against a coffin. "If you will take these two the price will be three thousand each and the difference yours, for patronizing my shop."

Chuy wasted no time considering this offer. "Many thanks," said Chuy.

"The mining company will be billed the regular price of four thousand," said the manager. "Please sign this invoice."

After he left the Urna del Oro, Chuy stopped at the used-car lot and sought out the proprietor. "I will be here on Saturday for my car," he said.

"And you will bring with you the balance of the down payment, four thousand pesos," said the owner of the Volkswagen.

"Do you take me for a man who plays jokes?" said Chuy.

The taxi became a familiar sight to every settlement on the way from Ibarra to Concepción. Men plowing furrows and women baking bread watched as the red car appeared on the level stretches of road between vineyard and farm as suddenly as a drop of blood pricked from a vein. Goats and children fled from Chuy's path and pigs escaped by their native cunning alone.

If he had no other customers Chuy would crowd five men into the Volkswagen and, for two pesos each, drive them from the plaza of Ibarra to their shifts at the mine. Sometimes when he passed the Evertons' gate the two Americans were standing there and waved. Through the suffocating fumes of his exhaust they could see Chuy waving back.

"That car needs a ring job," said Richard.

"Chuy Santos was singing," said his wife.

For indeed it turned out that Chuy could sing. He sang all the Mexican songs ever written. When he proceeded from verse to verse of "Adelita" he transformed himself into Pancho Villa's soldier serenading the camp follower he loved. Chuy sang "Ojos Tapatíos." *"Todas las flores suspiran de amor,"* sang Chuy, and the roadside weeds seemed to languish as he passed. *"Bésame,"* sang Chuy, waiting for his passengers to emerge from the surgery in Concepción. *"Bésame mucho,"* and people on the sidewalk stopped buying newspapers and counting change to listen.

So that before long it was not only the people of Ibarra who recognized Jesús Santos Larín but many in Concepción and on the road between. And recognized the red Volkswagen, too, and even admired it, aware that it traveled on errands of mercy.

But Chuy had postponed the ring job. His exhaust continued to blacken the air and enshroud the two ghosts who trailed behind.

8

Parts of Speech

During her third Mexican autumn, when there was still a nuns' school in Ibarra, Sara walked through the plaza and along the alameda every Thursday to take Spanish lessons from Madre Petra. A few years later, accredited government teachers would supplant the nuns, and a new cura would pasture his cows in the convent patios and store his fodder in the classrooms. After that, there was no school where the children of Ibarra could learn both to spell their names and understand religion.

While Richard spoke more and more fluently in the accents of the miners who worked with him, Sara continued to speak incorrectly and without embarrassment her own flawed version of the language. When at last she noticed the grammatical precision of Mexican children barely able to walk, when she heard them utter their first word, "Mamá," and follow it soon after with the subjunctive, she arranged for weekly sessions with the madre.

To reach the nuns' school and its *sala,* narrow as a closet and cold as a cave, Sara picked her way between the ruts of a wagon road to the edge of the village. Once there, she had to pass two dozen adobe houses whose doorsteps lined the ditches as close as park benches bordering promenades. From behind fences of organ cactus patched with tangles of thorns, the family watchdogs ran out to bark. On the morning of her first lesson many housewives, unprepared, failed to reach their doors in time to observe her. But every Thursday after that they were waiting on their thresholds at eleven o'clock to watch her pass in one direction and again at twelve to see her return by the other. At each separate house, greetings were exchanged.

As a result of this, Sara said "*Buenos días*" twenty-four times on her way to school and "*Buenas tardes*" twenty-four times on her way home.

Madre Petra was seventy years old and had rheumatism. She walked with a cane. After inquiring for Richard and hearing Sara's quick answer, "He is well," the nun explained the parts of speech.

"These are nouns, señora." The madre pointed at the page with her left hand, from which the third and fourth fingers were missing. An accident with a door, Sara thought, or a windowpane.

"These are the verbs," said Madre Petra. "This is a list of possessive pronouns." Then she read examples of them all as if in English there were no such things.

The two women sat on stiff chairs at a blue table under pictures of the Sacred Heart, the Virgin of Guadalupe, and the pope. Sara, even at midday, was buttoned into a sweater. The nun wore a plain black dress and flat black shoes. A square of black cotton covered her head. Gone were the starched white wimple and bib, torn loose by the constitutional reforms of 1857, snatched off by the Revolution of 1910. Sara made slow sentences.

"My house is one kilometer from your school. Our well is dry. A burro brings our water from the Drunk Man's Spring."

"This water you and your señor boil and drink."

"No, it is too muddy. We drive to Loreto to buy bottles of pure water and tanks of butane gas. The water from the spring is for the bougainvillea and the Castile rose." Sara averted her eyes from the nun's maimed hand. "Loreto is a town so new it has no history, it has no trees. Have you been there?"

"Please write a sentence using the preterit tense," said the madre, and Sara put down in her notebook, The father of my husband was born in Ibarra and lived here as a boy.

Outside the single window a peach tree, still in October leaf, insulated a small patio and the *sala* itself from warmth. Under her scarf the nun's eyes gazed serenely out of her creased face, two stillnesses at the center of a hurricane.

"Where were you born?" asked Sara.

"For your next lesson please write a paragraph on an event of the coming week," said the nun.

As simply as this, without method or rules, the line of skirmish was drawn between the two women, one resolved to close off the past, the other to reject the future.

It was noon and the children dismissed by the mother superior had gathered to form a frieze at the window. Whole classes crowded at the entrance to watch the American woman leave, and the boldest among them followed her as far as the plaza. A few told her their names. Most of the rest clasped their homework to their chests in silence. But there were one or two who for no reason burst into such sudden laughter that they stumbled and fell down on the road.

By the end of a month Sara had written paragraphs about the explosion of the water heater and the strangling of the drains by pepper-tree roots. She read her compositions to the nun.

Madre Petra made corrections. "Your house, as well as the copper mine, suffered from disuse during the years since your husband's family left Ibarra."

Sara stared through the window at the peach tree which interfered with daylight as effectively as a palm-thatched roof. "But this house," she began. "The one Richard's grandfather built," and she tried to find words. "The walls and floors of it," she began again, and wanted to say, Richard scarcely sees their cracks and splinters. She was at a loss to explain. "And this town," she went on, and sensed its desolate, flat, earth-colored presence behind her. "Ibarra," she said, and stopped. She had wanted to say, If my husband could choose any place to live on the face of the globe, this is where he would put his finger.

"Let us turn to irregular verbs," said Madre Petra. "Please conjugate the verb, to know."

"*Sé*," said Sara. Then she said, "*No sé.*"

Later the same morning she interrupted a discussion of geography to ask, for the second time, "In what part of the country were you born?"

The madre hesitated. "On an hacienda."

"Which one?"

"The hacienda called Cinco Cerros." And, in case she had implied wealth of her own, added, "My father was a groom in the stables."

"And were there actually five hills?"

"Señora, you must try to roll your *r*'s," said the nun.

That evening Sara told Richard that the nun was born on an hacienda between five hills, and each one named for a bird. So that there were the Eagle, the Dove, the Vulture, and the Quail, and one more, the Lark. The original owner, who was granted the land from the king of Spain, believed the names would bring the birds. But of them all only the vulture flew over the hills.

Richard listened to all this. "You've learned more words," he said.

"Is it possible to visit the hacienda?" Sara asked the madre at her next lesson.

"The hacienda perished with the family who owned it."

"But the five hills, where are they?"

Madre Petra closed her notebook. "Until next Thursday," she said.

"The Spaniard and his descendants lie twice buried, in the ground and under their fallen walls," Sara told Richard that night in the kitchen. He measured rum into two glasses and filled them with ice.

"Twice buried," he repeated. "Fallen walls." He sat on the kitchen table and handed his wife a glass. "The madre's a poet," he said. "*Salud.*"

Week by week, between the study of accents and adverbial clauses, the indicative and conditional tenses, between diminutives and *ísimos,* Sara pried at the doors the madre had locked behind her. At the end of three months, in December, she pried one open.

When she asked if the hacienda workers were allowed holidays, the nun looked up from the page she was correcting and said, "Yes. There was a particular celebration every year, though I did not see the first one. I happened to be born the same day as the hacienda owner's only son. The fiesta that took place then was described to me so often I used to think I remembered it." She returned Sara's notebook and, to her pupil's surprise, went on. "Because of a coincidence all my birthdays were observed with fireworks and songs meant for someone else. Until the revolutionaries came." Then she found a list of abstract nouns and the lesson continued.

Sara believed there was more to be told. Details had been omitted. What of the flags and the tissue-paper garlands, the tuberoses on the chapel altar? Band music that shook ripe figs from trees?

Later on she described these things to her husband. "The *hacendado* himself hung a cedar wreath around the coat of arms carved above his door. The *mayordomo* fired off a thousand rockets between one morning and the next."

Richard examined her face. "Are you sure this is what Madre Petra told you?"

Sara thought of the convent *sala,* its sparse furnishings, the nun's seamed face, her crippled hand.

"It's what I heard her say."

As the lessons progressed Sara became uneasily aware of the erosion of areas she herself had sealed off. Within these guarded places were hidden all matters connected with Richard's health, and with the counting off of days and the sharpening of fear. When she spoke again of a trip to Loreto, the madre said, "It must be troublesome to drive so far simply to procure drinking water and gas." Without thinking, Sara answered, "This time I went alone. To place a telephone call." She was astonished to hear herself go on. "To a doctor in the United States."

Madre Petra was concerned. "Have you been ill?"

"No." Then, instead of suggesting, as the nun would in her place, Let us review the idioms, Sara recklessly continued. "I called about my husband."

"Is the señor ill?"

"No," said Sara. "He is working as usual at the mine. But last week he had an infection and a fever."

"You do not trust the doctors in Concepción to care for don Ricardo."

"They are excellent and highly trained. But the North American doctor is a specialist." And she almost added, impelled by her familiarity with the words, A specialist in diseases of the blood. *Enfermedades de la sangre,* she translated to herself.

"I will pray for him," said the madre.

Sara protested. "But he is well now." Through an open classroom door she heard the voices of children reciting multiplication tables in unison.

"Did the *hacendado's* son like to ride?" she suddenly asked.

The nun was caught by surprise. "Yes. From the moment the child Alejandro was first handed up to his father, Captain Velasco de Aragón, and the two rode down the avenue to the gates." The madre was quick to forestall further questions. "Señora, those years belonged to another life. The old images have faded, as God intended."

But on her way home Sara sketched in new outlines and filled the spaces with primary colors. At dinner she described the child's first ride to Richard. She said that when the captain's son was still an infant he rode in his father's arm through plantations of corn and alfalfa, through pastures where humped cattle buried their heads in grass, and up to the bullring. Here the father lifted his son to watch the apprentices wave red rags at the yearlings. At the house, servants collected on the steps to see for themselves if it was a braver child that returned than the one who had started out.

Richard tried to break in.

"No, let me tell you." Sara paused for the words she needed. "When the boy was six, he rode every day on his pony with the groom, Madre Petra's father. From the tops of the hills named for birds he looked out over the twenty thousand *hectáreas* of land and the house, built like a pink stone fortress, that would be his. He saw Indians clearing the plain, watched them chop cactus and walk barefoot through the spines."

Richard's hand was on her arm to stop her.

"But wait," she said. "When they returned to the house, the groom lifted the child down to his mother. 'What did you see?' she asked. And the boy said, 'Two rabbits and one iguana.' "

Richard stared. "Is that what the madre told you? In those words?"

"Almost," she said.

They had finished their fruit and their wine. Sara pulled Richard back as he started to leave the table, but she confessed to no fabrication. She simply held him there.

"Are you all right?"

"Yes," he said. "Why?"

By March and the twentieth lesson Sara had found out that Madre Petra lost two fingers of her hand when she was thrown from a horse.

"Did you ride much?"

"Only rarely, behind the stables."

"How old were you when the accident occurred?"

"Eighteen years. Señora, please give an example of the subjunctive used in a phrase contrary to fact."

"If it were still winter, the tree would not have flowered." Both women looked outside where a fading mat of petals covered the space between the walls.

"The haciendas were no better than feudal estates," said Sara. "It was time for a revolution."

"We in religion do not discuss the politics of Mexico," said the nun. "Is your husband in good health?"

"Naturally," said Sara. She did not say, Three more years remain of the time the doctor promised.

That night she told Richard, "As a girl Madre Petra helped her father exercise the horses. She rode sidesaddle in a long green skirt and embroidered blouse. She wore a man's sombrero."

"How do you know?" Richard sounded impatient.

They were sitting on the porch under Orion and a sky of other stars. When there was no answer, Richard went on. "Even assuming some of it's true, the rest is your invention."

His annoyance was clear. Sara stretched her hand toward him.

"The madre asked how you were."

"Did you tell her?" said Richard.

Sara studied with Madre Petra for ten months, her lessons interrupted twice by vacation weeks and twice by visits to the North American doctor. In Morelia, Michoacán, where the vacations were spent, streams rushed down hillsides and wild orchids grew from trees.

"Morelia is a city of carved wood and stone," she told the nun. "In spring the streets turn purple with jacarandas. For each rainstorm we have here, there are five in Morelia."

"Then, thanks to God, here in Ibarra we are permitted more sun."

Sara thought of reservoirs drying in from the edge and street dogs panting with thirst. "The animals," she said, and had started to speak of their plight when a new idea came to her.

"Perhaps your accident happened when one of the captain's hunting dogs frightened your horse."

"No," said the madre. "Not a dog."

"Were you alone? With no one to help you?"

"I was not alone." The nun looked from the *sala* window into the curling summer foliage of the peach tree, which had already been stripped of its hard pale fruit. "Is the North American doctor satisfied with don Ricardo's recovery from his recent infection?" asked the madre.

In the second before she answered the nun's question Sara had time to travel two thousand miles and enter the hematologist's office, time to sit for half an hour with the silent relatives of other patients. When Richard emerged from the laboratory rolling down his left sleeve, he held a slip of paper in his hand. Outside the office he and Sara read the report. "Only 22,000," they said of the white count. Or, on another occasion, "58,000. But there's the new medication."

Resuming her place in the convent *sala* after this second's lapse, Sara answered the nun. "Yes, he is," she said. "The doctor is quite satisfied."

She told her husband at dinner it was not a dog that had caused the madre's horse to shy. Therefore it was a rattlesnake or a coyote. The girl Petra was thrown, not in the exercise ring behind the stables, but somewhere out on the plain that stretched to the five hills.

"I see," said Richard.

"She was not alone at the time," his wife went on. "Eighteen years old and beautiful as the Malinche of Cortés. Her father saw to it that none of the laborers' sons approached her.

He broke the nose of one and loosened the teeth of another."

"That's what the madre told you," said Richard. He pushed back his chair.

"Listen," she said. "The only son of Captain Velasco de Aragón was a boy Petra's father couldn't hit." Sara watched a candle burn bright, dim, then bright again. "This is what happened." And she explained to Richard that on the day of the accident a horse was saddled and ready to mount when the *hacendado's* son sent the groom off for a riding crop. When Petra's father returned, the horse was gone, also his daughter, also the captain's son.

"You heard this from the nun." His voice had hardened.

Sara leaned toward him across the table. "But surely you can see that this is how it must have been."

Richard stood up. His eyes had turned marine blue and the old scar across his cheek stood out white against his skin.

Sara was late for her next lesson and half ran the kilometer between her house and the school. She stumbled into ditches and slid on gravel, and finally tripped over the root of a stump and fell to her hands and knees. Her notebook and dictionary lay open in the dirt, exposing their rules and definitions to a red flycatcher in passage from a roof to a huisache tree.

From where he lay against the threshold, Remedios Acosta's blind old dog, El Tigre, lifted his head to listen. Remedios herself stepped from her dooryard to the road. "What a barbarity," she said. "Look at your torn skirt. Look at your scraped palms."

Five minutes later, sitting discomposed and grimy in the habitual twilight of the *sala,* Sara told the nun that the lesson after this one must be her last.

"So you believe you understand the language and its irregularities," said the madre. She laid both her hands with their eight fingers on the table as if it were a trunk she had packed and locked.

"You have taught me the usages most important for

communication." Sara noticed that the leaves of the peach tree were powdered with the dust of June. "I must stop because during the next weeks visitors are coming, geologists and engineers."

"And when will you travel next across the frontier?"

"Not for several months." And once again Sara removed herself to the doctor's waiting room two thousand miles away and watched Richard come out of the laboratory rolling down his sleeve.

"Don Ricardo is well then," said the nun.

Sara listened for a child's recitation from a classroom but the doors were closed. "On the hacienda, when you were a girl, did you ever ride as far as the hills?"

"The horses were for the pleasure of the *hacendado's* family."

"Was the captain's son a good rider?"

"I used to see him on his buckskin," the nun began. Then she stopped and said only, "Yes. Both were fine horsemen, the captain and his son."

"Did you ever ride the buckskin?"

"Señora, it is as difficult to recapture the past as it is to prefigure the future."

At eleven o'clock that night the Evertons were reading in bed. Sara closed her book on one finger and said, "Now I have found out everything."

"Good," said Richard, without looking up.

"About the madre and the *hacendado's* son."

Richard laid his open book, pages down, on the blanket. He said, "I see."

"The day the groom discovered the buckskin horse and both of them gone was in July and hot. Mirage pools formed and dissolved on the plain." Sara said that Alejandro, as he rode off, had pulled Petra up in front of him and that her skirt whipped back like a green flag against his leg. Her hair came loose, her hat blew off, and the groom's daughter held tight to the captain's son until they reached the farthest hill, the one where the lark was never seen. Under an oak behind this hill Alejandro and Petra lay together until evening.

Richard made no comment.

"All one afternoon they lay there," said Sara.

When Richard spoke, there was something unfamiliar in his tone, an edge of outrage. "It's unthinkable that the madre told you this," he said. "Either in these words or any others."

"But let me tell you." Sara sat straight up and faced him. "It was on their way back to the stables that a coyote broke out of the brush like a running gray mist and crossed in front of them. The buckskin shied and they were thrown. Alejandro released the reins, but Petra couldn't let go. That's how she lost two fingers."

Richard turned away from her. He said, "I'm married to a clairvoyant," and picked up his book. They read for half an hour without speaking, and both at the same time put out their separate lamps.

For five minutes they lay silent in the dark. Then Richard spoke. "Do you believe the doctor will find a cure for me?"

Sara drew a long, careful breath. "He might."

"Don't count on it," said Richard. He turned and reached for her. "Please don't count on it."

On the Thursday of her last lesson Sara cut a sprig of mint and a rose from her garden and tied them with a twist of purple string for the nun. At each house she passed that morning, the woman sitting at the door or sweeping the empty dirt in front of it said, "Wait." Then each of them, understanding the flowers were for the madre, picked a nasturtium or a lily from her row of pots and thrust it out to Sara. There were so many of these offerings that when she entered the *sala* and presented them to Madre Petra they seemed to kindle in her hand.

Sara read her homework, a paragraph describing preparations for the visitors. At the nun's request, she composed a sentence including both the perfect and imperfect tenses. "While I was driving to Loreto yesterday, a bird flew into my windshield and was killed."

"You have had to telephone again from Loreto," said the madre.

Sara picked up a fiery geranium, considered it, and put it down. "When did the revolutionary armies seize the captain's house?"

"Only a few days after my accident. My hand was still bandaged."

"Couldn't the hacienda protect itself behind its own walls with its own guns?"

"Señora, I remember this. That when the first rebel shot was fired, the Indians who had worked whole lifetimes for a sack of corn and one peso a week ran in from the fields waving pitchforks and hoes. Side by side with the insurgent cavalry they attacked the house of Velasco de Aragón."

"And the captain's son, was he saved?"

But the madre only said, "That same day the hacienda priest, whose parish was about to be stripped from him, took me to the nuns in the provincial capital. It was there, señora, more than fifty years ago, that I learned the rules of grammar I have been teaching you."

Outside the *sala* the peach tree scattered down its wilted leaves. Inside the room the two women seemed to have nothing more to say. The silver ringing of the mother superior's bell announced noon, and half a minute later the window was fringed with children's faces.

Madre Petra paused at the *sala* door. "I prayed for your husband in our chapel this morning. For his lasting good health."

"You are kind," said Sara. But she was not grateful. She was angry. She considered the nun's prayers an intrusion, a threat to the act of will she herself daily performed on Richard's behalf. Remote as from another planet, she heard her own voice stiffly thank the madre for the lessons, her time, her patience.

As Sara walked away from the school with the second and

third grades trailing behind, the nun called after her. "Review the idioms with your husband. Practice the parts of speech."

By the time the last child had dropped from the procession and the last "*Adiós*" been spoken, Sara's fury had subsided.

But no more than halfway home here was Remedios Acosta at the roadside, holding out a glass jar. It was filled with a cloudy liquid and rich beads of fat. Floating in it was a chicken's foot, crusted with scales.

"Broth for don Ricardo," said Remedios. "To prevent another attack of grippe."

Sara acknowledged the jar as she had the madre's prayers, in a flat tone that was not hers. And to the same extent that she rejected the prayers, she rejected the broth.

Beyond the edge of the village and as if in answer to her dilemma she encountered Remedios's blind dog, El Tigre, rubbing his back against the rough bark of a tree. When she spoke to him, he turned slow, white-filmed eyes in her direction. But she called his name until he followed her behind a wall of rubble. Here she opened the jar The dog lapped ravenously at its contents, but in the end she had to spill the liquid out and reach in with her fingers for the hen's foot. El Tigre swallowed it with a single contortion of his throat and his tail wagged of its own accord

"Now you will see again," she told him, and hid the jar under some broken adobes.

She had passed the water carrier and his burro at the Drunk Man's Spring and almost reached the corner of her own high wall when she began to narrate to herself the details of the storming of the hacienda. As though Madre Petra had described it all, Sara knew that five hundred shouting insurgents had galloped in, half of them bareback. Within ten minutes they had killed the guards, two house servants, and an Indian *peón* who crossed the line of fire as he rushed from the threshing room to join the revolution.

The *hacendado,* Captain Velasco de Aragón, was disarmed at

his iron-grilled outer door. From here he witnessed the ravaging of his house and the liberation of his serfs. He saw his mother's portrait slashed and bottles from his wine cellar broken open on the keyboard of the Bechstein piano. After the rebels had drunk, they handed the bottles to the Indians, who washed the dirt from their tongues and the grit from their throats and for the first time laid their hands on cut velvet and set their feet on tapestried rugs.

Velasco de Aragón, held at gunpoint, looked on as the ragtag troops led his horses, tossing and dancing, from the stables. The groom, as he had on occasions of house parties, carried out silver-trimmed saddles, two at a time. Alejandro had come to his father's side to watch the new masters mount.

When at last the buckskin was brought to be saddled, the captain's son stepped forward. He still believed his word had power. He shouted, "Stop!" A dozen pistols took aim in warning. Alejandro, as if he had inherited immunity from his ancestors, ignored them. "Get back," ordered the soldiers of the people's army. He advanced in spite of them and they shot him.

At this, the captain, too, disobeyed commands and ran out to his son. Because of his own obstinacy, he also was killed. Hours later, when the girl Petra was taken away by the priest, the two still lay not far apart on ground that had blackened with their blood.

By now Sara had arrived at her gates. Between them and her front door she confronted and stripped off illusion. The scene she just created may have revealed itself as myth. Or it may have been that for the first time, having found herself too occupied before, she noticed how a month's drought had reduced the countryside. Up and down the face of the hill, goats cropped dry stems and thorns. The arroyo had run dry. Long after a truck passed on the road, dust hung in the hot, still air.

She would say no more to Richard of the hacienda's pink

bastions and its hopeless fields and paths. And, together with one fantasy, she renounced another.

Until this moment she had refused to consider the sort of future that included hospital rooms and nurses, that threatened emergencies and an ambulance. She had denied a whole vocabulary of words: radiation, transfusion, hemorrhage. Until today she had convinced herself Richard might be spared them all.

Standing here at noon on the long covered porch, with her lists of double negatives and dependent clauses, she relinquished her right to have her way. None of it would happen as she had willed it. The magic pill would not be found. Richard would not recover.

And she knew it was unlikely that some windless morning or brilliant afternoon he would simply get up from the desk or come in from the road, lie down on the window seat, the bench, or the bed, and without even closing his eyes say, "Now."

9

The Thorn on the Blown-Glass Lamp

"A geologist and an engineer are coming at the end of July," Sara told Lourdes. "They will sleep in the room with the round straw rug. I have just made their beds. Why were these under the pillows?" She opened her hand.

"Two blue buttons," said Lourdes. She tucked them among the tangle of raveling spools in her sewing box.

"The Americans are removing the charms from every corner of their house," said Remedios Acosta. "They have no faith in them. Not in the threads and pins any more than in the holy objects of the church."

She was sitting on her doorstep to observe the excavations for the president's new drains and knitting as if her fingers had eyes. Two women with baskets and an old man on a crutch had gathered in front of her to receive this information.

"Everything María de Lourdes left in the drawers and cupboards to ensure their safe return after a month's absence has been discovered by the señor and señora," said Remedios, "and by now thrown out with the rubbish."

"What were these things?" asked the bystanders.

"Lourdes will tell you." And Remedios's knitting needles stabbed with precision at the yarn.

All that Remedios said was true. The day after their return in May from a trip to California Richard Everton noticed a bent hairpin on top of his slide rule and Sara a slice of stale bread between the folded dish towels.

She found Lourdes hanging out socks behind the house.

"What are these?" she said, and displayed the objects, one in each hand.

"A hairpin," said Lourdes, "and a slice of bread."

"How did they get among the towels and on the señor's desk?"

"Who knows?" said Lourdes.

That evening the Evertons, sitting on a colonial bench in the *sala,* both at the same time noticed a red thread extending the length of the bookcase from *Viva Mexico* to *A Handbook of Metallurgy.*

When Lourdes arrived from the village the next morning Sara met her in the hall. Without speaking, she held out a red twist in the palm of her hand.

"That is embroidery thread," said Lourdes.

"Why on the books?"

"Who is to say?" Lourdes reached for the thread and pushed it deep into her apron pocket.

Remedios Acosta said, "The books of the Americans are written in English and no one in Ibarra, not even the cura, can be sure what is in them. Lourdes says the señor and señora read their separate books, then stare out the window for ten minutes at a time. They look through tree trunks, the stone wall, and the hill across the road." Remedios went on to explain this behavior to her friends. "The señor is concerned for the success of his mine and whether he will run out of ore, but the señora has other thoughts. We will see her soon in the clinic or the schools, presenting her ideas about window screens and boiled milk."

The bell in the church tower tolled for midday mass and Remedios rose.

"Why screen the windows if one cannot screen the plaza where most of our time is spent? And we have only to look around us to see aged men and women who never thought to boil their water or their milk." Remedios took a few steps in the direction of the church, then paused to speak of the government's recent campaign against polio.

"It is true that many mothers brought their sons and daughters to the doctor. But what of all the rest who sent their older children off to the hills and hid the little ones under the bed?" Remedios covered her head with a saffron rebozo. "In the same manner," she said, "these parents will resist the señora's school enrollment program."

A Canadian geologist and a Lebanese engineer who was born in Durango arrived at the Evertons' house on the last day of July and stayed for a week. Every morning the geologist stood beside Sara in the kitchen as she scrambled eggs over the butane gas burner. He spoke at first of the woods and lakes to which he would return and, after a few days, of his wife, voted most beautiful by her graduating class and now, a decade later, forty pounds heavier.

"She eats in secret," he told Sara as she transferred the eggs to the plates. "She hides chocolate creams behind the spices."

In the dining room the Lebanese engineer and Richard talked in Spanish about levels and flooding, about pumps, air compressors, and drills. Richard made notes on graph paper. He wrote down everything the engineer said and when one page was filled with figures he started another.

Sara and the geologist brought in the eggs. As she took her place at the table Sara examined her husband's bent face for signs, if not of optimism at least of lessening care. But his eyes were still the eyes of an explorer who had struck out across the desert without water in the direction of a receding mirage. Richard took a third cup of coffee and added the columns again. If his thoughts had been handed to her in print, Sara would have read them no more easily than she did now. To buy the recommended equipment he must ask the bank for another loan, and he already knew he must borrow to meet next month's payroll which supported a hundred men.

They left the table and the engineer approached Sara as was his custom after every meal. "A thousand thanks," he said, and made a formal bow.

She handed her husband a paper bag that held six bananas and three sandwiches of meat and hot *chiles*. The men intended to stay out on the hills all day.

"You are too gracious," said the engineer.

Sara envied them their hours on the July hillsides, wandering through shrunken cactus from one withered slope to another. Paralyzed with drought, the whole landscape would lie around them in suspension, the gullies adrift with dust, the dry grass sheltering seeds as small as grains of salt, ready to sprout up green the day after the first rain. But now there would be no flowering weed or crawling snake to distract the three men. The sun, stationary at high noon, would lie hot on their backs, and they would breathe air so still and thin it would only half fill their lungs.

"This air is affecting us all," Sara said to an empty room. "Everything is too intense, too quick, and too perilous." She looked through the wall toward the mountain, Altamira, where she imagined Richard pulling himself by scrub oak branches up the steepest incline.

Moving to the window, she saw Luis, the gardener, at the top of a pepper tree, hacking at dead wood with a machete. She went outside and stood below him.

"Shall we transplant the small jacaranda today?"

"That work will be better done in two weeks," said Luis.

"Why?"

"Because of the moon, señora."

One morning the Canadian brought four pinto beans to the breakfast table. "These were between my shirts," he said.

Richard passed them to Sara. "You figure them out. Tell us what Lourdes means this time."

Health to us all, Sara wanted to say. Rain and a fine crop of corn in the valley. Tunnels lined with copper in the Malagueña mine.

"Well, what?" said Richard. "What do these things portend?" He spoke sternly from across the table, then laughed for the first time in three days. If he had been sitting beside her, and the other two gone, he might have kissed the palm that held the beans.

"It means this," Sara said to the Canadian. "That you will travel safe and return here often. That your wish will come true."

The geologist's eyes were on her.

The chocolates will be gone, she promised him silently. Your wife will be thin.

"The visitors have been here for a week," Lourdes told Remedios, "searching for metal with their maps and instruments." The two women were sitting on a bench in the plaza, waiting for the church bell to ring vespers.

"With nothing more than machines and books they expect to find ore," Lourdes went on. "With pills alone they expect to cure don Ricardo of the grippe."

"It is not grippe," said Remedios. "It is his heart. He has an illness of the heart."

The last dinner with the engineer and the geologist turned into a celebration, not of the discovery on the hills of gold overlooked by the Spaniards, but of traces of copper and hints of silver rich enough to bring back hope. While the men tramped over the slopes, avoiding dwarf cactus that could pierce their boots, they had stumbled on unexplored outcroppings and chipped off rock samples with their picks. That evening the geologist brought his sample to the dining room and kept it at his place while he ate his chicken and drank his wine. Later in the *sala* he held it in one hand while he lifted a brandy glass with the other.

Meanwhile Richard composed in his mind the final draft of his letter to the bank regarding a loan. Already he could feel the thick envelope, bulky with the favorable reports of professionals. He began to talk to the engineer about the clearing of tunnels and the laying of track.

The geologist sat apart in a corner of the room under the blown-glass lamp. He was so still, so absorbed, he might have been holding, instead of unproven ore, the philosopher's stone that could turn base metals to silver and gold, and prolong life as well. He had banished his wife to the woods beyond the Canadian lake and a single metamorphic relic was his universe.

Sara understood this passion that beset geologists. Their minds were heavy with theories shaped by fire and water, their pockets weighted with residual bits of evidence chipped from road cuts and canyon walls, identifiable, able to be pigeonholed in time that stretched back five hundred million years. She understood that the rock in the Canadian's hand was likely to endure intact long after the bones of the four people in this room would be discovered set in sandstone among snail shells and ferns.

At midnight, three hours after Sara had driven Lourdes back to the village, the men got up from their chairs.

The geologist spoke for the first time that evening. Pocketing his piece of ore, he said, "Thanks. Good night."

At breakfast Sara and the Canadian stood together for the last time over the thickening eggs.

"If no one was with her, my wife would eat all these and the eight slices of toast besides," said the geologist.

Sara only said, "But you will soon be with her," and divided the eggs on four plates.

By midafternoon the conferences had ended. The visitors loaded their duffel bags and instruments into a battered Jeep.

The geologist had lined the floor on his side with ore samples. "Many thanks," he said, and shook hands with the Evertons while his eyes searched out faults and dikes on the scarred hill across the road.

"I will hold this visit in my memory." The engineer bowed twice and took the driver's seat. He had no sooner started the motor than the thumping of drums and the rattling of bells ruptured the quiet outside the wall.

"What's that commotion?" said the geologist, jolted against his will from the Mesozoic era into the present.

"A procession," the engineer told him, and all four of them looked down the driveway to the road.

At the head of the procession marched a child wearing the tunic and long skirts of an altar boy. He struggled to support a staff topped by a gilded cross that swung and dipped above his head. A few paces behind him strode the cura in his habit, surplice, and stole. Strung out behind the priest followed a dozen male dancers wearing only breechcloths and feathers. Bracelets of bells rang from their wrists and ankles. Their hands beat drums that hung from their necks and their bare feet pounded the dust of the road. Each danced a tight circle of his own and the advance of the procession was slow.

"There's Paco Acosta and Pancho Reyes," said Sara, recognizing friends among the Indians and controlling an impulse to wave.

Behind the dancers trailed a crowd of men, women, and children. From its ranks a familiar figure detached itself and entered the Evertons' gate.

"Lourdes, what is it? What is happening?" asked the Americans.

"As you see, señores," said Lourdes, "the cura is leading the *matachines* as they perform a rain dance. They have danced all the way from the plaza and will dance as far again to the chapel of Tepozán. There the cura will conduct a service and pray for rain."

The Lebanese, the Canadian, and the two Americans lifted their faces to scan the cloudless sky.

Rain started to fall before midnight. At breakfast the Evertons looked out on streaming tiled paths and hanging pots that dripped from the wall.

Richard opened the newspaper, published the day before in the state capital, delivered to Ibarra by the evening bus, and brought to the house by Luis this morning. He looked first at the metal prices of the preceding day, and then at the weather forecast.

"Listen to this," he said. "A tropical storm that will break the drought is expected to reach here by evening." He glanced at his wife. "What do you think? Did the cura pick up a copy of the *Heraldo* in Concepción yesterday morning?"

"No," said Sara. "It's a coincidence."

Remedios Acosta told her friends, "The same day the geologist and the engineer left, don Ricardo walked to the mine in the rain and now he is in bed with a fever. This is the third time in one year he has had an infection. We will know it is serious if the señora drives away by herself to place a long-distance call to the North American doctor."

She measured the blanket she was knitting for her first grandchild. "When the time for the birth comes, I myself will assist Paz. Only if there are complications will Polo, the *curandero,* be summoned."

Remedios's steel needles shot off spears of light. "If the Americans had not spoken so often against *brujos* and *curanderos,* I would take Polo to the Casa Everton today. But I already know that don Ricardo would choose to perish, and his wife permit it, before either of them would receive a *curandero* at their door."

She had been speaking to the grocer's wife and sister, but now she rose abruptly and stuffed her knitting into a straw bag.

"Perhaps I will walk up there before the summer is over," she said, "with a few leaves and flowers from my own plants, known to cure such illnesses as send don Ricardo to his bed. It is possible that the señor and the señora will accept these herbs, since they have the same ones growing in their garden."

Remedios started in the direction of her house. "But they think these plants are weeds."

Long before Remedios brought the curative herbs, Richard's fever had dropped to normal. He had been notified of the bank's decision that its money would be safe with him and he spent all the daylight hours at the mine. On the afternoon preceding a new moon Luis transplanted the small jacaranda, which not only survived its uprooting but, three months out of season, bloomed.

"I've seen that color in hyacinths," said Sara. "Or in a church window somewhere."

"No, not quite," said Richard. "But I saw a streak of it yesterday in a new cut on the fifth level."

By the time Remedios came, Sara had transferred her energy to the house and was rearranging furniture and lowering pictures. She emptied drawers and reorganized them. This was done without the help of Lourdes, whose wish it was that the señora would cease her dusting of objects and investigation of corners. Lourdes would have liked the señora to spend the day in the garden, digging and pruning, the occupations that suited her best.

But Sara remained in the house and even dragged a ladder into the *sala*. Holding a soft cloth, she mounted the steps to dust the blown-glass lamp. The lamp was shaped like a very large melon, its sections bound by wrought-iron strips, and no two people agreed about its color. "It is green," one would say. "It is gray," said another. But it always reminded Sara of a shallow ocean wave in September at low tide.

From the top of the ladder she clung to the chain above the lamp and wiped at the glass with her cloth. Almost immediately she discovered that one section was cracked along its length. Then she noticed at eye level a matchstick or nail or twig on top of the lamp. But it was none of these, she found as she lifted it off.

It was a thorn, and not the thorn of a nopal cactus or a rose, but a thorn cut from the pointed tip of a maguey leaf, cut by a knife and whittled into a two-inch stiletto. With the thorn in her hand she descended the ladder.

Lourdes was boiling ears of corn.

"I have found this thorn," said Sara, "and I have also seen the crack in the blown-glass lamp. I believe the thorn was placed there to prevent me from noticing that the lamp was damaged."

Lourdes said nothing.

"I am sure it was an accident," Sara went on. "Perhaps it happened when you were reaching for cobwebs with the long broom. All of us sometimes break things. What I cannot understand is your belief that this thorn could keep me from finding out."

Lourdes turned down the flame and covered the pot. She faced the American woman.

"It is true that the thorn failed to prevent your disappointment," said Lourdes. "But señora, consider this. The engineer and the geologist who visited here a month ago succeeded in finding the means to keep the mine from shutting down. Then don Ricardo himself let it be known that he had received good news from the bank. And as you will remember, the señor recovered quickly from his recent illness. All of these things happened while the thorn was on the lamp."

Sara did not reply. With Lourdes's eyes upon her, she crossed the kitchen to drop the thorn among the crumpled paper of the wastebasket.

Within an hour Remedios appeared on the porch with a handful of pungent weeds.

"Please accept these plants," she said. "They have been known to cure sickness since long before the Spaniards came. Next time don Ricardo is ill, try this one," and she pointed to a tough gray stalk.

"Thank you," said Sara. She laid the coarse leaves and shriveling flowers on the red chest in the hall. Then she found her garden clippers. "I want you to have cuttings from my geraniums," Sara said.

At five o'clock Lourdes and Remedios walked out the gate together. Sara, alone in the house, examined the herbs on the chest. Remedios had left no directions for their use, no clues as to whether they should be taken internally, applied externally, steeped in vinegar or honey, eaten cooked or raw. But if Sara wanted to know, she had only to ask Lourdes.

She filled a tortilla basket with Remedios's plants and took it to the *sala*. Here she set it down next to the fragment of a pre-Columbian figure. Still life with idol, she would tell Richard.

At six o'clock he was still not home, nor at seven. When evening darkened into night, Sara went to the kitchen and lit a lamp. She found the contents of the wastebasket untouched, the thorn plainly visible against a paper towel. Sara looked at her watch. Seven-thirty, and the mine offices closed since five.

Oh, where is he? she wordlessly asked the stove and refrigerator.

Ten minutes later he came into the kitchen and caught her standing at the window with the maguey spike between her thumb and finger.

"What's that?" he said, and took it from her hand.

Sara described the discovery on the blown-glass lamp. "Lourdes believes it will protect the house and the mine."

"Good God," said Richard. He tossed the thorn into the basket of trash.

"What next?" he said. "What next?"

10
The Night of September Fifteenth

Believing as they did in a relentless providence, the people of Ibarra, daily and without surprise, met their individual dooms. They accepted as inevitable the hail on the ripe corn, the vultures at the heart of the starved cow, the stillborn child. But when they heard that Basilio García had killed his brother, Domingo, everyone in the village said, "It is a lie."

At this time the brothers lived with their mother in a house that was dissolving with the rain and scattering with the wind. Domingo was ten years younger than Basilio and still had his first teeth when his brother began to bring home money that he earned. Their mother, Concha, surrendering each slack day to the next, sat on her doorstep and allowed the hens and chickens, and even the goats, to enter the house. Rice soups and sorrow had made her so fat the mattress of her bed sagged like a hammock. She still mourned her husband who, three months before Domingo was born, went to the city to find work, encountered love instead, and died of a disease.

On a gusty March afternoon when Basilio was twelve, he walked behind the hill of San Juan through whirlwinds of topsoil to the Paradiso mine, which had not operated since the Revolution. Here he climbed down the shaft on the loose rungs of old ladders to the first level and filled a sack with rocks that were lying near the opening. The next day he took a candle and a bigger sack. At the end of a week he showed his pile of rocks to don Emilio, who bought ore.

Don Emilio looked at them and said, "Choose the best and put them in one sack," and when this was done, he said, "The Paradiso is mined out above and flooded below. If you want to recover some high-grade ore, go to the Socorro dump. I will buy anything this good or better." And he tapped his foot against the selected rocks. He lifted the sack into his truck and paid Basilio five pesos. "From now on, it must be weighed," said don Emilio.

When Basilio was fourteen, don Emilio gave him a pick and a helmet with a lantern. Basilio stood with a dozen men in the shadow of the hoist tower, where fraying cables clung to a rusty drum, and climbed after them down forty meters of ladders to the second level. When he had broken off as many rocks as he could carry, he attached his sack to a head strap and climbed back up the ladders.

At the end of the day, Basilio and the others—who were all grown men, fathers and grandfathers—watched don Emilio weigh the ore each one had brought to the surface.

"You ask why I cannot pay more," said don Emilio. "Remember that the owner of this mine receives a percentage. Remember the cost of transportation to the smelter. And if you follow the metal prices, you will see how they swing, up one month and down the next." But none had followed the metal prices. Among them only Basilio could read, with his finger under the letters and the sounds often trapped in his mouth.

Four years earlier, when Basilio was ten and still not enrolled in the nuns' school, the mother superior Yolanda had called on Concha, who offered her a pitching rocker while she herself sank low on the unresisting bedspring. The composed, exhausted face of her visitor reminded Concha of a saint from whom she might expect an indulgence. A remission of want, perhaps, or pardon of sloth.

The madre said that Basilio must come on Monday to join the first grade, that he must read and write and calculate numbers, that he must stay through the fifth grade and stand on the graduation platform, a credit to his mother and his teachers and to God who protected the school.

On Monday, in a classroom where rain, wind, and dust entered as if by invitation through shattered windowpanes, Basilio shared a desk with Pepe González, six years old. Basilio cramped his knees and sat doubled over on a small blue chair. He learned a song about a crow and another about nighttime. At the end of this song the children put their heads on their desks and pretended to sleep. Basilio, unfed since yesterday, might have rested there for an hour had not the madre addressed him personally and recalled him to his shame.

From the madres Basilio learned to make words on lined paper with his clenched pencil stub and to divide three dozen oranges by twelve children. In the grocery he deciphered the labels of flour and cooking oil, and in torn comic books could read much of what ballooned from the quacking bill of Donald Duck. He understood the sign PELIGRO on the exposed curves of the mountain road and on a box of dynamite.

With this knowledge Basilio discontinued his education in the middle of the third grade and began his career. The mother superior Yolanda visited Concha again. "You must think of his future."

"I will tell him to be at school Monday," said Concha, but she did not.

In the case of Domingo, things were different. When the younger brother was still five years old, Basilio ordered him, "Come on," and led the way to the nuns' school. If the boy missed his classes, to wander with the goatherd and his animals over the hills or to wade in the arroyo after a thunderstorm,

Basilio took him back the next day and watched from the door until he opened his book. Domingo learned the rules of grammar and how to reduce fractions, and when he graduated from the fifth grade received a medal from the mother superior.

Again Basilio said, "Come on." His brother followed him to the federal school across the loose dirt of the playground and entered the sixth grade. Four years later he graduated first in his class and recited a patriotic poem at the exercises. His mother, massive and awed in spotted black, wept out of pride and uneasiness.

At this time Basilio was twenty-four and in love with Carmen López, eight years younger. On Saturday nights, when he sat shaved and clean near the bust of Juárez in the plaza, she would find a place under a lamp so close he could see the fresh red enamel on her nails. Or she would pass slowly in front of him, glancing down in a way that made her lashes fringe her cheeks. From these signs Basilio knew of her interest. He began to imagine Carmen as his partner in one or another of a series of passionate encounters.

In order to impress her father, Basilio started to save his money. Gaspar López was don Emilio's cousin and secretary to the mayor. He was a consumed-looking man who suffered from chronic belching. He tried to conceal the true and incurable nature of his affliction by carrying about with him an open, untasted bottle of beer. Gaspar would lift the bottle, pretend to swallow, put his hand before his mouth, emit a burst of air, and say, "Pardon me."

Because of his government position and connection through his cousin with prosperity, Gaspar expected his daughter to bring him a son-in-law of some importance. Such a person would merit winning Carmen's various charms, not least among them her arresting eyes and stunning breast.

Basilio now worked on the fourth level of the Socorro mine and was able to carry up fifty kilos of copper ore at one time in the sack that lay on his back and hung from his head. He bought a strongbox and hid it in the adobe wall behind his bed.

"What is that key you wear around your neck?" asked his mother.

"It is the key to the storeroom at Socorro, where my lantern is," Basilio said without hesitation.

In the fall Basilio took his brother, Domingo, to the federal preparatory school in La Gloria, ten miles away. They rode on the bus over the mountain, past the ruined monastery where the cells stood open to seasons and to storms, through fields planted in alternating rows of corn and *chiles*, between ditches where cows grazed on sunflowers and nettles, to the entrance of the school.

"This is my brother," said Basilio to the director. "He will register in your school now, attend for the full three years, and go on to the university in the capital." When they were alone outside, Domingo said in protest, "I am fourteen, which was your age when you went into the Socorro." And Basilio said, "I promise you. In the end you will be glad of all this," and he waved in the direction of the brick buildings behind. Then the brothers returned to the village on the same bus that had brought them and that parted, as a boat parts water, the luminous greens and yellows of late afternoon.

Every week, when he was alone in the house, Basilio counted out Domingo's bus fare from the strongbox, then locked and hid it again. As his savings grew, he addressed Carmen with smiles and a few words each time they met. In response, Carmen's eyes fastened on his and her sweater seemed to reveal more explicitly the contours beneath.

One evening Basilio presented himself to her father. Gaspar López sat alone on a bench in the plaza. In his hand was a bottle of beer.

When Basilio announced his proposal to court and marry Carmen, Gaspar raised the bottle and, discarding its function as a disguise, swallowed much of the beer. Shaken by the convulsion that followed, he replied unsteadily. He said that Basilio was an honorable man and a hard worker. He said that Carmen, hardy lily though she might be, was still no more than a child. So trusting of men and so desired by them, how was such an innocent to choose? Gaspar swallowed and belched behind his hand.

"Pardon me," he said. "As her father I hold her future like a blind moth in my hands. Her husband must be a person of esteem. This is acquired by education and wealth." He belched again. "Pardon me."

Basilio outlined his plan, to save his money, buy tools, lease an idle mine, sell ore to the smelter. In short, to shape himself to don Emilio's mold.

There was a pause while Gaspar weighed parental background against prospects, past against future. Then he said, "In that case, you may call at my house."

Three years later Basilio's savings lay piled like certificates of bliss in his strongbox. He called on Carmen López at her father's house and gained such confidence that she was allowed to stand alone with him outside the door just before he took his leave. Basilio's hunger was acute. He pressed Carmen to him and kissed her hair, her eyes, her mouth, and what he could reach of her breast. Carmen responded with such energy that Basilio felt his bones begin to melt.

"Pardon me," said her father from the threshold.

In June of this year Basilio's brother, Domingo, graduated, in a starched white shirt and polished shoes, from the preparatory school in La Gloria. He delivered a speech on the brilliant expectations of the future. Basilio sat with his mother in the second row. Concha, tightly confined by a new dress and pinched by new sandals, wiped her eyes and nose on her shawl and said, "The poor child, who has never known his father."

During the summer don Emilio lowered the ladders to the

fifth level of the Socorro, where an unmined vein was disclosed. Basilio held back half his pay and told his mother that he had dug into a fault. He watched his strongbox fill. In July the younger brother was employed to type correspondence for the mayor. He sat in the reception office of the *presidencia* at a small desk near the larger one of Gaspar López.

One day Carmen came to bring her father a slice of guava paste. Domingo rose when she entered and stood, smooth-haired, close-shaven, and white-shirted, until she left. The next day she brought two slices of guava paste and stayed for fifteen minutes, sitting on a corner of her father's desk and swinging one slender leg while her skirt crept slowly up her thigh.

Basilio worked overtime now, loading don Emilio's truck and driving it ninety kilometers to the smelter. Don Emilio sat next to him in the cab and said, "Why so fast, not so slow, blow your horn," according to highway conditions. One headlight of the truck shone up into the tops of cottonwood trees beside the road and the other picked out potholes and sudden animals on the pavement. Basilio imagined himself driving his own vehicle, heavy with ore, across this nocturnal landscape that lay sometimes shrouded under stars and sometimes revealed by moonlight.

More and more frequently Basilio opened the strongbox and calculated. Separated in one rubber band was the money to cover his brother's entrance fees and books at the university. Once enrolled, Domingo would support himself by the clerical work he was sure to find.

Basilio divided all the rest in three parts. One part was for adobes, lime and cement to build a house, one part was a cash reserve to satisfy Carmen's father, and the final third was the down payment on a truck. Basilio counted and sorted the bills a dozen times and then he consulted his brother. Basilio showed Domingo the strongbox and explained his plans—the dowry, the house, the new business.

"How does it strike you?" he asked.

Domingo said, "You have thought of everything."

For two months Basilio rode the Sunday bus in search of the vehicle destined to be his. He went once to each of the nearby towns and twice to used-car lots in the state capital. On the first of September he told Domingo he had found the truck, fourteen years old but in top condition. The owner had agreed to repair the brakes and retread two tires.

"There will be something to celebrate on the sixteenth besides the independence of Mexico," he said to Domingo. "Please say nothing to Carmen and her father. Let them find out when they see the truck."

On the tenth and again on the thirteenth of September Basilio ran at five o'clock from the Socorro mine to the plaza, where he caught the bus for Concepción. At the outskirts of the city he jumped off near the fenced dirt yard of the dealer he had chosen and each time found the repairs were yet to be made.

The dealer had one white blind eye that was fixed in a round, unblinking stare and one smaller brown one that darted from corner to corner like a caged mouse. This eye flickered to the right and to the left of Basilio when the dealer announced the truck was not ready.

"It is essential that I have it this week," said Basilio. "I am starting a mining operation." And the white eye was fixed upon him.

"In three days," said the dealer on the tenth, and when Basilio returned on the thirteenth, he said, "The afternoon of the fifteenth, without fail."

The bus trips and the transportation of don Emilio's ore to the smelter occupied every evening of this week except one. When Basilio called at her father's house, Carmen López, fragrant and ripe as a splitting grape, had little to say. At the moment of parting, under stars that were smothered here and there by clouds, Basilio clung to her as if he were a man drowning in a stream and she the willow branch that might save him.

"Pardon me," said Gaspar in the doorway, and later Basilio

could not have sworn that Carmen's arms had embraced him or that they hung like empty sleeves at her side.

On the fifteenth, Domingo suspended loudspeakers from the roof of the *presidencia* and, with the help of the postmaster's grandsons, decorated the peeling façade with flags. He attached and tested the microphone through which at midnight the mayor would utter the familiar salute in celebration of the end of Spanish rule. Strings of red and green light bulbs festooned the plaza, and under Gaspar's desk were twenty rockets contributed by don Emilio. In the patio of the nuns' school the mother superior Yolanda, preparing for tomorrow's program, allowed her skirts to fly as she led astonished five-year-olds in the squares and circles of folk dances, and at the federal school the director rehearsed the marching band in a straight column of fours.

Concha, mother of Basilio and Domingo, rested on a bench in front of the *presidencia* and ate a tortilla she had discovered in her apron pocket. She watched Carmen López approach Domingo, crossing the cobblestones in her platform shoes and skirt so tight that her buttocks were seen to pivot, one at a time, at each step. Concha put her fingernail to her teeth and sighed.

An hour before midnight Basilio arrived in the village at the wheel of his truck. He drove directly to the plaza, where he found his brother at a table under the arcade. As Basilio opened the door, a sudden eruption from the jukebox in the cantina assaulted the trees so that they swayed and the walls of houses stiffened.

"Get in," said Basilio to Domingo, and they rode twice around the square with all the townspeople turning to watch. When the truck stopped, Basilio's friends from the Socorro mine touched the fenders as they might the withers of a patient, spavined horse.

Then Basilio drove home along a street that drained to the

center and that he remembered from the day, rather than perceived in the dark. But when he parked the truck in front of his house, he clearly saw how the vehicle loomed, unaccustomed, clumsy, and noble, against the night. He took out his strongbox and gave Domingo the money for the university. After that he held for a moment the two thick packets that remained. They burned his palms with their promises, of leasing an idle mine—the Gloriosa, the Purísima, the Bonanza; of entering into friendly negotiations with the smelter regarding deliveries of ore; of exchanging courtship for consummation. Thoughts of the impending possession of Carmen produced within Basilio a rising ferment. Domingo watched him lay the truck keys next to the money and conceal the box once again in the wall.

The brothers started toward the plaza on foot, but Domingo had forgotten something, his pliers, perhaps, or some other tool. He turned back. "Don't wait," he said. "Go on."

During the next fifteen minutes Basilio searched the square for Carmen. The crowd seemed to have become sober and dull. Mongrel dogs snarled and chased through leaves that had dropped out of season from the trees. Babies wailed and older children fought for places on their mothers' laps. A dozen painted bulbs had already blown out.

Basilio pushed his way to the rostrum, where the mayor was preparing to deliver the traditional message of liberation. Gaspar López was not in his usual position a few steps behind, poised to spring forward at a word. Nor was Domingo on hand to adjust the amplifier.

In answer to Basilio's question, the mayor burst out, "They are not here. They have failed me, the municipality of Ibarra and the republic of Mexico." A rocket exploded prematurely on a hill in back of the town.

Basilio, pierced by the first thrust of suspicion, ran to his house. When he saw that nothing more than the night filled the space where his truck had been, he investigated his strongbox. The money was there. Only the keys were gone.

Out on the street again, he observed his neighbor, old Juana, sitting on her doorstep. She had wrapped herself in the blanket from her bed and was smoking a cigar. She looked at Basilio, pointed her cigar to indicate the direction the truck had gone, then shifted her attention back to the plaza, which she located by the pale glare in the sky above it. Of its sounds, the cries of vendors and the yelping of dogs, the occasional maledictions and fragments of song, Juana, a deaf-mute, knew nothing.

Basilio ran on, in the resigned and obstinate manner of a man whose destination continually recedes before him. He stumbled into potholes and fell against a tree stump and an abandoned oil drum. Arriving, as he must, at the house of Gaspar López, he saw that his truck stood outside with the motor running. Domingo was at the wheel and Carmen sat beside him. Her father was pulling at the driver's door with his precise, clerk's hands, and demanding to know Domingo's intentions and whose vehicle this was. Appealing to God to intercede, Gaspar rushed into his house and returned with a rifle.

By now Domingo had the truck in gear and was moving ahead. "Stop!" shouted Gaspar. He shot at a tire and missed.

At this moment, which was midnight, the mayor's voice, much distorted, issued from the loudspeaker, exclaiming, "*Viva la libertad! Viva la república! Viva México!*" and a succession of rockets went off at close range.

Basilio seized the rifle. "Domingo!" he called out. "Hear me!" and he pursued the truck until it gained momentum. "Hear me!" he cried again across the distance widening between them. As he plunged down the rutted street, Basilio aimed his gun over the cab and fired three times. At the third shot the truck veered to the left, rolled into a gutter, and stalled. When Basilio opened the door, his brother fell out. There was a small hole in his back and, where the bullet had torn its way through, a much larger one in his chest. In the plaza the mayor concluded his address and, unaware that Domingo lay dead on the ground, blamed him publicly for the malfunction of the amplifier.

Basilio was taken into custody that night and had to wait six months for his prosecution to be scheduled. The lawyer who was to help him at his trial asked if he had any money, and when he learned how much was in the strongbox, said, "Good. We will plead manslaughter and hope for a five-year sentence. Are you in agreement?"

Basilio nodded. He was certain that five years would scarcely be noticed among the vast reaches of time that spread before him.

11

Christmas Messages

It began like any other winter day, with the oyster light of dawn exposing the ravaged streets and broken house fronts of Ibarra, but already, between midnight and six o'clock, two men of the village have died. The body of one lies in his own blood on the clinic floor and the body of the other half sits, half reclines against the shuttered cantina door.

In their chapel across the arroyo the nuns are on their knees and the sacristan of the parish church is toiling up the last steps of the bell tower. Five blocks from the plaza Paz Acosta, thirteen, is delivering her first baby. But there are complications.

Farther on, beyond numb December fields and a forsaken farmhouse, the eastern light, turned opal by now, enters the bedroom of Richard and Sara Everton and falls on their sleeping faces. Sara wakes, turns from the window to her husband, and sleeps again. This is their fourth winter in Ibarra. They know all its dusks and daybreaks.

These Americans seem no more aware of Christmas than the two dead men or the girl who has already been in labor for twenty hours.

But by twelve o'clock tonight there will be something to mark the day.

At six in the morning the bus driver, who had spent the night in his parked vehicle, discovered a body outside the cantina. He stopped the grocer and his family on their way to mass.

"Here is a man frozen to death," said the bus driver.

"It is Victor, the potter, and not frozen," said the grocer, and he summoned two passing youths to help. Between them they carried Victor by his stiffening arms and legs across the plaza, past the post office, to the entrance of his house. His wife, Trinidad, came to the door barefoot and half dressed, her tangled hair falling into her unfastened blouse.

"Here is Victor," said the men.

Trinidad gazed at her husband's face, the glaring eyes, the twisted lips, the sickly skin. Gazed as she might if Victor were a stranger from another town dead of a stroke or an attack by thieves.

Then she pointed across the room to a bed partly covered by a rumpled quilt.

The bus driver, the grocer, and the other two laid Victor down, but his knees remained bent and one hand fixed in the air. As they left the house the grocer, looking back at the potter, noticed a few empty bottles under the bed.

"He is still thirsty," said the grocer to the bus driver, and the two youths nodded. "But the cantina is closed," said one. "Until noon," said the other, as if Victor might even now compose his limbs, regain his senses, and take note of the opening hour.

As soon as she was alone Trinidad bolted the door. Then she called, "Luis," and the Evertons' gardener emerged from the kitchen with his denim work pants over his arm. He approached the bed.

"*Dios,*" said Luis, and put his hand on the quilt that half an hour ago had warmed Trinidad's broad thighs and his own spare frame. He regarded Victor's lifted arm and contorted face.

"A friend to me always," said Luis, and he lit the candle Trinidad had brought to burn above the dead man's head.

She had found her shoes and was wrapping herself in two shawls, first a green one, then a black one.

"Where are you going?" asked Luis.

"To tell the cura and the doctor."

"Then let us get rid of these bottles," said Luis. "Those two are opposed to alcohol in cases of cirrhosis." He crouched in his long gray underwear to reach under Victor.

Trinidad pulled the two shawls over her head. "God arranges these things," she said, and opened the kitchen door into a square space of dirt where some aprons and a man's shirt were drying on a cactus under the wan sun. Beneath a shed in one corner stood Victor's kiln, in another the pile of dung he used as fuel. Lined against the wall were a dozen unbaked clay flower pots.

"These pots were to be a Christmas present from don Ricardo to his señora," said Luis. He tossed the bottles over the wall and crossed the yard to inspect the pot designs. All were favorites of the señora and conformed to the order he had placed himself. Each had a scalloped rim and was circled with a band of decoration that Victor had pressed into the wet clay, rings of fern leaves and shells, stars and swans.

Luis pulled on his pants. "I will have to notify don Ricardo."

Before he left he stood once more with Trinidad at the bedside. "The American would have paid whatever Victor asked. One hundred pesos for the lot. Two hundred pesos." As Luis spoke these words he imagined he saw the dead man's countenance cast over with the shadow of regret.

By the time they were on the street the reluctant sun had risen high enough to light up the purples, mauves, and sea blues of the church's mosaic dome.

"Will you go first to the church or to the clinic?" asked Luis. But Trinidad made no reply as she walked in the direction of the plaza with the long green fringe of one shawl showing below the short black fringe of the other.

In the house of Remedios Acosta the girl Paz lay shuddering on a cot. She had suspended herself on the thin thread of a moan as if it were a lifeline that could save her.

At two in the morning Remedios, having used up the poultices and plasters, infusions and drafts of her own contriving, called in Polo, the *curandero.* But he too, after four hours of potions and compresses, of turning Paz over from left to right, of making her sit, stand, and walk, was unable to end all these preliminaries and induce the birth.

"Should I send my son to bring the government doctor?" Remedios finally asked Polo. But they hesitated. Such a summons would mean the *curandero* would have to pack up his sack of miracles and leave. The doctor might blame Remedios for not calling him sooner. He might say, "Paz must go to the hospital in the city." Or, "The baby is already dead." He was almost certain to say, "Who is the father?" And this was a question no one could answer.

Besides, there was another consideration. The matter of conceding to the Americans, particularly the señora, who all along had recommended monthly checkups and the doctor present at delivery.

However, at seven o'clock in the morning Remedios, persuaded by the hoarse and incessant moaning, defied the *curandero* and dispatched her youngest son, Horacio, for the intern, newly graduated from his university classes and only five months in Ibarra.

"Run to the clinic," she told him. "If the doctor is asleep, pound with a rock on the door." Then she remembered the day. "But to a doctor that makes no difference," she said. "La Navidad."

Horacio was scarcely on his way when Luis arrived at the house of the Americans. The Evertons had not expected to see their gardener on Christmas. Richard answered the door in his pajamas with his wife behind him in a cherry-colored robe.

The three stood on the porch of the low white house and faced east to benefit from the first tepid rays of the sun while Luis presented his news.

"My friend Victor died in the night," he said. "Of cirrhosis. Before he could fire the pots you ordered."

"I regret his death," said Richard. "But the quantity of alcohol he swallowed would kill anyone." And he remembered coming home with his wife from a weekend away to discover Victor unconscious and spread-eagled across their drive. The potter's sombrero lay tilted at his side, the brim hanging loose from the crown. Sara had remarked that the presence of the hat indicated something more significant than custom. It impressed her as a mark of incorrigible dignity. "The fact that in this condition he thinks to put on a hat," she had said to Richard.

"Did the doctor attend Victor?" he asked Luis now on this cold, still morning, and was told there was no time.

"When I saw him Victor seemed to be sleeping," said Luis, who had already come to believe this was true. "On his own bed, with his wife of twenty years nearby."

Then he spoke again of the flower pots but by now Richard had forgotten them. He was wondering if Victor's death would be registered as suicide. But dying, except in cases of violence, was always suicide according to Richard, who considered that the collapse of a man's will was the immediate and invariable cause of his death.

"We are expecting the doctor for lunch at one o'clock," he told Luis. "Unless, of course, there is an emergency to detain him."

The new widow, Trinidad, and the Acosta boy converged upon the clinic at the same time. But there was no need to shout and pound. The door swung open by itself and there in front of them on the floor was the doctor with a hole in his forehead and a pistol not far from his hand.

"*Jesús,*" said the boy under his breath, and the woman bent to touch the doctor's throat, which was cold and without pulse.

The black and bloody hole in the doctor's head made Horacio think of a rabbit his uncle once shot on the hills with his old army rifle. As for Trinidad, she may have been thinking of youth, and young men in particular, for the doctor was in his twenties, and handsome. Or of privilege, for he had a profession that might eventually have made him rich.

Or she may have been comparing her husband's outraged stare with the serene gaze of the doctor, who looked straight up at a crack in the ceiling and through it into pure emptiness beyond.

The Evertons had gone back to bed after the visit of Luis, for it was still just past seven in the morning. The wool robe and the pajamas were slipping inch by inch from the foot of the bed to the floor.

"Is this our best Christmas?" Sara asked.

"Best Christmas, best Halloween, best Fourth of July," said Richard.

One hour later they were still in bed, and when Luis returned to knock on the door a second time there was some delay before they answered. The Americans intend to wear these garments through the day, the gardener remarked to himself, for the señora was still wrapped in red wool and the señor his half-buttoned blue pajamas.

"The doctor has shot himself," said Luis without preamble. "In the clinic, where his body must remain until the authorities certify his death and discover who his parents are so that they may be informed."

The Evertons neither spoke nor moved. They looked over the stone pool, the olive trees, and the wall to the bare, dormant hillside beyond.

After a long time Richard Everton said, "The señor cura knows the names of the doctor's parents and how to find them."

As soon as Luis started back to the village Sara said, "It was the music. Having to give it up."

"The music, yes," said Richard. "And something else besides. The child dragging himself around on a dirt floor because his mother refused the polio vaccine. The bead necklace to cure pneumonia. The mint leaf pasted on the tumor."

The Evertons were dressing in front of a fire. Richard had directed his words to the floor as he pulled on his shoes. Sara watched him put a slide rule in his pocket and attach a ring of keys to his belt as if, the days being short as they were, he meant to spend all Christmas in his office at the mine.

He went on. "To the doctor it must have been like emptying the sea with a thimble. The pregnant Acosta child wearing that belt of corn. Victor and his raw alcohol diet."

"He made the most beautiful pots," said Sara. "He was the Michelangelo of potters." She pushed back the curtains and looked out on a landscape dimmer under this faint sun than under the full moon of September. Even the weeds and the nopal cactus seemed to be in hibernation. Sara believed that the landscape, by its own force, had arrested time.

"But it was mostly the music," she said later, and remembered the day the doctor had brought his parents to meet the two Americans. The cura had come, too, naturally included on such an occasion.

They arrived at the house in late afternoon at the end of a summer rainstorm when everything shone wet outside, tiles, leaves, berries, and the drenched Castilian rose. From the porch they had looked down toward the village, where wood smoke, fanned from kitchen doors by aprons, rose as high as the clock on the church. The runoff of rain dripped like subsiding tears from channels in the Evertons' roof.

By way of presentation the doctor said, "My parents," and then he said no more. But when they were in the *sala* having tea and sherry the cura enlarged upon the introduction.

"The doctor's father is a musician," said the priest. "He is first cellist with the National Orchestra." And the doctor's father bowed as if to applause for the solo part in *Don Quixote*.

"And his mother," the cura went on, "until her recent retirement sang mezzo-soprano in the National Opera." Now the mother bowed, and flowers tossed from an invisible balcony seemed to fall at her feet.

"We are honored," said the Evertons.

"Do you, also, play an instrument or sing?" Sara asked the doctor. He shook his head. His father turned to stare at him and his mother opened her mouth to speak, but neither of them uttered a word.

"There is no room for a piano in the clinic," interposed the cura. Sara immediately looked at the intern's hands and saw them at a keyboard, saw them with a scalpel. He might be an artist in both professions. Oh, choices! Sara thought, and considered the ones of the six people gathered here, the singer, the cellist, the doctor, the priest, and the other two, the nonprofessionals, who had simply chosen Ibarra.

Here in their house, five months later, Sara and Richard drank their Christmas coffee and mourned the musicians' son. He was too young, they told each other, to have made such an intimate friend of death.

At noon Horacio Acosta peered through the windows of the Evertons' house until he discovered the señor carrying an armload of wood to the fire and the señora sliding a plucked bird into the oven. He knocked on the kitchen window.

When he was admitted he said, "There is a message from my mother. Paz has a son." He looked around the room at jars and kettles and at the market basket on the pine table. This basket held oranges, papayas, and a pineapple. "Paz howled and shrieked all yesterday, last night, and this morning."

"And the doctor couldn't help," said Sara, confronted by an image of the white-smocked pianist on the clinic floor.

The boy shook his head. His hands were in his pockets and his eyes were on the fruit.

"Take a papaya," said Sara. And as Horacio started away she said, "Take another." Just as he reached the door she called after him, "Take the pineapple," and before he left she had handed him the whole basket.

She knew from conversations with Remedios during the past months that this baby had no particular father. For if Paz herself could not identify him, how could anyone else settle on this youth, that older bachelor, or one of those married men who were sometimes seen with strange women at the *cine* in the city?

In the kitchen Sara invented a composite father for the infant, a father with the wide eyes of the baker's Pedro, the high cheeks of the mason's Chon. Paz's baby would have the flat ears of the police captain and the round chin of the mayor. Out of all these features Sara constructed a representative child, the first of a series of such children Paz would bear. For at ten Remedios's daughter had displayed clear intimations of heroic and legendary charms. By the age of twelve she had set her foot on the path made smooth by Helen, Guinevere, Salome, and Isolde.

Sara went to find Richard. "Will there be more messages?"

"No more today," said Richard, as though he had the power to declare and execute prophecies. As though he could see into the future and, according to his whim, change its course.

As it turned out, he was right. No one else came that day to knock on the Evertons' door or tap on their windows. But that in itself proved nothing. There may have been other births, deaths, and defections. But these events, if they occurred, went unreported to the Americans, at least until a later day which might dawn warmer, with a yellower sun, and enough light to cast the shadow of a tree.

Since four o'clock a heavy gray ceiling has strung itself from hilltop to hilltop over Ibarra, stifling wind and muffling sound. At ten minutes before midnight, for the first time in sixty years, snow begins to fall. With a hiss on a lantern, a whisper on a branch, a shiver on a windowpane, it covers the corn fields, the rutted lanes, and the scarred dwellings of the town. It shrouds the bus and the red taxi parked in the plaza. It fits coats of frost to a pair of burros left out on the slopes to graze. By tomorrow's glittering sunrise, ice will drip from rain spouts and every maguey spear will carry its burden of white.

Dogs sniff their way tail down and cats prowl wary. Boys scratch the date with nails into adobe walls and great-grandfathers limp on canes to the open doors. Women hold up their children and say, "Look." This is something to remember, something they cannot expect to see again. Snow.

12

LUNCH WITH THE BISHOP

By the last Sunday in January, when the Evertons were to meet the bishop, the snow had long since melted, but the recurring cold was so intense that to take a breath of air between the teeth was to bite ice.

"What shall we talk to him about?" Sara asked her husband. "Without sounding like infidels." She shivered at the doorway of the cura's residence adjoining the church.

"We are infidels," said Richard.

Inside the house, even the crowding together of fourteen people, twelve black-robed priests and the two Americans, failed to temper the chill of the *sala.* Neither the bishop nor the cura was in sight, and for a time the Evertons stood by themselves near the door, waiting for a sign that would point to an avenue of communication. They each took a glass from a tray, sipped at its contents, and coughed.

Then Sara identified a priest across the room. "There's Father Octavio," she told Richard. "The old one, the one who's shaking." They watched drops of brandy scatter from Father Octavio's glass and fall about him on the floor in amber beads.

Because of accounts the cura had given her, Sara recognized the old priest by his stooped frame and the border of white hair that fringed his scalp. Now she attached his biography to him. Father Octavio had lived eighty-two years and still sat once a week in his own church behind the curtains of the confessional to hear and forgive the minor and the monstrous sins. He still presided at communion. But Ibarra was eighty kilometers from his parish, and much of the road unpaved, and the bus unheated. Sara saw him move close to the window as though he expected God to blow on the pale sun, causing its flames to burn hotter and its rays to thaw his toes, two of which were visible through slits he had cut in his shoes.

"He's eighty-two years old," Sara told her husband. "By now he must know everything."

Outnumbered six to one by clerics in the narrow *sala,* the Evertons, wearing two sweaters each and the invisible armor of their agnosticism, felt the alcohol at work against their throat linings, their diffidence, and the currents of air that froze them to the glacier-green tiles of the floor.

"We'll have to start talking without introductions," said Richard, and he and Sara turned to a young priest in dark glasses who stood as silent as themselves near the door.

But at that moment their host, the cura, came into the room with a bottle in his hand and a brown topcoat buttoned over his habit. He greeted the Evertons and circled the room, filling glasses.

"I have looked in the church," he told his guests. "Twenty children are still to be confirmed." He raised his glass to Richard and Sara. "Health to our guests from across the border."

At this, all the priests toasted the two Americans. They did this out of courtesy, having neither clue nor curiosity as to why the strangers had been included in today's gathering, or happened to be in Ibarra on its saint's day, or had come to know the parish priest. Two Protestants, thought the visiting clerics, and they drank to the Evertons.

While Richard talked with a young priest about the soccer finals, Sara approached Father Octavio.

Instead of trying to find out all he knew, she only asked, "Is your church far from here?"

The old man stared at her out of sunken eyes whose pupils had faded as much as black can ever fade. She saw he hadn't understood and she tried again.

"How do you like Ibarra?" she asked, separating the words and pronouncing them with care.

Father Octavio heard this question and nodded, spilling more brandy.

Sara, observing him so close, began to believe this was the oldest man she had ever seen. He's twenty years older than I thought, she told herself. He's at least a hundred and must expect each sunrise to be his last. In another corner of the room Richard and the young priest were laughing.

"My husband and I came to live in Ibarra exactly four years ago," she said so loudly that several heads turned in her direction. She expected the old man to say, "Why?" and had prepared a sentence about Richard and the Malagueña mine.

Instead, Father Octavio only remarked, "God in his wisdom ordains."

Sara fell silent and moved toward the wall that separated the *sala* from the nave of the church. She would have liked to watch the confirmations, see the boys and girls in laundered white approach the bishop, the altar, and the crowned figure beyond, Virgin of Bethlehem, fair-haired, light-skinned, blue-robed *patrona* of Ibarra. Over them all, from a pair of columns, leaned two seraphim, brown-faced and fierce-eyed as infant Montezumas. And dark as the seraphim were the grave, starch-shirted boys who yesterday had hailed Sara on the road, and the veiled, ruffled girls she knew by name.

Half of the boys were Jesús, but all of the girls were María. Sara already knew from their mothers of the lace that would be worn by a Mary of Hope, the beaded collar of a Mary of Sorrows, the embroidered skirts of Marys of Refuge, of the Angels, of the Trinity; of Lourdes, Fátima, and Light.

Now the cura, on his rounds with the bottle, paused in front of her and, as if he guessed her thoughts, expanded them. "And many not often seen at mass are filling the church today, among them some regular customers of the cantina. I noticed Luis, your gardener, praying—a man who usually spends Sunday unconscious in the park."

An image rose before Sara of Luis kneeling at a pew, his face bruised and scabbed from last night's brawl, his gentle bloodshot gaze fixed on the children and the flowers.

"And visitors from out of town as well," continued the cura, "who have come by bus or bicycle from the ranchos of La Emancipación and Bombiletes, from Loreto and Concepción."

These were places Sara knew. The two ranchos were part of the cura's parish.

But Loreto, a town of tractors and fertilizers to the north, and Concepción, the state capital to the south, lay beyond its bounds. Loreto was connected to the rest of the world, as Ibarra was not, by railroad tracks, a telephone, and a *cine.* In Concepción the bishop's cathedral occupied all the west side of the plaza.

Once Sara had seen him step out of his car at a side entrance and bless the shoppers, storekeepers, and children selling *chicles* who collected to watch him pass. He walked through the crowd with such natural benevolence that Sara thought what she had heard of him might be half true. He might be half saint.

Everyone in the cura's *sala* was a little drunk now. The visiting priests and the Americans had become immediate old friends. Their host had proposed so many toasts, to the health of his guests, to the memory of former priests of this parish, to the restoration of the baptismal font, that the Evertons supposed he might next lift his glass to the saint of Ibarra, herself.

"Excellent brandy," Richard remarked.

"It is local," said the cura. "One year old and artificially colored." He poured a little more in the American's glass.

The draft from the open door caused a minor seizure in

Father Octavio. The tremor traveled across his shoulders and set his head in motion like a mandarin doll, first nodding assent, then shaking denial. The cura, observing the spasm, guided him to the red silk sofa. As soon as the old man was established there, his host once again left the room to review the progress of the confirmations.

In his absence a silence fell. The assembled guests might as well never have been introduced, never have raised their glasses in unison. Sara looked at Richard, suspected he might be catching cold, and drew him to the window. Like Father Octavio she believed there was warmth to be absorbed through the glass from the leaden sky.

"You're taking care of me again," said Richard.

"I suppose I am."

"But I've decided not to die this year."

"All right," she said, and standing so close the back of her hand touched his, they gazed toward the blue-garlanded plaza where preparations for the evening's carnival were still under way. On the cantina side three men were bolting together sections of a Ferris wheel that, lashed to the bed of a truck, had rocked up the mountain this morning. Already assembled in front of the *presidencia* was a merry-go-round of twelve horses. In spite of the wooden blocks wedged in to steady them, both the wheel and the carousel tilted at angles on the cobblestones. They appeared destined to collapse, perhaps when filled to capacity. A few years ago the Evertons would have supposed a tragedy was inevitable. But now, like everyone else in Ibarra, they were certain that the sun would set, the moon would rise, and no accident occur tonight.

Sara watched a red car swing at the top of the wheel. "We could take a ride later on."

"Good idea," said Richard.

But they knew they would not. After the bishop left, they would return to their house, light their lamps, light their fire, and in this way reduce the world, spiritual and temporal, to a bright square space between four whitewashed walls.

Now the cura was back and calling to the kitchen for a tray.

"Hurry up," he told his guests. "His Excellency is coming and he doesn't drink."

Only seconds after Manuela Reyes, the murderer's daughter, who had come to help for the day, stumbled out with the glasses, the bishop entered the *sala*. Each of the priests, except Father Octavio, who was napping on the sofa, kissed his ring. The Evertons shook his hand. As soon as they met, Sara fitted to the mild, purple-sashed man all she had heard about him from the people of Ibarra. And things she had not heard she fitted to him, too.

Although this was the bishop whose seat was the cathedral of Concepción, although he had presided at the wedding of the governor's daughter and was seen being driven from parish to parish by a chauffeur in a black Buick, he had been born in a village poorer than Ibarra. Born of parents who died of unknown causes, Sara imagined, or, to be more accurate, starvation, but not before they had committed their son to a lifetime of service and three meals a day in the Holy Church of Rome. Sara thought they had done the right thing. Their son was known to be a man of inflexible dedication and he had enough to eat.

Paulita, the cura's aunt, had left the kitchen and now, unassuming as a shadow, slipped into the room and kissed the bishop's ring. So small and thin she scarcely displaced air, she folded Sara in an embrace that was suggested rather than felt.

"Come with me," Paulita said, and with hands as urgent as a child's she pulled Sara through the door. The patio outside barely accommodated two tables set for lunch, a number of flower pots, and a leafless elm. Hanging from a branch of this tree was a parrot in a cage.

"This is Enrique Caruso, whom you have not met," said Paulita. "Speak to the señora, Enrique."

"Buenas," said the mottled green bird, omitting the *tardes* in accordance with local custom.

"Enrique has a vocabulary of twenty-seven words," said Paulita, and Enrique, examining his visitors from beady profile, used another. *"Vámonos!"* said the bird.

"Pretty thing!" exclaimed Paulita, and touched the cage briefly, withdrawing her finger before Enrique could fasten his beak on it.

Behind them Manuela Reyes arranged stalks of scarlet gladiolus down the length of one table. She laid the flowers in place with the same ceremony she would have assumed if she were to honor a hero's monument with a wreath.

When lunch was announced, the bishop preceded the others into the patio and gravitated naturally to the head of the table that had flowers. Richard and Sara were seated at his right and left, the cura stationed himself at the other table, and the twelve padres found chairs. Father Octavio, roused from dozing, sat opposite the bishop at the first table.

All stood while His Excellency thanked God for what they were about to eat. In the middle of the blessing, Enrique Caruso said "*Buenas*" again and repeated the word until Paulita hurried from the kitchen to cover his cage with a towel. Then Manuela served fresh fruit in a stemmed glass to the bishop and in fifteen saucers to the rest. With spoons chilled by the intemperate air around them, the cura and his guests ate slices of papaya, banana, and melon from regions of Mexico that steamed under a savage sun from one winter to the next.

Tortilla soup followed. During this course the Evertons learned that the bishop had attended the last ecumenical council at the Vatican. Now Richard and Sara had something to say, of stones and drains and arches, for they, too, were once in Rome. But as they opened their mouths to praise ruins, Father Octavio spoke from his end of the table. "How was His Holiness then?" the old man asked over a trembling spoon.

The bishop replied that the pope had been dying by degrees and that his doctors were powerless to relieve his pain. "The cancer had begun to tear at him with a beast's claw," said the bishop.

"A martyr of God," said Father Octavio, spilling as much soup as he swallowed.

Sara looked across the table at her husband, who apparently recognized no similarity between the pope's illness and his own. Or he might have been thinking of the mine, of new tunnels and pillars, of how a Roman architect would have solved problems of mass and stress.

The bishop continued his recital of horrors. "In the liver. The lungs. The esophagus."

Sara suddenly intervened. "Was it spring when you were in Italy?" she asked, and she began to speak the names of flowers. The bishop regarded her patiently, without comprehension.

Sara spoke again. "Italy is my spiritual home," she stated, and the priests at both tables turned their faces in her direction. Not a Protestant after all, they decided. A recent convert.

"April," said Sara. "April in those medieval churches. The tubs of white azaleas in front of the altars. Hiding the altars."

The bishop put down his spoon and lifted his calm right hand. "A church has no season," he said, "and an altar no disguise."

Sara had finished her soup and sat with her hands folded under her napkin for warmth. When conversation stopped, she looked into her husband's face and, in order not to exclude the others, said to him in her spare and simple Spanish, "One day we will go back to Italy. True?"

Richard, instead of contradicting her, immediately agreed. "Yes, true," he said. "As soon as we have more time."

Sara, watching his eyes darken, deciphered their message. I have joined you in make-believe, they said. It's a game more than one can play.

But the clerics smiled at his positive response. They too, it might seem, had travel plans and could adjust their itineraries to his. Sara, anticipating the proposed, impossible trip, pictured them all eating together in a restaurant on the Pincian Hill.

Manuela had no sooner brought the next course, rice with chicken, than two dogs pushed through the cura's iron gate and bounded into the patio. The Evertons recognized them as the postmaster's mongrel, El Bandido, and the baker's bitch, La Mariposa. The bitch was in heat and, like her butterfly namesake, scarcely settled in one spot before she was off to another. She teased and flirted. El Bandido pursued. At one point she ran under the first table past Father Octavio, the other priests, and the Evertons to the feet of the bishop, where she paused as if for absolution. El Bandido was waiting and continued the courtship until together the dogs broke a flower pot and Manuela chased them into the street with a broom.

As the plates were changed again, for salad, Richard invited the bishop to visit his mine, preferably two months from now when a new vein would be exposed. "The blasting away of underground rock reveals a new world," he told the bishop. "A place no eyes have seen."

Feet walked, hands touched, Sara silently added. For, as if Richard had spoken these words himself, she understood he was describing Eden. She glanced at the bishop.

He apparently had noticed no connection. "My schedule is such . . ." he began, when his attention was drawn to some beggars who had found their way through the gate left open behind the dogs.

Sara recognized all three of them and, seeing them together for the first time, started to compute their individual and collective ages. The total shocked her. Add in Father Octavio and the sum of their years would be three and a half centuries. What was it that made them live so long? Was there a trick, some sorcery? Sara believed the answers might be among the things Father Octavio knew. She translated into basic Spanish the questions she would never ask.

First of the mendicants to reach the bishop's side was old Inocencia, bundled into a magpie assortment of raveling garments. Like the two others, Inocencia expected no alms from the prelate, only his prayers for her soul and his blessing on her career. These he seemed to bestow when he touched her bowed head.

Next came Juana, the deaf-mute, who sank to the tiles at his feet and pointed to her mouth and ears. The bishop, allowing her to kiss his ring, invoked God's compassion upon her.

Old Pablo was the last to approach, shuffling on his knees from the gate to His Excellency's chair. Once there, he exhibited the naked stump of his right arm. The details of the accident that caused the loss of his hand were well known in Ibarra. It occurred through the intervention of his father, who cut it off when Pablo was an infant. Like the bishop's parents he had managed to ensure for his son a lifelong profession.

By now the guava paste had been consumed and the lengthening shadows had produced a heightened and more piercing chill. All rose but Father Octavio, asleep at the end of the table, his chin resting on the folds of his stained habit. The bishop woke him with an invitation to ride in the Buick back to the capital. Father Octavio, knowing himself to be the object of divine providence, stood up and departed with new energy.

For the bishop the saint's day of Ibarra was an annual commitment. "We will meet next year," he said to the Evertons. And added, "God willing."

"Next year, then," said Richard.

"Yes," said his wife. "Next year."

The patio was empty now except for Paulita and Sara, who took leave of each other near Enrique Caruso's cage. He had been forgotten.

"*Pobrecito!*" said Paulita, pulling away the towel.

"*Atención, por favor!*" said Enrique distinctly. He reeled over on his perch and regarded them from upside down.

Manuela was removing the red flowers from the table as carefully as she had laid them down.

"Now take them back to the altar," Paulita told her, and the girl, who was scarcely bigger than a child, bore them off, carrying the stalks across her arm like a sheaf of fire-tipped spears.

The Evertons, as they walked past the church, saw the three beggars on the steps. They were counting their money and appeared content. They had not been so rich since this time last year. The coins that made their pockets sag would satisfy every requirement of the foreseeable future, if the cold let up, if they could patch their roof and their shoes. If the laurel leaf on the brow cured the headache and the string around the throat cured the cough. If they survived the night.

13

CALLING FROM LORETO

One Sunday, not long after they came to Ibarra, Richard asked Sara, "How about the movie at the Rex?" But when they thought of Loreto's treeless walks and goose-necked street lamps and of the modern church, half rose, half bottle green, that faced the Cine Rex, they decided not to go.

Loreto was nothing more than a vacant place in the desert until the Ildefonso dam had brought water there ten years before. Then the sandy floor of the flatland that had lifted in coils at every gust of wind settled back and turned first to weeds, then to corn, then to alfalfa, and finally to the magenta bougainvillea in the plaza.

Although the streets remained unpaved and the painted plaster on the houses was already scaling off, the people of Loreto had all the water they could use and lights were everywhere, a sky of wires. The train stopped daily at the station. Conveniences included a telegraph office and, more important, a telephone switchboard, located in a motorcycle showroom just off the lobby of the Cine Rex.

Here Amparo, the long-distance operator, sat all day in headphones, twisting her hair around a pencil while she joined and severed connections. It was Amparo who from the start put through Richard's calls to the geologist and the machine shop and, later on, Sara's cries for help to the specialist in California.

Loreto was up-to-date. Just as Ibarra was old in everything—church, city hall, custom, and resignation—Loreto was new.

On a certain April morning Sara drove down the mountain to Loreto. She passed farms and reservoirs and the field at Bombiletes where young men, dressed in the pink-and-purple shirts and torn denims of civilian life, performed their army drill on Sundays. She crossed a shallow stream, left more farms behind her, and turned sharp left at an ex-president's gilded bust. Jolting over raised train tracks, she left her car on the packed dirt outside the Cine Rex.

At the switchboard, Amparo was sipping Squirt from a bottle. Behind her, a well-fed rancher in new boots and a tooled sombrero crowded himself and a lighted cigar into the glass booth. Near the window, a youth, pockmarked and sallow, kicked the tire of a motorcycle. So only these two are ahead of me, Sara thought, and neither is from Ibarra. There is no one here to report back to the village that I'm calling a doctor in California. No one to tell a neighbor, "Don Ricardo is ill again."

Sara gave Amparo the number. "Person to person with Dr. MacLeod." She spelled the name. "As soon as possible, please. I have to get back to Ibarra."

The operator glanced into Sara's face. "Ay, señora. Your husband has had an accident."

"No," said Sara, and met Amparo's stare. The operator leaned over her notepad, causing two black wings of hair, which she wore parted in the middle, to fold over her cheeks.

Sara realized that, with perseverance and a certain amount of luck, Amparo could connect the Loreto caller to the telephones of every continent. Theoretically, she could communicate as easily with the Vatican as with the hamlet of Jesús María, a few kilometers down the road.

"Not an accident, exactly," Sara said.

She sat in a narrow, stiff chair and stared through the plate-glass window at the church across the street. Years ago she had gone inside and seen near the entrance a notice banning the films shown at the theater. PROHIBIDO! warned the placard. "The following pictures are not to be seen," and over the bishop's signature it listed all the attractions advertised in the lobby of the Rex. These films involved gangsters, bandits, monsters, and actresses who could by merely breathing personify sin.

Once or twice recently, Sara has had to call Dr. MacLeod in the evening, when the women of Loreto sat on their doorsteps with their children scuffling at their feet. On these occasions lines of men stood at the ticket window and, whenever a patron entered the theater, sounds of violence burst out, gunfire, stampedes, collisions, a woman screaming.

"It's hard to hear you because of the cowboy film," she told the doctor one night and he, oblivious, continued to repeat his instructions. Or, as Sara saw it, to portion out his magic.

The rancher, his dying cigar in one hand, was still shouting into the phone about pumps and fertilizers, and the scarred youth still examining motorcycles when the door from the lobby opened and Remedios Acosta walked in. Sara, abruptly stripped of privacy and presuming an emergency at home, watched her approach. Remedios is here with news, she told herself. The latest news from Ibarra. Richard is dead.

But Remedios only said good morning and explained she had come to telephone her aunt in Rio Azul. This aunt was expected to arrive in Ibarra tomorrow.

"For a visit," Remedios said. "But she is eighty and traveling alone. She will have to take three buses."

After placing her call, she took the chair next to Sara and regarded her with contemplative eyes. They sat in silence until

Sara felt compelled to speak. "I'm also here to make a long-distance call."

"Where to?"

"California."

"To your relatives," said Remedios.

Sara chose not to correct this assumption. She gazed through the window at passing traffic, an old man and a sleeping child on a burro, two bicycles with a pair of street dogs after them. Remedios spoke of small things, the irregularity of mails, the price of tortillas, the indisposition of the cura. She mentioned a doctor's name. Dr. Vásquez.

"There is a new intern at the clinic," Remedios was saying. "Very young, very inexperienced."

Sara, a line of her defenses crumbling, only nodded.

"Then you have already met the new doctor." Remedios waited for an explanation.

Sara, however, did not speak of her most recent meeting with Dr. Vásquez, early this morning at the foot of her husband's bed. Instead she said, "Three weeks ago, when he first came to Ibarra." With Remedios's eyes on her, she continued, "I went to the clinic to talk to him." And still under scrutiny, added, "About family health in Ibarra."

Remedios, as though she had witnessed the meeting, said, "Then you know that this doctor tells mothers of families how to prevent the next child."

"Yes," said Sara. "I know." And she recalled the intern's bare office, where only his framed year-old diploma from medical school decorated the walls. She had faced him across his desk. "All these babies," she had said, and spoken of shortages of schools, food, houses, jobs.

Dr. Vásquez had regarded her gravely.

"But perhaps dealing with this problem is against your faith," she said. And he answered, "It is not."

As Sara walked away that morning, the doctor watched her from the clinic door. By the time she reached the plaza, five children were following her. Even after they were out of sight, the sound of their talk and high laughter carried back to where he stood.

From her place next to Sara at the switchboard in Loreto Remedios spoke as though for the pope. "God's gifts," she said.

When, at seven o'clock that morning, Dr. Vásquez had been called to the Evertons' bedroom, he took Richard's temperature and gave him an injection. The intern surveyed his patient from the foot of the bed. Sara stood there, too, expecting signs of immediate improvement. Richard was thin, having lived on broth and juice for three days. Now Sara waited for him to say, "Please bring me toast and a boiled egg." Or, "I need graph paper and my slide rule."

Dr. Vásquez examined the quiet profile of his patient's wife. When at last she looked in his direction, the set of her mouth and the absence of tears in her intent wide eyes confirmed his suspicion. The sick man's wife believed doctors had supernatural powers. She believed this of the American specialist and of Dr. Vásquez himself.

He started to say, "I must make clear to you the serious nature of your husband's illness," but instead merely presented a report. "Señora, you will wish to know that three women of the town are now using contraceptives."

When she seemed not to have heard, he went on. "This is a small beginning. But even these three cases could mean a dozen less children on the streets of Ibarra."

At this she faced him. "Twelve less," she said, and Dr. Vásquez watched her make internal calculations. She was subtracting from her delights the boys and girls who followed her across the plaza; eliminating the ones who trailed her from their doorsteps to her gate.

In the motorcycle showroom off the lobby of the Cine Rex, Amparo twisted a strand of hair from her shoulder to her ear and at the same time turned a crank to signal Gloria, the operator in Concepción.

Amparo cranked and said, "Gloria? Speak louder, please. I need lines to San Felipe and Rio Azul. To San Francisco, California." Then, in a lower voice, with more concern, she spoke of her boyfriend, Chico. "He is still in León. In the cheese factory." Amparo lashed her hair to the pencil. "We haven't talked for a week."

There was a silence while Gloria spoke. Amparo answered in a voice that was barely audible. "No, I called him."

Now the door of the telephone booth slammed open and the rancher pushed the width of himself and his big sombrero into the room. Immediately, the pockmarked young man crossed to the booth, closed the glass door behind him, and began whispering into the phone.

"Will you have coffee?" Sara had asked the intern that morning, and for a few minutes they sat at the *sala* window with their backs to the ash tree, in early leaf, and the greening stubble that ran down from the garden wall to the edge of Ibarra.

"Where were you born?" she asked the intern, as she had once asked Madre Petra. As if this were information she must have.

"On an island," he said. "In the middle of a lake," and he named the lake which was five hundred kilometers south of Ibarra.

"Richard and I know that lake. And the island, too." She listened for confirmation from the bedroom and heard none. "We've been around it in a launch," she told the doctor.

"It's a small island," he said, assuming that as tourists the Evertons had expected more. "Small, and with sides like cliffs. Halfway up one of these cliffs is my father's house."

Sara imagined she remembered the Vásquez house on the far side of the island, where a few stunted peach trees lined the shore and Richard had pointed out a pair of mallards feathering the water between the reeds.

In the showroom, flies buzzed in circles from wall to wall and flung themselves against the windowpane. The man in the booth went on talking. Sara found herself thinking her husband's name. Thought Richard twice, as though the seven letters had mind and heart, could breathe. Remedios had loosened the shawl she wore over her head and exposed her flat wide cheeks, flat wide brow, and the absorbed gaze between. She directed one remark after another toward Sara who, rather than discover the failings of the intern, closed her mind to the stream of talk and silently began to count off seconds in groups of ten. She willed these tens to pound against the glass door of the booth, but the man inside ignored them.

Sara had measured off two minutes and started a third when Amparo spoke Chico's name again. The operator, her face shadowed by her hair, was bending over the mouthpiece and mourning Chico in a murmur only Gloria could hear.

Sara lost count when the voice of the woman next to her became entangled with the numbers. Remedios was describing a thimble. "Engraved," she said. "With a wreath of leaves and my initial. Silver," she said, and believed she had Sara's attention. "I was named for my mother. The thimble was hers and should be mine. Daughters before sisters, do you agree?"

Before Sara could answer, the glass door opened and the young man left the booth wearing the contented look of a person who has just been promised money.

"Where is the salesman?" he asked the three women, and gestured toward the motorcycles. As soon as Amparo told him, he disappeared into the theater lobby.

Sara approached the operator in time to hear her say to Gloria, "Shall I call him again tonight?" Amparo looked up and pulled three plugs from the switchboard. "There is a delay on the international line," she said.

Sara, back in her chair, sensed an omen at work in the

room. The names of these people, she thought. If there is any power in names, no bad fortune can fall here now. A woman named Remedios is beside me and my call is being put through by Marys of Help and Glory. The name of the man who just left the booth is probably Miguel Angel.

As though signaled, this Miguel Angel returned with the motorcycle salesman, a shabby, pensive man with a toothpick between his teeth. Together they moved from one to another of the four machines. The salesman, his toothpick dipping, explained he had no printed list of prices. He kept them in his head.

Miguel Angel, who had already examined and re-examined the motorcycles, now seemed to be noticing them for the first time. He hesitated among them. At last he pointed to one painted royal blue and lime, the biggest of the four. "This one," he said.

The salesman, searching slowly through his mental list, discovered the price and pronounced it so that all could hear.

"*Virgen purísima!*" said Remedios.

Discussion ensued, and compromise. But the cost was still too high. Miguel Angel would have to place another call. He reached Amparo's desk at the same moment she waved to Sara.

"The doctor in San Francisco, California," announced Amparo.

"The doctor," repeated Remedios, confirming that she had heard.

Sara stepped into the close air of the booth. As soon as she heard the hematologist's voice, she said, "Richard's had a fever for three days." But the connection was poor and she could scarcely understand Dr. MacLeod. She strained to catch his words. "Under what name is that sold here?" she asked of each medication, but the specialist in California could not say. He described the pills and injections by formula and she wrote these down syllable by syllable on the back of a receipt for flashlight batteries.

"Please repeat what you said. There's a man buying a

motorcycle just outside." And she continued to copy his words, filling the paper from top to bottom and around the edges.

Then the doctor stopped talking and at the same time the interference on the line cleared.

"Call me next week," said Dr. MacLeod with extreme clarity, and Sara could think of no way to keep him on the line.

She said, "Thank you." He hung up and left her clinging to the phone.

Ten minutes later Sara was still waiting for her bill; Remedios and Miguel Angel to be summoned to the booth. The salesman had gone, leaving behind him an unspoken consensus that more than a second call would be necessary to raise the money to buy the motorcycle. Miguel Angel would have to make a third call, and a fourth, and even then might fail.

Remedios had further comments on Dr. Vásquez. "The intern was born on an island in a lake." Sara nodded. So far Remedios had told her nothing new.

But there was more. "His father mends fishing nets. That is his profession," said Remedios. "As it was the profession of his father's father and grandfather. The intern is the first man in his family not to be a mender of nets." With these words she succeeded in implying that the traditional occupation would have suited Dr. Vásquez better than his present one.

"The intern has not cured the rheumatism in Madre Petra's knee." Remedios brushed at a fly with the fringe of her shawl. "Or the cura's chronic cough. In the case of the storekeeper's broken finger . . ."

Sara stopped listening. Instead, she invented a short film of Richard and herself back at the island. The first frames show them circling it in a launch. "Stop here," they tell the boatman when they are half around it. Midway up the cliff old Vásquez stands at the threshold of his house. Below him the hillside is webbed with nets strung from poles. Richard and Sara sit on a bench at the stern of the boat and turn their backs to the lake, whose surface shifts with the wind from one blue to another.

They notice the fishing nets veiling the slope, the path that twists and slides from old Vásquez's feet to the water's edge. He waves.

Now they are jumping out into mud and hyacinths. They climb the precipitous hill without pausing to take an extra breath. They are nimble and wiry as goats.

Remedios had entered the glass booth and left the door ajar. She was explaining distances to her aunt, and the amount of fares. She named the bus lines, the Yellow Arrow, the Eagle, the Central Transport. Remedios would wait for her in the plaza of Ibarra. She did not say, "To help you from the bus with your needlework and thimble." But she expected the silver thimble. Expected it to be hers before tomorrow night.

Sara left her seat abruptly and went to Amparo's desk. "I must ask you again for my bill. I have to leave immediately." The operator held up her left hand with thumb and forefinger a fraction of an inch apart, to signify only a second more.

"So you think he will call me," she said to Gloria.

Sara interrupted. "My bill," she said. "Please."

On the other side of the room Miguel Angel stood between motorcycles like a man with a match among explosives. His hand rested on the seat of the one he had chosen. In the booth Remedios continued to review the bus routes with her aunt. "The Yellow Arrow, the Eagle. I will meet you."

It became clear to Sara that at this moment each of the four people gathered at the switchboard wanted one thing in the world, and that thing only.

On the street a hay cart, drawn by a teamed horse and burro, made its lopsided way between her and the church. Sara saw a woman enter, then another, then an old man with a bandaged foot. She knew they had come to reinforce their faith, to pray for salvation and a place in heaven.

Outside the Cine Rex a moment later, she stopped and looked up. Above her, the supplications from the switchboard and from the church rose, thinner than wood smoke, in two separate columns. Sara watched them collide over the radio antenna on the roof of the mayor's office. Here they mingled until caught up by a sudden gust that scattered them to the outskirts of Loreto and as far as an unplowed field beyond.

14

THE PRIESTS' PICNIC

Later on, when Sara tried to assemble the scattered images of that autumn afternoon in order to point and say, "It was like this," she found she could not. Until time had passed, she almost believed there was nothing to tell of the priests' picnic.

Except that it took place on November twentieth, the anniversary of the Revolution of 1910, when persecution dispersed clerics into all paths of flight and all disguises. In those times, priests suspected of performing final rites or celebrating mass in secret were harried from the Pacific to the Gulf and caught, as often as not, scaling the wall of a barranca or slitting a passage through the jungle. And, even when they had burned or buried their habits, might be recognized wearing a farmer's grimy white cotton or a beggar's broken sandals.

Only its date might have distinguished the picnic, except that its site was San Antonio del Pulque, a name suggesting there might also exist in Mexico the communities of San José del Mescal and San Martín del Tequila, with a patron saint presiding over each.

On the nineteenth of November the cura of Ibarra invited Sara and Richard to the picnic.

"Why not ask them?" he said to his aunt, Paulita. "They will enjoy sitting on the ground to eat."

"Don Ricardo has had grippe again."

"And has recovered again," said the cura.

"They are not accustomed to our food. They are not Catholics."

The priest resolved the matter. "Give them two ham sandwiches and two cooked eggs."

On the morning of the twentieth a message was delivered to the Evertons' door by a boy wearing a carrot-colored shirt and patched trousers. His head had been shaved for ringworm and he still had his baby teeth. When he looked at the ground, his eyelashes lay stiff and black against his cheeks.

"One moment," said Richard, and read the note.

"I will wait for you at noon in my pickup at the bridge beyond the town of Los Ricos. From there I will lead you to the picnic." Below was the cura's signature, Juan Gómez, though the priest's name might better have been César Máximo Iglesias to correspond with the power he wielded over his parish.

"How old are you?" Sara asked the boy, and found he was five. Then she asked him who his parents were, but he only scuffed his feet in the dirt and picked at his scalp.

Richard wrote an answer to the cura. "We will be at Los Ricos at noon," and handed the paper to the child, who folded it over three times and ran off down the drive. From where the Evertons stood, only his bald head showed above the low wall and seemed to bounce along it like a ball.

"I think his father's the man who does odd jobs for the nuns," said Sara. "And his mother is that green-eyed niece of the postmaster." In this way she conceived and delivered a family to the unknown boy.

"You're imagining this," said Richard. "As far as we know, he may be an orphan."

"I don't think so. He reminds me of someone in Ibarra." She leaned over a geranium in a pot and started to pull off dead leaves. "We've lived here four years and this is our first invitation from the cura to the picnic. Do you suppose we've missed much?"

"We'll know after tomorrow," Richard said.

Sara spoke over her shoulder. "From now on, the cura will probably ask us every year."

Richard stared at her from the doorway. She was moving from pot to pot, her hand full of brown leaves.

"It will be like the January luncheon for the bishop," she went on. "Our being heretics won't matter if we fit in with the priests." Sara ignored her husband's silence. "This is the first of a series of picnics we'll be invited to. We'll always celebrate the Revolution with the cura."

Richard stepped toward her, letting the door slam behind him, and pulled her up to face him. The withered leaves spilled from her fingers to the tiles.

"Not a series," he said. "Not celebrate always." He lifted her chin to make her face him, but her eyes were on the leaves. "Look at me," he said, and waited until she did. "I only have another year or two. We both know that."

She touched the scar that ran from his left ear to his chin. "At least two. Maybe more."

"Not likely," said Richard. "The doctor estimated six years and we've used up almost five."

She still had her hand on his face. "He said at least six, and that means more."

Richard shook his head. "You're counting on miracles."

Sara gazed at him as she would at a stranger. What was it, after all, that made him exceptional? Not his straight eyebrows, not his wide mouth and stubborn jaw, not his unremarkable nose and ears. There were the eyes, of course, those mutant blues, and the voice. She moved closer in order to hear it through his chest as he talked.

"Sara, listen," he was saying. "You've got to stop making things up. Stop making each day up. See it."

"I do see it," she said.

"You revise it as it comes along. You revise me."

She pulled back to look at his face. "I don't," she said. "I see you now. Perfectly."

The drive from Ibarra to Los Ricos was a hundred-kilometer sampling of all the roads in Mexico. First the twisting descent down the mountain, then the paved highway to the state capital, then a gravel stretch through vineyards to a steep range of hills. From the top of one of these the Evertons descended abruptly to sink at the bottom among the foliage of avocados and limes. They lowered the car's windows to feel green air and, when they passed embankments, were brushed on the shoulder by long leaves of ferns.

Making his way between overgrown ditches, Richard drove more and more slowly. Sara glanced at him.

"Are you all right? Shall I drive?"

"Of course I'm all right."

"I know," she said. But inside her a woman not much older than herself stood alone in a dark, windy place.

What remained of the road to Los Ricos wound through guava orchards, whose fragrance invaded the car and clung there. Through an atmosphere of suffocating sweetness Los Ricos appeared in the form of a long corrugated shed that housed a fruit-processing plant. Two dozen men and women sat on the ground with their backs against its side. Farther on a rusty gasoline pump leaned hoseless toward a one-room structure that had lost its roof.

"Where do the people live? And where is the church?" said Sara. "Stop a minute."

On the far side of Los Ricos they paused and tried to find a wall or a window among the trees. But there was nothing. The guava processors must have arrived by truck or bus.

"Or by airlift," said Sara, and she imagined an old DC-3 marked EL AGUILA lift a door in its side and scatter down by parachute, like a hand sowing seeds, the men and women who still sat, hatted and shawled, behind her.

"Why are they here on a national holiday?"

"Maybe to march in a parade," said Richard. "For an audience of guava pickers, wherever they are, and that cat." For, from under a nearby sunflower, a bobtailed cat was pondering them with silver eyes. In this single minute that cat has learned everything there is to know about us, thought Sara, and felt against her ribs a welling up of fear. "And the priests," she said. "How will they celebrate?"

"Not how," said Richard. "Why?"

Beyond the next curve, beside an arched stone bridge carved with a coat of arms, they met the cura. He, his aunt, Paulita, and his merry assistant, Padre Ignacio, sat in the cab of the pickup, and five nuns occupied the rear. The eldest, Madre Petra, was seated on a straight chair with which she seemed of a piece, as if as a unit she and the chair had been removed from the convent and as a unit would arrive at the picnic place, to be installed without separation in the shade of trees, near a stream, among flowers.

"We have just arrived ourselves," said the cura, either out of courtesy or to head off apologies that would only consume more time. He climbed down from the cab and the Evertons saw him for the first time without his habit, wearing brown gabardine trousers and a yellow-checked shirt. He walked to the back of the pickup and put his hand on a cardboard box.

"Rockets," said the cura.

As soon as they crossed the bridge the Evertons' car was caught in a backwash of dust produced by the worn ruts and the cura's spinning wheels. Whenever the American guests fell back to breathe, the pickup disappeared into a grove or beyond a field. At last the priest stopped. As the dust subsided, the Evertons gradually made out the five black shapes of the nuns. The madres' faces were clean and calm, as if when they took their vows they had renounced dirt as well as lust and greed From her chair Madre Petra waved.

"We are the last to arrive," said the cura, and the Evertons saw parked around them half a dozen veteran Dodges and

Chevrolets, survivors of the years, the roads, and their owners' volatile moods.

The cura pointed and said, "This way." With deliberate steps he led the party single file up a path slippery with shale.

At the first bend they came upon San Antonio del Pulque and its nine houses that seemed to have tumbled down the hillsides like blocks and come to rest against whatever boulder or stump detained them. Cows and goats and a few lean men balanced on the thresholds. At the foot of the slope a chapel slanted toward a laurel tree. Its door gaped open and swallows dipped in and out under the lintel.

Once past this settlement there was nothing more to see except endless rows of the maguey cactus that demanded nothing in the way of care. Without spade or manure they endured drought and flood and continued to decorate the landscape with symmetrical spikes until their leaves were cut for fiber and their juice drained off to ferment.

"Look at this view," said Sara, believing Richard to be tired.

They stopped between two rows of plants and followed them with their eyes to a horizon of blue-green bayonets. Then they rejoined the others, circled a stony rise, and were there.

In front of them, as if produced by wishing or a dream, was a grassy clearing below an earthen dam. It was shadowed at one side by a grove of oaks and bounded at the other by the overflow from the spillway. Here twenty or thirty people strolled about on a flowering carpet of yellow weeds.

"Where's Madre Petra?" said Sara, for she had not seen her on the trail.

Richard pointed to the oaks.

Across the clearing, Sara saw the old nun still in her chair, sitting in the shade of trees, near a stream, among flowers.

As soon as the cura arrived, he lifted the carton, cried "Rockets!" and everyone cheered. But to the Evertons the cause of the celebration remained unclear, whether it was the stripping of ranches, mines, and vineyards from the Roman Church, or the subsequent laws that prevented priests from voting or holding passports. Or whether it was simply the place itself, the sudden grass, the improbable oaks, the thin running of water. Two of the men had taken off their shoes and were wading in the spill from the dam.

Aunts and nieces spread out cloths and covered them with mounds of tortillas and kettles of beans. They set down buckets of *mole.* Padre Ignacio, who regularly demonstrated by example that there was room in religion for many of the other satisfactions, was drinking from a jug. Wine dripped from his chin and stained his red silk vest. The cura of Ibarra abruptly turned away, removed his shoes, and went to the creek to wade.

It was then that Sara glimpsed an orange shirt among the tree trunks. "There's that boy," she said to Richard, and pointed to the deepest shadows, where the child sat on the box of rockets behind the nuns. "How did he get here?"

But, for that matter, how did any of us get here, she almost asked, and she looked at the people around her. What eruptions had shaken them loose from earlier patterns of living, lifted them to the fearful brink of choice, only to deposit them at crossroads poorly marked? Except for the merest accident, these five nuns might be designing hats or nursing babies, and all these priests owning drugstores or driving buses. She herself might still be living in a shingled American house with a boxwood hedge in front. Living there with Richard, who came home Mondays through Fridays at six from his company, which manufactured light-duty pumps, and who seemed scarcely to have heard of mines or Mexico. Until the night he came into the kitchen with a box of photographs. All of them had been taken by his grandparents and all were of Ibarra.

Before a week passed, the headframe of the mine, his grandmother in a hammock, his grandfather on a horse, his father at four playing marbles with a Mexican boy his age—these pictures and a dozen more were propped on top of cookbooks, on the spice shelf, along the windowsill, next to the toaster.

One morning a few weeks later he filled his coffee cup and Sara's and said, "I have an idea."

That accounted, in a way, for their presence this afternoon at the picnic where food was now being spooned onto plates and introductions made.

The cura, wearing shoes again, took them up to each of his friends. "Don Ricardo is restoring Ibarra to prosperity," he told them. "He is providing a veritable fountain of work."

So many congratulations followed this remark that no one heard Richard say that he could employ only one hundred and forty men. That the future of the operation depended on the copper market and the price was falling. His wife stood a short distance away while he tried to explain the odds for and against success to men who pumped his hand as if they themselves were miners and newly employed after a layoff. "Risk is involved," he tried to say.

He stubbornly resisted their faith in him. Listen to them, they may be right, Sara wanted to tell him. You may find new ore. You may have enough time. Shading her eyes with her hand, she estimated the number of priests gathered in the clearing. Twenty, she guessed, and to this figure she added the five nuns. Perhaps if they all prayed at once, she thought, to their God who saves baptized babies, converts, and, for all she knew, bootstrap operations, perhaps an angel or a lesser saint might hear. San Antonio del Pulque might hear.

"The best-known San Antonio," said the cura, as if she had asked, "is San Antonio de Padua, whose day is celebrated in June." He paused, perhaps to savor the aroma of *chile*, garlic, and spices rising from the pots on the ground, or perhaps to watch his aunt, Paulita, approach with two plates.

"Here is your food," said the cura. "Sandwiches and cooked eggs."

With lunch the afternoon fell away from any pattern and into fragments. The serving of food, rather than cementing individuals into a party, separated the picnickers. They isolated themselves in groups of two or three and spoke in broken phrases.

"How do you like your . . ." said the cura, but he went off to refill his plate and left the unfinished sentence suspended in the air over the place where he had just stood.

A tall, beak-nosed man, whose black turtleneck sweater fit his muscular torso like a sheath above a wide black leather belt, approached the two Americans. He took Sara's hand, then Richard's in his enormous grip and spoke, without introduction, as to old friends.

"We all need holidays like this," he said, and his restless eyes surveyed the clearing. "The country air makes us wish . . ." Still gazing past them, he suddenly changed the subject. "May I invite you to visit, when you can, my . . ." Here he lapsed silent, as an ivory-skinned girl, light-footed and sinuous as a cat, wound her way past him.

What would we visit? Sara wondered. His chapel, his icon collection, his hybrid rose? She wanted to ask him to mark the route on a map, but the cura had returned with his second helping and was saying, *"Muy rico."*

Richard looked at the priest's food. "Perhaps we might . . . If there is enough—"

"Have you noticed . . ." said the cura, and waved his fork in a circle so that the tines seemed to rake up all the assembled faces, the ones that were mostly Indian and the ones that were mostly Spanish, into a jackstraw heap of flashing eyes and smiling teeth and deposit them at his feet.

Sara took a step backward, away from the faces. She clutched at Richard's hand just as he lifted it to point to the dam. "In last summer's thunderstorms . . ." he began. But now came a clatter of hooves behind them and they turned to see Padre Ignacio riding a mule bareback down the slope. Trailed by a landslide of stones and gravel, the cura's assistant reined in at the edge of the grass, called for wine, and, still mounted, let it overflow from his mouth to his lap and into his shoes. He waved his arm in the direction of the nuns. But the four younger sisters looked down at their own folded hands and Madre Petra had closed her eyes against the sun. Therefore she saw neither Padre Ignacio wave nor the strong restless man in black pull the ivory-skinned girl to him and start dancing. Nor did Madre Petra know that the girl moved as though in her sleep to the rhythm of her partner's singing, moved first her right foot, then her left, and that she danced, if this was dancing, in one place and with both arms around his neck. The nuns, with their eyes cast down or closed, could not notice that the man's hands were first on the girl's shoulders, then her waist, then her hips, pressing her to him through a pleated skirt as thin as gauze.

The nuns neither saw nor heard Padre Ignacio's summons. But, in any case, his commands were not directed at them. He was waving to the child on the box of rockets.

The boy, clearly reluctant, stood up at last and made his way, step by slow step, past the nuns, around the clusters of people on the grass, in front of the Evertons, and to the mule's side. Padre Ignacio extended a hand and swung the child up.

Sara saw that soft drinks had stained the orange shirt, and a taco fallen on it, and some sauce. His face, too, was smeared with food. And Sara noticed something else.

From where she stood, the man and boy sat astride the mule in profile, their features silhouetted against a sky bluer than the interior of heaven.

"Look," Sara said to Richard, "how much alike. . ." and together they noticed that the priest's long upper lip and knobby brow were duplicated in smaller scale on the boy. Padre Ignacio's flared inquisitive nose was reproduced on the child, also the unblinking stare. But what seemed bold in the man appeared simply patient in the child, who swayed unsteadily on his perch, clinging to the mule's stubby mane, while the priest tipped out his wine.

Padre Ignacio was about to put the jug to the child's mouth when the cura, who had been standing at some distance, approached the mule and lifted the boy down.

At this the child began to cry without a sound, peering into his own tears, grown blind and dumb in his relief.

"The resemblance," Sara said to her husband. "They could be father and—"

"Or brothers," Richard said.

"But there's more than forty years between them. Even in this country, even in a family of twelve . . ."

Richard told her to be still. The cura had advanced into the middle of the clearing and displaced the dancing couple. He raised his hand for silence.

"It is time," he said.

Whether it was the words, or the shrinking in of the afternoon, or a gust of air from the north, something at this moment caused Sara to button her sweater to the neck.

The cura spoke to the weeping child. "Come on," he said. "It is time for the rockets."

Chosen to fire them off was a youth whose head drooped to his chest and his hands to his knees. He appeared spent.

The cura addressed him as Cuco. "Light the fuses and step back, Cuco," he said. "Stay whole today and they will recognize you in the seminary tomorrow."

The nuns called him Refugio. "The child is following you, Refugio. Take care of him," they said.

Everyone except the two dancers, who had vanished among the cactus, and Padre Ignacio, still on the mule's back, gathered in the clearing and faced the hill. With the sun at their backs, they gazed up at the ascending pair. Cuco, as melancholy from the rear as face-to-face, climbed as if the boulder on the summit were a burial site and the box of rockets on his shoulder an infant's coffin. Behind him the boy crawled as often as he walked, reaching out to weeds and clods of dirt to prevent a fall.

Arrived at the appointed place, Cuco kept his back to his audience while he set down the box and laid out the rockets. After that the celebration had to be delayed until the child, scuffed and breathless, reached the older boy's side and picked up a rocket.

"Refugio," called out the nuns in modulated tones.

Cuco pushed the boy away and lit a match. The ensuing blast brought reverberations and a smell of powder from the hillside, shouts of approval from the onlookers, and a rush of beating wings above the oak trees, where a flock of doves, unseen and unheard till now, soared steeply upward and were lost.

"Are you accustomed to rockets?" the cura asked the Evertons, and they nodded, remembering childhood July Fourths, when daytime explosions were merely a noisy prelude to the whispered starbursts of Roman candles after dark.

Without incident, except for a stunning volume of sound, Cuco detonated five rockets.

"How many are there?" Richard asked the cura, and discovered there were ten.

Cuco fired off the sixth, seventh, and eighth. With each explosion the child covered his ears and retreated another step. He had not foreseen so much noise and this burnt smell. He had expected to find a magnificence in it all.

Padre Ignacio began to issue orders. "Give the boy a match," he shouted. "Let him light one."

"Refugio," the nuns protested in their crystalline voices.

Cuco obeyed the higher authority. He beckoned to the child, who shrank back and tried to hide behind a sparse mesquite. Cuco, impatient to finish his job, grasped the child's hand and pulled. But the boy snatched with his other hand at the objects he passed, twigs, the edges of granite rocks, a cactus branch. Cuco dragged him by force to the scorched boulder, pointed toward the ground, and lit a match. The child shook his head and Cuco lit another.

Now the cura of Ibarra, watching from below, called out. "Refugio," he called. "Let the child go."

But Cuco, half deaf by then, failed to hear the priest and held out another match. This time the boy, finally resigned to the harm he knew would follow, accepted it. He lit the fuse and the rocket fired. Its explosion knocked him to the ground, and Cuco too. From the hillside rose shrieks that would echo there until nightfall.

Four men stumbled up the slope and moments later, in a headlong descent, brought the accident victims down. At the same time, the man in the black sweater came running from the maguey fields and, when he reached the clearing, made it his private clinic. "Stand back and let them breathe. Get all the cold water you can. I need scissors or a knife." Richard handed him a jackknife and one of the priests found a machete. Later on, Sara would say, "That machete. Why did he bring it? Where did he hide it?" But that was after the picnic.

Two nuns were kneeling by Cuco and the child to cut away cloth from burns. Next to them the girl who had danced tore strips from her skirt to soak in the pots and casseroles spilling over with water from the dam.

Madre Petra rose unsteadily from her chair, took a step forward, and said a prayer. Then she put her arm through Sara's. "They will recover," she said, "but scarred. Look at Refugio's shoulder. Look at the child's face." Leaning on Sara, the old nun explained the authority of the man in black. "He was a medical missionary once, in the north, among the Tarahumaras." The madre took another step and considered the pair on the ground.

"Now God has made them his special charges," she said.

Padre Ignacio had pushed through the crowd and was standing next to the child. "*Qué tal?*" he called out in hearty salutation.

The child stared up through wet lashes.

"In a week you will be spinning tops," said Padre Ignacio. The boy closed his eyes.

In this first dusk the clearing seemed less spacious than before, less green and flowered. It was turning itself back to what it was, a ragged plot of weeds between scrub oaks and a ditch.

Cuco and the boy were carried off on stretchers made of coats and limbs of trees. Sara imagined the procession filing through the magueys and sliding down the trail at San Antonio del Pulque, attracting no attention from the inhabitants. An observer would think boys were burned with dynamite every day and borne lurching down the path each evening.

The cura sought out the Americans. "This was not the happiest of our picnics," he told them. "But it was not the unhappiest. Five years ago a priest was shot by a radical on the bridge at Los Ricos and once one of the padres had a heart attack here, in this quiet place, on a day much like this one, full of sun and fellowship."

As the Evertons shook hands with the guests that were left, each man asked to visit the mine.

"By all means," said Richard. "But make it soon."

Sara, without speaking, looked at the ground, at the charred boulder on the hill, and at the sky. Out of the fading blue wash above her reeled a cloud. It was the doves, dropping on fixed wings into the oaks.

Along the dim path straggled the last of the picnickers. Sara walked in front of Richard without a word until they reached the houses of San Antonio del Pulque.

"They've never heard of time," she said. For the men in the nine doorways were leaning, reclining, and examining their situation in identical attitudes as before.

When the Evertons came to the road, they saw that only their car and the cura's truck were still there. In the back of the pickup Madre Petra was already stationed in her chair, surrounded by her four sisters. In the cab, next to Paulita, a picnic guest, turned priest again and wearing a clerical collar, sat in Padre Ignacio's place. It appeared that the assistant priest of Ibarra had been left to find his own way home.

The Evertons started the return trip ahead of the cura. They looked for an armed revolutionary on the bridge and for scraps of bunting in Los Ricos. But the road was as empty as the countryside. The guava processors had left the iron shed.

"Did I imagine them?" Sara asked.

"Not this time," said Richard. "And there's that cat." He pointed to the derelict pump.

Under it crouched the silver-eyed, bobtailed animal, clawing feathers from a thrashing sparrow.

A kilometer or two beyond Los Ricos, at the moment the evening turned dark enough for headlights, Sara looked at her husband and offered to drive.

To her surprise he stopped the car and changed places. In less than a minute he was asleep with his head nodding toward her until it touched her shoulder and was lifted with a jerk. "Turn up your lights," he said at these moments. Or, "Keep to the center of the road when you can to avoid cattle at the sides." Then he was asleep again.

She went on in silence although she had things to say. "Am I going too fast?" she might have asked. "What time is it? How far have we come? Are we almost there?"

It was while she was driving in the middle of a lane edged with reeds that a horn sounded twice behind her. She pulled to the right, Richard woke, and the cura's pickup passed them.

In the beam of the raised headlights the nuns could be seen meditating in the back of the truck. The Evertons watched the cura negotiate a bend, saw the pickup careen, Madre Petra's chair topple, four pairs of arms extend to set it straight.

Sara simultaneously reached for her husband, as if otherwise he might slide from the seat, through the door, into the night, and under the wheels.

When they rounded the curve and came up behind the truck, Madre Petra was once more upright in her chair. Her hands were clasped and her head was bowed. She may have been asleep. Or concerned with the soul of Padre Ignacio and the recovery of the boys.

But nothing is sure. Perhaps she was simply praying to be alive for next year's picnic, and the one after, and even the one after that.

15

THE BAPTISTS

From the beginning it had been known in Ibarra that the Evertons belonged to no church, neither to the true church nor to any of the others. But in the years since then the townspeople had become accustomed to the sight of the American couple walking along the steep brink of dams, on the narrow-gauge trestle across the arroyo, or in front of the bus when it was already in motion, as if they had faith, particularly Catholic faith.

So it was merely to share news that late one morning the parish priest stopped Sara Everton as she walked past the village church. The cura stood bareheaded in full sun, his crucifix and the metal rims of his glasses reflecting light.

He began with the formalities. "Your husband is well," he said, "and the mine prospering." Pronounced with clerical authority, his intended questions became statements requiring no response, neither the truth nor the lies.

The priest came to the point.

"A Baptist minister is coming to Ibarra," he said.

"What for?" said Sara.

"To visit his relatives."

"Are the relatives Baptists?"

"No. They are Catholics, as he himself once was." The cura

looked past the bust of Juárez in the plaza, over the cantina and the convent and the slack flag on the *presidencia,* and beyond them all to the circle of hills seared to their zinc and copper veins by the hot winds of Mexican spring. Then he lifted his gaze and it seemed to Sara that he was hoping for a sign, one that would be visible to her as well. She, too, often looked up, but only to follow a pair of black butterflies, or a sparrow and a hawk.

"Do I know the relatives?" she asked.

"They are Inocencia Casillas, the Baptist's aunt, and her two nephews, the Baptist's cousins."

In her mind Sara placed Inocencia against a series of familiar backgrounds, among the crowded market stalls in the city of Concepción, under the portico of the cathedral, in the narrow doorways of Ibarra.

"With three nephews, why does she beg?"

"To her, begging means more than a plate of stew or a pair of shoes. It is her profession." The cura started to walk away, then turned with a reminder. "She begged from you, señora, even when her son, Blas, was employed at the Malagueña by your husband." He paused halfway up the church steps. "Inocencia is ill," he said. "This morning I gave her last rites."

Sara remembered the beggar's pinned and knotted garments, her quick eyes, her bird-claw hand. She deserved a luxury before dying, a sack of sugar or a goose-down quilt, a long red coat. But it was already too late.

A small whirlwind from nowhere carried dust across the cobbles, lifted Sara's light hair, blew grit into her eyes, and reached the top step at the same time as the cura.

"The Baptist wants to see his aunt before she dies," he said. "He will arrive tonight, bringing with him his wife and daughter. From El Crucero, Chihuahua, on the United States border."

"Perhaps he became a Baptist when he married one," said Sara.

"No, she was a Catholic." The priest regarded Sara as though, even after their long acquaintance, he still believed she might put her thoughts in order and explain apostasy. She noticed this look, interpreted it correctly, and started to move on.

But the cura spoke again. "It is probable," he said, "that the three Baptists will walk up to your house to call on you and your husband."

"Why?" said Sara.

The priest, without answering, glanced at the clock in the tower and moved toward the church. From its entrance he addressed her once more.

"Next Sunday is the day of our Señor of Tepozán," he said. "If you will look from your house at noon, you and don Ricardo will see the procession on its way to the monastery. Eight men will carry Christ's statue on their shoulders."

Sara had already seen this figure, paler than flesh and larger than life, sealed in its transparent coffin in a windowless cubicle off the west transept. Through the glass the body had a greenish cast as if, once life had bled away, neither faith, nor revelation, nor an artist's skill could restore its natural colors. It reposed, stabbed and nailed on a purple cloth, and stared into the twilight of day and the black of night that followed.

"We will be at our gate to watch you pass," said Sara, and the cura entered the church.

"Do you remember Inocencia, the beggar?" Richard said at dinner that evening. "She has died. Of old age, according to the miners."

Or of snuff and pipe tobacco, thought his wife. Or of carrying a bucket of well water for half a mile on her head, morning, noon, and night since the day she learned to walk.

"How old was she?" Sara asked. "Was she ninety?" From the age of ninety, which many people attain, she subtracted Richard's age of forty-six. According to Inocencia's longevity, half his life should lie ahead instead of the doctor's predicted and now shrunken span. Sara looked at her husband's dark head, bent over a mango he was slicing from the seed. He showed no remorse for the cruel thing he'd done, to allow himself an illness that had no cure. Her anger passed, giving way to fear. Fear, for the time being, passed.

"Inocencia probably never knew how old she was," said Richard. "But she was at the mine last payday, begging from the three o'clock shift."

Sara stared through the window and saw, instead of the darkness outside, the gnarled old woman toiling up the steep ascent from the plaza to the Malagueña gate.

"And her son killed only three months ago," said Sara, recalling the exhibition of bravado presented in January by Blas Casillas, a mature man. On that occasion he rode his bicycle from the mine to the town with failing brakes, catapulted headfirst into the stone façade of the *presidencia,* and was dead before the mayor could get up from his desk.

There are more violent ends in this village than in a provincial capital, thought Sara. Scarcely a week passes without a broken head, a severed leg, a fatal burn. Or is it only that everything shows in Ibarra, is on display like the buttons and spools of a notions shop?

Richard took two pills from his pocket and swallowed them with wine.

"You forgot them at noon," said Sara, and felt a momentary sinking, as if a strand of the rope to which she clung had begun to fray. It was too insubstantial to hold her, this rope, woven as it was out of a doctor's life-or-death pills and her own unreasonable expectations. She could feel it sag.

Richard glanced at her, rose from his chair, pulled her up to him, and kissed her on the wrist, on the throat, and, without stopping, on the mouth. In this way he closed the door on her foreboding.

"You're a mind reader," said Sara.

"I've had chances to practice." He turned as he left the room. "Blas Casillas was a good miner. He was more at home working through an ore body than he was on his own doorstep." Then he unnecessarily reminded Sara, "You shopped with me in Loreto for his coffin."

On that day winter was resurrected and the Evertons awakened to a light that lay like ashes on the landscape, draining off the green from the jasmine and the red from the patio tiles. Icicles as long as pennants hung from burst pipes outside the bathroom and the kitchen. No water ran in the house that day, and, outside in the courtyard, the earthen jar, so wide and high it could have hidden a bandit from a soldier, was sealed with three inches of ice.

The Americans had been drinking coffee in front of the dining-room fire when Remedios Acosta, a Casillas neighbor, tapped on the window.

"Blas is dead," said Remedios the moment she was inside. When the Evertons nodded, she went on, "I have come on behalf of Inocencia. About the coffin." She surveyed the room, noticing the windows, which might better have been boarded up for privacy, and the hearth piled with logs thick enough to barbecue a goat.

"The mine will cover all costs," said Richard.

"The coffin will fit in your car," said Remedios, and, when the Evertons agreed the station wagon would hold it, the affair was settled. As they opened the front door for the visitor to leave, the air from outside struck across their faces like a blow.

"This is the coldest day I have ever known," said Sara, forgetting all the others.

"Even so, it is best to buy the coffin immediately," said Remedios.

The Evertons, their wheels caught in the frozen ruts of the road, had covered half the distance to Loreto when they reached a decision. They would buy one of the cheaper boxes for the dead man and give Inocencia the difference in money.

"It's what Blas would want," said Richard, and Sara nodded. Behind them lay an extended space where they had lowered the back seat to make room for the coffin.

But in Loreto at the unlit, narrow shop with FUNERALES ORTEGA painted over the door, the proprietor argued that this was not what Blas would want.

When Richard pointed to a plain gray box, Ortega said, "That one is not suitable," and moved along his stacked display, mentioning woods, metals, fabrics, and hinges.

"I must insist," Richard said at last, and Ortega, still protesting, helped him load the gray coffin into the car.

On the way back to Ibarra between stiff roadside weeds, the station wagon, weighed down by the box, barely cleared the crown of the road and occasionally scraped it.

"We should have come by wooden-wheeled cart," said Richard.

"Pulled by white mules," said Sara.

"A matched pair," he said.

And to herself she added, Wearing black plumes.

From out of the crowd who filled Inocencia's door two men came forward to help carry the coffin of Blas Casillas. But when they saw it, these two brought up four other men and together they pondered at the back of the car. From within Inocencia's house issued a scent of incense and an echo of prayer.

Finally one man said, "It is gray."

"It is a woman's color," said another. Then they all said, as if they had rehearsed it, "It is a woman's or a pauper's coffin."

When Richard explained his proposed cash present to Inocencia, the six men made no reply and in silence leaned against the car to let time pass.

"Is it possible to ask Inocencia herself?" said Sara.

"She is in grief."

In Loreto one hour later, the proprietor of Funerales Ortega without comment exchanged the gray box for a finer one at eight times the cost. "The mother of the deceased will be happy with your choice," he said. "It is the same model selected by the families for the owner of the *cine,* the assistant stationmaster, and the tax collector."

Now old Inocencia, the beggar, was dead.

"Must we shop again in Loreto for a coffin?" Sara asked her husband the day after she heard the news.

"Not this time," he said. "Inocencia died rich, the second richest woman in Ibarra. Next only to Chayo Durán." And Sara conjured up a picture of Chayo's *mesón,* where visiting engineers and government clerks sometimes boarded by the week without fuss or feathers, hot water, or an inside toilet.

Sara began to revise her previous image of the beggar. As though she had witnessed it herself she now saw Inocencia in the National Bank at the state capital. She observed the old woman's bent and ragged form at the teller's window and watched her unknot her *rebozo,* allowing pesos, centavos, tostones, and quintos to scatter over the counter. These coins rolled across the floor as far as the manager's desk, where they toppled on their sides to expose the faces of patriots.

"It was all found this morning," said Richard. "Kettles and tureens of coins, a mattress stuffed with paper bills."

How soft the beggar must have slept, thought Sara, and asked, "Who discovered the fortune?"

"Two nephews," said Richard.

"And they divided it."

"No. The cura came along and took it away in a flour sack for later distribution."

"These nephews," said Sara. "What do they do?"

"One is the sacristan of the church and the other is the chairman of Acción Católica."

"So they'll get the money."

"There's a third nephew," said Richard, "a Baptist minister from the state of Chihuahua. He'll arrive in Ibarra tomorrow."

"I know," said Sara. "Bringing his wife and daughter." And she saw the shades of the Baptists advance up the driveway without touching the ground and settle, wraithlike, into three porch chairs.

On the following Sunday morning the Baptists came, unaware that Sundays were the only days the Americans had to themselves without the cook, the gardener, and the water carrier, without interference and encounters. The Baptists could not know that Richard and Sara were awakened from sleep at daybreak by the singing of an uncommon bird outside their bedroom window, or that at nine o'clock they were still in this bed that had part of a choir screen for a headboard. Or that for these hours they had lain so close it seemed doubtful that custom of any kind, opening curtains, getting dressed, eating breakfast, could pull them apart and deposit them, naked, on opposite sides of the bed to feel for their slippers on the splintered pine floor.

During this time they spoke occasionally.

"That bird is singing the scale of C major backward," Sara remarked. "C, B, A, G, F."

"It's a cenzontle," he told her.

Half an hour later he said, "The whole thing's settled." And when she asked, "What?" Richard said, "The two Catholic nephews will inherit Inocencia's money. The cura has eliminated the Baptist on grounds of neglect. He hasn't visited Ibarra for fifteen years."

Sara raised herself on one elbow to look at her husband's face. "Did the other two help her?"

"Of course not. The sacristan is paid in sacks of rice and bottles of cooking oil, and the chairman of Acción Católica has nine children." With his left hand Richard pulled his wife's head down to his.

"There's that bird again," she managed to say.

The three Baptists could not have suspected, when they pushed open one side of the heavy wooden gate, that the Evertons had closed it last night for the sake of privacy. Or that they would discover the American couple still at breakfast when they arrived, still drinking coffee on their porch with their feet up on a pair of carved stones.

"It is eleven o'clock by my watch," said the Baptist minister, who during the next hour spoke only Spanish in spite of his years on the border. He was a short, square man, tightly buttoned into a suit that was warm for May. Introducing himself, his wife, and young daughter as the Peraltas, he went on to describe his Chihuahua mission which, although short of funds, had already separated two hundred souls from idolatry and the kissing of rings and brought them to the floating off of sin by immersion.

"Have some coffee," said Richard, and Sara brought cups.

Then she said, "We regret the death of your aunt, Inocencia, especially so soon after the accident that killed your cousin Blas."

"God save them," said the Reverend Peralta, and fell silent.

"You are admiring these stones," said Sara, and touched them with her sandaled foot. "They are pediments of columns discovered in the rubble behind the church and were given us by the cura of Ibarra."

During the pause that followed, the child looked down at her hands clutched in the lap of her somber twill skirt. The preacher's wife, short, robust, and wearing half-mourning for Inocencia, stared beyond the village that lay below them, in the direction of the tilting headframe of the idle Gloriosa mine.

Richard's glance followed hers. "Perhaps you would like to visit the Malagueña mine," he said. "We have it back in operation. Of course ladies are not allowed underground. They are considered to bring bad luck. If an accident occurred after a woman entered a tunnel it would be blamed on her."

"God reveals his will in mysterious ways," said the Reverend Peralta.

"That reminds me of a most unusual bird," said Sara. "Do you know the cenzontle?"

The Baptists, startled, put down their cups on a leather table. "May we see your house?" said the minister, and he rose as if appointed guide and led them all into the *sala.* Once there, the visitors sat side by side on a sofa that faced the adjoining bedroom and the tangle of sheets. Sara pulled together the sliding doors.

"Sunday is the time for Protestants to worship together," said the Reverend Peralta, and he suddenly stood and took a Bible from the pocket of his brown serge suit. His wife and daughter also rose and all three bowed their heads.

"The Lord is my shepherd," said the minister, and the Evertons, still seated, listened to the Twenty-third Psalm being recited in their living room with the same stupefaction they would have felt if Karl Marx, returned to earth, had come here to stand under the blown-glass lamp and recite his *Manifesto.*

"Though I walk through the valley of the shadow of death," intoned the reverend, and the words, converted in the Evertons' minds to English, reached them through layers of half-forgotten childhood practice and long adult disuse.

This can't be happening, Sara told herself. Not to us, not in this room. He is committing an act of trespass if he is trying to save our souls. Or is that what he's after? she wanted to ask her husband. For an instant her eyes met the Baptist's serene, acquisitive glance. Wishing she could induce an interval of deafness, Sara looked past the minister and through the long windows to the ash tree, among whose branches the cenzontle hid.

Richard, too, gazed through the windows and examined the dry hills beyond the garden wall for outcroppings of ore that might have extruded overnight.

The Reverend Peralta saw that their attention had strayed and addressed them separately. "Señor," he said. "Señora," and waited until their eyes turned reluctantly toward his. "My daughter will sing." When the girl continued to sit rigid in her place, he spoke her name. "Rebeca," he said, and when still she made no move to rise he spoke her name again and put his hand under her elbow to bring her to her feet.

Rebeca, pushed from behind, advanced two steps into the room. Her sorrowful young face was framed against the ochers and crimsons of a weathered painting on the wall behind her, a representation of the Virgin of Mercy presiding over purgatory.

"Look. The two girls are the same age," Sara said in low

tones to her husband. "The Virgin and the Baptist child."

The reverend, overhearing but not understanding her words, nodded and smiled as if she had said, "This is charming," or "I believe."

"Sing! Sing!" the father commanded the daughter, and Rebeca swallowed twice, twisted her fingers, stretched her flower-stem neck, and began.

"O come," she sang. "O come." But with these words her tremulous soprano died away. After a brief agony of silence she retreated and sat down.

"She has embarrassment," said her father.

Sara looked outside and attempted, by merely staring, to lift a branch of the ash tree, reveal the cenzontle, and will it into song.

The Reverend Peralta opened his Bible at random, like a dealer cutting cards, and announced his sermon. *"Fe. Esperanza. Caridad,"* he said, and Sara repeated to herself, *Esperanza, Caridad,* as if to practice rolling *r*'s.

The preacher watched her lips move. Now he has seen a sign, she thought. He believes we will be born again and give money to his mission. Then he can return rich, after all, to El Crucero, Chihuahua. She regarded the Baptist, whose eye was on her and whose voice was swelling with admonitions and examples. He has classified us as impulsive people, she realized. For if not impulsive, why would we have come here to Ibarra to raise up a mine and a house from ruins and isolate ourselves among papists?

"Charity," repeated the reverend. His glance fell on Richard, who had found a pencil and was filling a small notebook with calculations. Sara's remote gaze lay on a stand of organ cactus across the road.

Now the preacher's discourse and her eagerness to escape it seemed to raise her, as if by levitation, to a plane just below the beamed ceiling. From here she looked down on them all. On the Reverend Peralta, sweating in his zeal and his serge suit; on his wife, black and gray as a mockingbird out of respect for Inocencia's hoard of alms; on Rebeca, lost and bewildered on the crisscrossing paths of two worlds. First among us all, thought Sara, this girl ought to be born again, into pink dresses, hair ribbons, and beads.

From her vantage place Sara examined her husband and observed with surprise how thin he was, how his tan seemed brushed on his skin. If we were to be born again, she thought, we would choose to be born in this house, in that bed that is still unmade. Born to work this mine, whose name should be the *Quién Sabe,* and to live in this mountain town of one thousand souls. To hear church bells at dawn, the mine whistle at noon, and at first dark the jukebox in the plaza. All we would want out of being born again is this place to live and die in, as we are living and dying in it now. Then she amended her words. As Richard is dying in it now, in spite of the hematologist's pills, in spite of me.

A moment later she descended to her chair and said, "What time is it?" She had remembered the transfer of Christ's effigy to the monastery chapel of Tepozán and her promise to be at the gate.

The Reverend Peralta, interrupted in midparable, recovered quickly enough to say, "Almost twelve o'clock. If we were in my mission in El Crucero, Chihuahua, the collection would be gathered at this time."

But Richard merely totaled a column of figures and, without reaching for his wallet, returned the notebook to his pocket.

Sara said, "We must stop now. For the procession."

The Baptist, who had spent his childhood in Ibarra, was familiar with its feast days. "Do you believe in the myth?" he asked her. "That Christ appeared in a tree and said, 'Build a chapel for me here.' "

"I don't believe in myths," said Sara. "But I can imagine, under certain circumstances, improvising an altar to the gods."

The preacher bowed his head and said a prayer. He spoke the words with little hope, like a vendor who continues to call his wares when, up and down along the street, the shutters are closing for siesta.

The Baptists and the Evertons reached the gate at the moment the procession came into view, trailing a backwash of dust and faint song. The cura walked in front and, without turning his head, acknowledged the group at the side of the road. Behind him eight men carried on their shoulders the wooden pallet bearing the patron of Tepozán.

"They are making a parade of Jesus," said the Reverend Peralta.

Rebeca stared fearfully at the ground, her mother toward Chihuahua, El Crucero, and home.

Immediately behind the effigy came the cura's current assistant, old Padre Javier, trailed by three dogs, and after them the sacristan and the chairman of Acción Católica.

A question occurred to Sara. "What color was Inocencia's coffin?" she asked her husband.

"Not gray." He was watching some miners he knew walk by. "Gray would have been only half suitable."

"I think it was mauve, or amber, or ultramarine," said Sara, laying Inocencia to rest in shades the beggar never dreamed of.

Hearing the old woman's name, the Baptists had turned to look at the Americans. The preacher spoke. "If I had been able to establish my church in Ibarra, my aunt would have been the first convert to my congregation. But, since I moved away, I had no opportunity to guide her. So she remained a pagan."

As the townspeople passed the gate and disappeared around a bend in the road, Sara once more revised her image of old Inocencia. She no longer saw her begging at market stalls or secreting coins in jars but as a wanton girl, barefoot and merry, drifting on tides of perfumed air from sacrilege to sacrilege.

"A pagan," said Sara, and thought she heard snatches of profane song echo from the empty sky.

"Yes," said the reverend. "A pagan. So to speak." He beckoned to his wife and daughter and, stumbling now and then in the potholes of the road, led his family in the direction of the village. He turned back twice to look after the procession, which, out of sight by then, was approaching the arched entrance to the chapel and the worn stone floor where he had knelt as a child.

The Evertons started toward their house and locked the gate behind them. A moment later they were on the porch, sitting in two leather chairs as if they had never left them. Again their feet rested on the carved stone pediments.

"At this instant we're a kilometer from the Catholics at Tepozán and a kilometer from the Baptists in Ibarra," said Sara. "And who can tell how far from Pan and the dryads?"

She gazed toward the wide valley below Ibarra. Its arid expanse was patched with fields already plowed for rain.

"Where does that leave us? So to speak." Now she was facing Richard, memorizing him.

At first he seemed not to have heard. His eyes followed the ring of hills to the south, San Juan, Santa Cruz, La Capilla, then turned to the mesas on the eastern horizon.

Still not answering the question, he reached into one of his pockets for an ore sample, into another for a magnifying lens, and leaned close to examine the rough fragment.

Eventually he said, "This is probably Mesozoic."

"A million years old," said Sara.

"One or two hundred million." He gave her a split rock that was the size and shape of a primitive stone hatchet.

She was unable to let it go. The jagged wedge lay lighter in her hand than the shell of a quail's egg or the dust of a Damascus rose. It was still between her fingers when the procession passed again, bound this time from the monastery to Ibarra. The Evertons made no move to witness the return trip. Instead, they lingered on the porch as if they had nothing to do in the world but sit in the sun, close their eyes, hold stones.

16

The Doctor of the Moon

In early November there was an emergency. Sara left Ibarra at midnight, arrived in Concepción at one, and for the rest of her life could recapture this hour whole and bright, polished as it had been with fear. Time failed to blur the images, and five years later, or even ten, glimpses of them would intervene between her and a gathering of people, a display in a shop window, her own reflection in the glass. She would never afterward stand under a full moon without seeing corn shocks and chaparral, ditches flooded yellow with wildflowers, the chandeliered lobby of the Hotel París, and the telephone on the reception desk. Without hearing the doctor's voice as he answered.

"*Bueno,*" he had begun. "*Bueno,* señora."

When Sara realized a few minutes before twelve that her husband might die unless she found a doctor, she left the house and stepped into moonlight so radiant that the pepper trees along the drive stood in separate pools of shadow. Fermín, the watchman, was asleep at the gate. But at her approach he rose so quickly it appeared that naps made no difference to a man seventy-five years old.

"Please go to the clinic and get the intern. Don Ricardo is ill."

The old man turned his long somber face toward Ibarra, toward the plaza, the church, the *presidencia* and the clinic behind it, though all these things were a kilometer away and out of sight. "The *practicante,*" he said.

"Yes, the *practicante.*"

"It is Saturday. He has left Ibarra for the night." The watchman noticed the widening of Sara's eyes. "But there are doctors in the state capital and the taxi driver knows every one of them. Chuy Santos has delivered patients to them all."

"Then we must find him." And she brought the car.

The wide brim of the watchman's sombrero prevented him from entering. He stood at the door, turning his head one way and another until at last Sara said without patience, "Take off your hat."

Moonlight had narrowed the aimless streets of Ibarra. Sara drove past the cantina, the post office, down the single block of the alameda, and crossed the arroyo on the arched stone bridge. She was approaching the convent when the watchman said, "Here," opened his door while the car was still moving, and stumbled off into the shimmering dark.

Sara saw she had stopped on the basketball court in front of a row of houses that appeared abandoned, their windows boarded against burglars and night air. In one of these lived her cook, who now must be roused from sleep and asked to stay with Richard. He cannot be left alone, Sara told herself, though she could not imagine what the cook might do in the event of a worsening crisis.

Sara walked from one house to another, calling in front of each one, until at last a sliver of candlelight fell across a sill. Behind it stood the cook, blanketed and unsurprised, her hair hanging below her waist. As Sara explained the emergency each woman regarded the other. What thick braids she has, thought Sara; she is wondering why I'm not down on my knees to pray. But the cook was dressed and already sitting in the car when the watchman came back with Jesús Santos.

Chuy bowed to Sara and said, "At your orders," as if the hour were four in the afternoon and the destination a ladies' tea canasta. When he understood the purpose of the trip he said, "Well then, you need not go, señora. I will find Dr. de la Luna, the finest in Concepción, and deliver him to your door."

"I must go," said Sara, "to give him the details. So he will bring the right medicines." At this moment three words, "bag of tricks," entered her mind and lingered there. "And in case Dr. de la Luna cannot come . . ." She looked at the convent, the school, the row of eight houses, all freshly whitewashed by the moon. "In that case, we must find the next best."

Chuy Santos contemplated her. He saw before him a headstrong woman who believed she could bend providence to suit her. *"A sus órdenes,"* he said.

Ten minutes later the cook sat at the threshold of Richard's door, prepared to bring him water, bring him ice, bring him broth. But the patient remained unaware of her presence. He was an explorer in a hostile land, set on by savage tribes, pinned by lances to a burning wall.

As Sara turned to go, she saw the cook cross herself.

There was a wooden crate of pots and pans on the back seat of the red Volkswagen, also two baskets of green *chiles*, and a birdcage made of twigs. Chuy saw no need to explain this cargo which was to travel with them the eighty kilometers to Concepción and the eighty kilometers back. Sara got in beside the driver, who leaned over to slam the door, said *"Vámonos,"* and started off.

When they had skidded twice on the gravel surface to miss hobbled burros grazing by night, Sara said, "Why don't you blow your horn?"

"It is out of service," said Chuy, and flung the car down the mountain on a zigzag course.

At the bottom of the grade the taxi veered south on the paved road and traveled a line so direct that Concepción might have been a magnet and the Volkswagen an iron filing. The pavement rolled out ahead of them and rolled up behind them and in its unwinding cast out along its edges half a dozen hamlets of a few houses, a silo, and a soft-drink stand. Between these huddled clusters a patchwork of stripped fields and harvested orchards pressed up to the pavement as if passing traffic might renew them. But until the red taxi reached the outskirts of the capital, it was the only car on the road. As far as Sara could tell, it was the only car in Mexico, the only car on earth.

An overhead light which was never extinguished shone dimly on the tasseled green fringe that bordered Chuy's windshield and on the wax rose that hung from the mirror. It shed its faint glow on a plaster statue of the Virgin of Guadalupe that swayed on the dashboard. The beams of Chuy's headlights crossed at a point twenty feet ahead.

"Can you see where you're going?" Sara asked.

"I could find my way along this road drunk, blind, or crazy," said Chuy, and turned off the headlights to demonstrate his control. At this, the whole countryside was misted over with silver—the endless thoroughfare before them, the fields on either side, and all the wide desert beyond that swept to the hills. It was in this spectral light that a scavenger dog raced from a plot of land onto the road and was struck.

"Stop," said Sara.

"On what account?" The driver continued on.

"It may still be alive."

Chuy looked sidelong at her obstinate profile, the profile of a child afraid of the dark who will enter a crypt at night to prove he is not. If I tell her the dog is only hurt, thought Chuy, she may ask me to bind its wounds. If I say it is certainly dead, she may insist that I inter it.

"We must think of don Ricardo," he told her, "not of animals who have no souls."

From the birdcage behind came a twitter. He plans to sell these things at one o'clock in the morning, Sara supposed. Get rid of them all while I talk to Dr. de la Luna.

But Chuy was thinking, not of a sale, but of Big Braulia, a

pomaded woman of forty, wide and generous of mouth, breast, and thigh, the wife of a locomotive engineer. During her husband's absences, Braulia observed an independent schedule of her own. As soon as Chuy had introduced the señora to Dr. de la Luna, he hoped to visit the engineer's wife in her rosy-pillowed room behind the fruit-and-vegetable market.

He switched on the headlights. In their sudden beam the ditches that would line the road on both sides from here to Concepción flamed all shades of yellow with marguerites, marigolds, and daisies.

Sara was startled into speech. "Look at those flowers!" And was shocked by her words, on this mission, at this time.

"There will be fewer tomorrow," said Chuy. "Tomorrow is All Souls' Day. These you see will be cut to lay on graves."

There was a silence while Sara watched the wild flowers spring into the light ahead. Then she asked Chuy the time and he glanced at the moon. "It is twelve-thirty," he told her. The taxi raced on, pulling to the left because of its alignment, knocking because of its cylinders, polluting the shining night because of its rings. The caged bird chirped twice and Chuy began to sing. "*Ay, ay, querida!*" sang Chuy.

Until this moment Sara had heard only scraps of song from Jesús Santos, torn phrases that trailed behind when the red taxi passed her in its rush up the road from Ibarra to the mine. But these scraps had been clues enough for her to guess that he could sing as he was singing now, in a voice to confuse rational discourse and stab the heart.

While her husband's fever mounted forty kilometers behind and Dr. de la Luna slept oblivious forty kilometers ahead, Sara listened to Chuy sing. He stopped at last and Sara, more affected by this voice, under these circumstances, than she could bear, failed to acknowledge the performance and simply asked, "Do you think it's dead?"

"What dead, señora?"

"The dog you hit."

Chuy sighed and struck the palms of his hands against the steering wheel for patience.

"By now that animal is in heaven with children who throw sticks for him to chase and old women who feed him bread."

On their left a solitary lantern hanging from a shed marked the town of Viudas. In the dark Sara recognized this place she had often seen by day. The streets of Viudas sloped and fell off into gullies, dragging with them crooked houses and the infants, cats, and grandmothers inside.

Chuy sang two more songs and had started a third when Sara spoke again.

"How do you know that Dr. de le Luna is the best in Concepción?"

"Because when Pepe Torres stumbled into the ore classifier, two doctors, first one and then the other, set his legs and at the end of a year he was still on crutches. Then Dr. de la Luna broke them again and lined up the bones as straight as a rifle barrel. Now Pepe can walk by himself."

"But my husband has no broken bones."

"Dr. de la Luna also specializes in don Ricardo's illness." And Chuy waited to hear what the illness was.

Sara said nothing, but against all reason began to believe this was true of the doctor. To the left of the road an expanse of chaparral and cactus made a horizon of its own and on the right the chapel dome of a derelict hacienda gleamed smoke-blue above stone rubble. But what if Richard dies before I can bring this expert to him? What if he dies before I get back, before I can tell him? Tell him what? she asked herself. Tell him about the dog, the moon, the flowers, the lost streets of Viudas. Tell him that Dr. de le Luna is a specialist in his disease. Tell him to wait. For the doctor. For me.

"Wait," she said to Chuy.

"What for?" he said, as he had the first time.

"The birdcage is about to fall."

Without decreasing his speed Chuy swept his arm into the back seat and set the cage straight, scattering seed and splashing water from a tiny cup. The bird beat its wings against the sticks that imprisoned it, ruffled its feathers, and clung to a dangling perch.

Chuy began to sing again in his resonant tenor about men whose women had left them for sailors, for bullfighters, for pimps.

If Richard dies tonight, Sara wondered, will I return to Concepción on this same road tomorrow to advise the coroner? Will I select a coffin at La Urna del Oro, drive back to Ibarra with it, and call Luis and Paco Acosta from the garden and the water carrier from his burros at the gate?

"Please help me with this coffin. Let me open the front door. Take it into the bedroom. Thank you."

When the taxi reached the plaza of Concepción the square was dark except for a single street lamp at each corner. Moonlight, filtered through the branches of jacarandas, illuminated the blue-tiled pond, the façades of the cathedral and the government palace, and the plate-glass windows of Woolworth's and the bank. Two dim bulbs burned at the Hotel París, one over the entrance and one at the far end of the lobby, over the reception desk, where the night clerk was opening a paper bag of food.

Sara stood with Chuy outside the hotel's etched-glass door and heard the cathedral clock strike one. "Please wait," she told him.

"I have a matter of business to attend to," said the taxi driver. "In the neighborhood of the market."

"You must be back in five minutes. Without fail." Sara, ignorant of Big Braulia, presumed that in this short time, in the early hours of the morning, Chuy expected to find customers for the pots and pans, the *chiles* and the bird. "If Dr. de la Luna agrees to come, we must go immediately to his house."

"His house is behind his waiting room and I have been there a hundred times," said Chuy. "I could drive there one-handed and backward and not miss a turn." He looked in the direction of the market, four blocks away. This talk will have to stop, he thought, or it will be too late. Too late for Braulia and too late to deposit at don Ricardo's bedside the finest physician in this state of Mexico.

Chuy pushed open the door of the Hotel París. "There is the telephone, señora. And the night porter to help you." For he believed that it was unlikely the American woman and Dr. de la Luna would be able to communicate. Only in Ibarra was her Spanish understood, and the doctor spoke very quickly in the idiom of Yucatán where he was born.

"Not a second more than five minutes. We must drive back with the doctor at once."

"*A sus órdenes,*" said Chuy.

Sara entered the hotel and walked the length of the lobby, which was painted in panels of coral and white, and hung with the framed faces of French royalty. The night porter was eating rice and *chiles jalapeños* rolled in a tortilla. With his free hand he reached for the directory under the desk.

There was only one Dr. Alonso de la Luna. She dialed and began to count. At the sixth ring a man's voice answered "*Bueno,*" and when she remained silent said "*Bueno*" again. She uttered four words, "Dr. de la Luna," and paused. "*Bueno, señora,*" the doctor said. Sara spoke the phrases she had memorized somewhere between Ibarra and Concepción. "My husband is ill, eighty kilometers away. I have a taxi to take you and to bring you back." When the doctor answered she understood only four or five of his words.

This is a man I've never seen, she reminded herself as she listened. I am handing Richard's life over to a stranger on the recommendation of a taxi driver. I am taking the word of Chuy Santos, who owns an old Volkswagen, can drive by the moon, sing like an angel, and sell a caged sparrow in the dead of night.

Leaning against the marble-topped desk of the Hotel París with the receiver clasped to her ear, Sara struggled to interpret the slurred dialect of Dr. de le Luna. "Please speak more slowly. What did you say? *Cómo? Cómo?*" And while she said "How? How?" to the doctor, an interior voice addressed Richard. Don't die, it said. Then, perceiving this imperative to be unreasonable, changed its refrain to, Don't die now.

The doctor was growing impatient.

"Cómo?" said Sara. *"Cómo?"*

"Tomorrow is November second, All Souls' Day," Dr. de la Luna would remark when he roused from dozing in the Volkswagen and noticed the road spilled over on both sides by the flowering tide of yellow.

These were words Sara understood. She leaned forward from the narrow space Chuy had cleared on the back seat when he returned to the hotel twenty-five minutes late. Her face was close to the doctor's. "Have you ever seen such flowers, such a moon, such a night?"

Dr. de la Luna turned his head and regarded her through heavy-rimmed lenses that magnified his eyes. This American woman with the pale flying hair and the gray eyes as big as a child's at the zoo is temporarily deranged. From what she has told me, her husband may or may not survive this fever. She is disoriented, Dr. de la Luna told himself. But the gray eyes were still on his.

"You are right, señora," he said at last. "There is splendor all around us." He unbuttoned his suede jacket, then buttoned it again.

She continued to lean over his shoulder. "How fortunate it is for my husband and me, for our peace of mind, that you are a specialist in his particular disease."

The doctor stared at her. "But I am not," he said. "I am an orthopedic surgeon."

Fear drained the light from the fields, the desert, and the hills. The horizon gathered and the landscape drew in. She felt the world shrink until it fit between her ribs.

As it turned out, Richard would not die that night in the house of his ancestors, in the bed with an altar screen for a headboard. He would die more than a year later in a San Francisco hospital on a winter day with air so clear and a sky so clean that Sara, standing at the window of his room, said, "If this were Ibarra and summer, today would be the first day after the first rain." The capped nurse who was on her rounds heard this and made no response. Richard made no response. As it turned out, he would die on a holiday, Washington's Birthday, so that the tray of juice and gelatin he would not touch was trimmed with plastic cherries and a paper flag. Richard, lying with closed eyes, looking inward, never saw the decoration appropriate to the day of his death. Sara would notice it and drink a cup of tepid consommé as she sat with her hand on his and listened for his breathing. When it stopped she felt nothing, unconvinced by anything as slight as this, the almost imperceptible difference between breath and silence, that he was dead.

And afterward, on her return to Ibarra, would be startled when miners approached her, took off their hats, expressed their sorrow. When a memorial mass was arranged on the first anniversary of Richard's death she sat bewildered at the front of the church. The people of Ibarra watched her enter and leave the nave dry-eyed, and said, "She is North American and not a Catholic." Outside the church Sara shook hands with the men who had sponsored the service—the mechanic, the carpenter, the welder, the foremen of the underground shifts.

"My thanks to all of you." But she was still not persuaded he was dead.

When the drive back to Ibarra proved after all to have an end, and they approached the house, the taxi's headlights revealed the watchman in his sombrero and two sarapes, standing at the open gate exactly as Sara had seen him last, at midnight. Beyond the *sala* the cook still sat in her chair at the bedroom door. Richard lay dying on his side of the bed just as he had lain there dying before.

When she saw this, Sara would believe that time had stopped.

The watchman would never leave the gate, the cook her chair, Richard this bed.

Dr. de la Luna performed his examination. "I will treat him now and leave instructions for the *practicante.*"

"Shall I send the taxi for you tomorrow?" Sara would ask.

"Send the taxi day after tomorrow at noon." The doctor turned from the bed and moved toward the door. "Unless . . . But then, in any case . . . In that event . . . "

He buttoned his coat and left.

Later on, she remembered of all that night only what mattered least. The midnight ride from Ibarra to Concepción, Chuy's reckless haste, the struck mongrel, the countryside washed of its meagerness by the moon, the ditches streaming gold with wild flowers. And through widening time, as she slept, as she woke, as she lived her day, came unsummoned glimpses of herself crossing the long lobby of the Hotel París to pick up the telephone.

In the end she had managed to make the arrangements after all. She finally understood Dr. de la Luna to say he would drive back with her to Ibarra.

"As you have described it to me, señora, we have nothing to fear. It is a simple case of pneumonia."

Sara realized the time had come to explain the situation. She waited a moment to practice the words before she spoke. "And there is the leukemia," she said, pronouncing it le-u-ke-mi-a, dividing the vowels, turning the *e*'s to long *a*'s. She only forgot that there is no *k* in the Spanish alphabet.

The doctor corrected her. "*Le-u-ce-mi-a,*" he said, stressing the third syllable.

"*Leucemia,*" repeated Sara, as though he had instructed her, "Repeat after me. *Leucemia.*" As though he taught first-year Spanish and said, "Please repeat these words. *Los ojos,* the eyes. *La mano,* the hand. *El día,* the day."

17

IMMENSE DISTANCES, EXTRAORDINARY EVENTS

When Richard had been dead for a month, Sara drove back to Ibarra to prune the oleanders and divide the mint, to set the cupboards and her life in order. But after she had crossed three American and five Mexican states, when she finally turned off the mountain road and approached her adobe house, memories of the recent past and suspicions of the future dissipated. There was only today, a March day in late afternoon with the ash tree in full leaf, a scent of lavender against the south wall, and Richard due home any minute from the mine.

Later on, when she lay down shivering in the warm night to sleep, she spoke out loud to Richard. She said, "How could you?" For he had somehow permitted himself to be removed, had left a space between them so vast it was impossible to measure and therefore seemed no space at all.

She slid her hand across the sheet to his cold, smooth side of the bed. And even if he had been resurrected to lie next to her again, holding the length of her against the length of him, even then she might have pulled back long enough to say, "How could you?"

In the three months since she was last in Ibarra, noons had turned hot and still, dawns slow, twilights endless. Each morning, as soon as the gardeners and the cook arrived, Sara said, "Please close the gate." Every afternoon at five o'clock she announced the hour.

"Hasta mañana," she said to Luis, who had come back to work in January, pale from the penitentiary where he had served a term for growing marijuana in the corral behind his house and selling it in cigarettes for five pesos each in front of the *presidencia.*

From the porch she called *"Hasta mañana"* to Paco Acosta, hired for the period of Luis's absence and still here. It was Paco who had a way with plants. Sara believed that whenever he walked under a tree it grew a new branch to shade him.

With the two men gone, there remained only Lourdes to send away. The cook was at the stove, stirring a pot.

"What is that?"

"A rice *sopa.*"

"I may not eat."

"Starving is for people who don't have this rice *sopa* cooked with herbs."

Sara grew suspicious. "What herbs?"

"Rosmarino, hierbabuena," Lourdes said. *"Salvia, laurel."*

Was she chanting? But Sara only said, "Five o'clock. *Hasta mañana.*"

When she was alone, she lifted the lid and searched the pot for unfamiliar twigs, a crooked root, an acorn, and discovered nothing. But she wants something of me, Sara thought. To turn Indian, to turn Catholic. To look to heaven and its saints, its new moon, and morning star for signs.

She took tea to the *sala,* played a Mozart record and a Brahms, leaned against striped cushions under the wide window, and watched the evening obscure Ibarra. Sometimes during the last year she had come here in the afternoon and found Richard stretched out on the window seat. On these occasions he acknowledged her by raising a hand and making room for her to sit beside him. Then she would tell him what she saw through the window.

"There's Luis, holding a broom and staring at the sun. He sees it's four-thirty, too late to sweep this patio. There's blood on his ear."

And Richard would say, "It's Monday."

"There's Lourdes, picking a handful of magic leaves. She's going to mix you a potion."

And Richard would say, "Add rum."

Then Sara, gazing at Ibarra, which was out of sight, would begin to improvise. "Paz Acosta is crossing the plaza in a tight yellow jersey and yellow pumps. She's climbing into the Coca-Cola truck. She's arranged to spend the night with the driver. There they go."

Richard made no comment. He had closed his eyes.

"Now I see Chuy Santos. There's a puncture in the left-rear tire of his Volkswagen. He's pushing a strip of rubber into the hole with a screwdriver. Now the red taxi has four good tires again."

Sara laid her hand against her husband's face and diagnosed to herself a low-grade fever. "The miners from the day shift are back in Ibarra. They've run into a vein of silver at the Malagueña. Enough to buy chalices, enough to pave streets. They're sending a delegation to inform you."

Richard opened his eyes. "Tell me the moment they come."

That was last year. Now Sara, accompanied by Mozart and Brahms, sat on the window seat and said, "Richard," out loud. She stayed there for an hour, while colors drained from tiles, from leaves, from the pink stones in walls. To the east, the mesas that rose one behind the other against the horizon turned in order from ash to smoke to midnight.

The music had stopped. "Richard," she said again, and listened.

The last few days of March, without change of climate or routine, became the first few days of April. Once or twice a week, on a tour of rooms, Sara pulled out a drawer, touched its contents, and closed it. She cleared the tracing paper, the slide rule, and the compass from Richard's desk and put them back. Under his magnifying lens she found an opened envelope, postmarked Peru. In the upper corner was the name of the Canadian geologist who had stayed here four years ago. Sara, lacking the energy for curiosity, replaced the envelope without reading the letter inside. She went into the north bedroom and stood in front of the carved pine *cómoda* that was taller than herself. She gazed at the scrolled wood of the doors and left them closed.

"I have heard from my coyote," Paco said to her one morning. In this way she learned that he intended to transfer his magic from her trees and patios to the happy groves of an employer of wetbacks north of the border.

The door pull of the *cómoda* was a brass wreath of flowers, tied with a brass bow. The month was May and Paco had been gone three weeks when Sara opened it.

Possibly she had expected its half-forgotten contents to swell and to multiply. Instead, except for a package of shotgun shells, the cupboard held only what she had stored there herself: a pair of blankets at the bottom, a roll of muslin, a pottery bird with the beak chipped off, and some boxes. She picked up the package of shells for no reason, unless it was that Richard was probably the last person to have touched it. In the first box were handmade Christmas ornaments; in the next two, jigsaw puzzles. American friends had given the Evertons these to help fill their days and nights. "What do they do there, all by themselves?" the friends may have said. Now it was, "What does she do there, alone?"

From the top shelf Sara lifted down a shoe box full of letters, clippings, and what appeared to be remnants of lists and notes. With a straw wastebasket beside her, she sat on one of the beds and started to sort the accumulation in the box. She pulled out a random scrap. It was a classified advertisement, in English, from a Mexico City paper.

"I traspass my apartment," wrote the author, still a novice at this second tongue. "Because of marriage. Marvelous decoration. Communicate rooms. Janitor shows."

She had read it to Richard one night to make him laugh.

Now she took an envelope from the middle of the box. It was a letter from Ajijic, Jalisco, postmarked a year ago and never opened.

"I found your name in the Anglo-American Directory," Sara read. "Can you help me? I have lived in Ajijic for three years but am anxious about some violent incidents and feel we are too many North Americans here. Should I change my residence to the Mexican state where you live? I am wondering how you enjoy your life there. Are there other Norteamericanas? Sincerely, Helga Ronslager."

Sitting on the bed, Sara composed in her mind the answer she should have sent to Ajijic last year. "Dear Helga Ronslager, you didn't tell me in your letter whether you intend to live in Concepción, which is the capital of this state and has parks, banks, Woolworth's, and a cathedral, or here in Ibarra, a less cosmopolitan town, a village actually, where several incidents have become known to me. In one of these, José Reyes killed two men in the cantina and soon after was stoned into submission on the hill of the Santa Cruz. In another, a helpless boy, an idiot, drowned in the tailings dump of the Malagueña mine. An intern of the government clinic committed suicide one Christmas day. Basilio García, who had enrolled his brother in the state university, shot him to death by mistake. Paz Acosta, the most beautiful girl in Ibarra, is a prostitute. Dear Helga, you must understand that these things happen everywhere.

"Very few strangers, particularly Norteamericanas, come to Ibarra. This is because the town is too small and remote to appear on any map. But I should tell you that, because of the altitude, our air is thin and clear. Also that, if you wish, you can read the newspaper by the light of the full moon.

"At the moment of writing, my husband and I are the only North Americans in Ibarra. Before long, I will be the only one. This is because of an incident I expect will occur within the next year or so. *Buena suerte,* Helga. Good luck."

Sara laid the letter and the clipping on the bed beside the shoe box. With the cupboard door still open and nothing yet discarded, she left the room and went outside to sit for half an hour in the sun.

That afternoon neither Luis nor Lourdes closed the gate. The Canadian geologist and his assistant, the Lebanese engineer, drove through it five minutes before the arrival of the watchman and the night. They stood on the porch with their duffel bags and waited to be invited in.

"Where's Richard?" said the geologist.

Sara lit candles and sat down to dinner with the two men at nine o'clock. This was after it was all done, the expressions of shock and the apologies, the proposals to travel on tonight, even after she had returned the shoe box to the *cómoda* in the north bedroom and spread the blankets on the beds.

"I wrote from Peru," the geologist said, and Sara remembered the letter on Richard's desk. "To say we'd come through here," he continued, "on our way north in May."

"Is it May?" said Sara.

The engineer tasted yesterday's reheated *enchiladas.* "Very rich, very delicious," he said.

The geologist had brought a rock sample to the table and placed it beside his glass.

"Did that come from Peru?" Sara asked.

"No, I found it on the road below your mine." The road reminded him of something. "This afternoon we missed a turn and came cross-country through El Portal."

She said, "Then you saw the child-sized chapel," and she remembered the filigree cross. "Richard and I came that way once." The Lebanese engineer lowered his eyes. Sara understood that from now on he would do this every time she spoke Richard's name. It was the engineer's way of mourning.

But as soon as she mentioned Richard, the geologist, as though barriers had fallen, asked who was running the mine.

When Sara explained that the assistant manager Richard hired six months ago was now the general manager, the geologist said, "We'll drive up there tomorrow to meet him." He tapped his piece of copper ore. "I hope there's more of this underground."

"I haven't been to the mine since Richard died," Sara said, and the Lebanese looked down.

The geologist examined her with his astronomer's eyes.

At breakfast the next morning everything was the same as when these men had stayed here before. The Canadian stood beside Sara in the kitchen while she scrambled eggs and the Lebanese remained in the dining room. With a pencil and paper he divided cables, beams, and drills by age and stress. The only difference was that this time he sat alone at the table.

"How is your wife?" Sara asked the geologist.

"She's the same," he said. "If she were here, she would eat all these eggs. Also the toast." He put his hand in his pocket to touch the ore sample. "She tried two diets but they failed."

"Do you still live at the lake in the woods?"

The Canadian nodded. "But I'm away a lot."

Sara lifted the pan from the fire. "How far is that lake from here?"

"About half the circumference of the globe." The plates were ready and he picked one up. "How about you? I expect you'll turn this house over to the mine and move away."

But Sara was already at the door, asking the engineer if he liked his coffee black. He rose from his chair to nod.

They left at noon. Sara made sandwiches of meat and *chiles* for them to take along. She filled their thermos with black coffee.

The geologist held the same rock he had carried about last night. Again tapped it. "You've got a lot of this on the sixth level," he told her. "The Malagueña's beginning to show what it's worth." When Sara remained unmoved, he tried to convince her.

"It's a hell of a sweet operation," said the geologist.

Sara looked down at the kitchen table and, without speaking, addressed Richard.

Listen she instructed him. Richard, listen. Did you hear that?

On a late afternoon in June, under banked clouds that promised rain, Sara looked up from her spading and found Horacio, youngest of the Acostas, standing silently at her shoulder. He said there was news of Paco and brought out from behind a corner of the house a loose-limbed, reluctant boy of about sixteen who said his name was Esteban.

"You have heard from Paco."

"No," said Esteban.

"So you don't know where he is."

Esteban said, "Yes."

Sara noticed the boy's large ears and feet, and the space left in his mouth by a missing tooth.

"You don't live in Ibarra," she said, and again Esteban said, "Yes."

Horacio, a round-shaped ten-year-old, intervened. "He is my cousin who lives over the mountain in Jesús María. He crossed the border with Paco."

"Yes," said Esteban.

Sara brought Orange Crush from the kitchen and the three sat together on the porch steps. From behind the western peaks came an occasional roll of thunder.

"How did you get across?" she asked Esteban, but he had

no easy answers to such questions. Words fell from his mouth slowly and one by one.

Sara had to draw him out. "So you met the coyote in Tijuana. At night he took nine of you along the frontier to a place where there was no barbed wire."

Esteban nodded. He said the coyote had a man on the other side to lead them through the canyons.

A drop of rain fell on Sara's face. "How far did you walk?"

Nine hours. At the end of nine hours they had met the van that transported them on unnumbered roads from one end of California to the other.

"So that's where Paco is." Sara felt another drop of rain. "What is he doing?"

"Grapes," said Esteban. He rose from the steps.

She watched a scattered shower spot the tiled path. "If the job is over, I expect Paco will be back soon."

Esteban, standing with his ears outlined against the portentous sky, shook his head.

"Then why did you come home?"

"There were too many days and nights between that place and here."

Sara looked after him as he made his awkward exit with Horacio at his heels. They were barely through the gate when the downpour started, beating impartially on the roofs of Ibarra and Jesús María, flooding the hen houses and corrals of both these towns, washing without distinction their gutters and their mosaic chapel domes.

That evening Sara sat at the *sala* window as long as she could see leaves drip and flower pots overflow. Then, instead of listening to another record in the dark, she went to the north bedroom, lit a lamp, and turned the brass wreath to open the *cómoda*. She took out the shoe box together with a pile of letters and papers that lay on top of it, an accumulation she had gathered since her March arrival. Depositing it all on the nearest bed, she began to sort.

She first picked up a fertilizing schedule she had made for Paco. This she set aside for Luis, although she knew his true persuasion lay in the circle of the seasons and the direction of the wind. She pulled out a black-bordered newspaper clipping. It was an announcement of Richard's death, placed in the Concepción *Heraldo* by a committee of miners. "With grief," said the clipping. "In esteem."

Here were three prescriptions signed by the hematologist in California. Here a packet of seeds marked phlox. Behind a recipe for oyster stew (use fresh bluepoint oysters) she found a twice-doubled piece of pink paper.

"What is this?" she said aloud.

The residual dust of dry leaves lay in its folds. Sara lifted one of the veined, scented skeletons. "Camomile," she said, and knew it was from Lourdes, knew it was meant to ensure impossible things, long life, a forgiving nature, faith.

There was too much here to sort in a single night. She began to refill the shoe box. When she found the accumulation was more than it could hold, she went to the closet for another box. She left the room in order, the doors of the *cómoda* closed, the shelves full.

But she had taken something with her and later on, in the kitchen, she spread it on the table. It was a road map so worn that the creases and the torn edges had been taped. On it an automobile route through the southwest United States and central Mexico had been lined in red, and stopovers circled. At one end of the road, in San Francisco, was Richard's specialist; at the other the Malagueña mine. The mountains and deserts and plains that the map, without illustration, implied, had been climbed and descended and traversed so often that Sara, years later and a thousand miles away, without needing to close her eyes could see the village with the ocotillo fences, the vine-covered boxcars switched onto sidings for family homes, the grazing land, the settlement without a well, the broken hacienda reflected in a lake. She could put her finger on the map and say, "Here's a blind curve. Here's a grade crossing. This is where we saw the Tarahumara Indian running beside the road."

She knew the distance, in miles and kilometers, between gas stations and between places to spend the night. All these motels, Sara thought, with their rooms waiting to be brought to life with toothbrushes, the local paper, slippers beside the bed. There had been occurrences in these places that, at the time, seemed scarcely memorable. But from this distance, from the kitchen of the house in Ibarra where she stood alone on a rainy night, they were exposed as remarkable.

One morning in Durango, while the Evertons were eating breakfast in their hotel, a man rode a horse into the vestibule, dismounted, took out a knife, and chased their waiter from the dining room. Once in Chihuahua Sara heard music long before daybreak and pulled Richard awake and outside to listen to a mariachi band of twelve serenade a pair of shutters that remained latched and bolted from the beginning to the end of an hour's songs.

She moved her finger on the map and remembered Ascension Day in Morelia. On that occasion there had been no need for her to wake her husband. The rockets that seemed to explode under their pillows at midnight lifted them simultaneously from sleep onto a balcony. Between the detonations, shouts and cheers racked the night. "It's like the end of a war," said Richard. Above the church, spotlights shone on a painted figure of the Virgin attached to an upright pole. In the midst of a succession of blasts, human screams, howls of dogs, police whistles, and a siren, bells began to toll for mass.

Tracing the marked route, Sara recalled the motel where Richard killed a cockroach, the one where he crushed two scorpions. As she folded the map she foresaw that future sorting might prove difficult, so faint and uncertain was the line that separated the significant from the trivial.

It occurred to her this evening in Ibarra, with rain at the

window and Richard four months dead, that nothing ever happened on either numbered or unnumbered roads that could be classified as unimportant. All of it, observed by dark, observed by day, was extraordinary.

18

Bring Stones

On a February day in the following year a stranger was delivered by Chuy's red taxi to Sara Everton's door. When the ice-cream vendor, a few miners, and the goatherd noticed this person passing them on the road, they knew with their instinct for endings that he had come to arrange for the removal of the North American woman's furniture, to count the tables and lamps and pictures and carry them across the border. By ten o'clock that morning the stranger, a lean, shrewd-eyed man who wore a brown felt hat indoors and out, was noting on a pad of paper the contents of the white adobe house.

Sara watched this man fill a page and start another. "Not everything in the house is to go," she told him. As he reached the bottom of the second page, she asked, "How did you get here so quickly from Michoacán?" She had not expected him before the middle of the day, or even late afternoon, if he missed connections. Seeing him point to a tall brass candlestick and the statue of Saint Peter, she wanted to say, wait. There has been a misunderstanding. It was never my intention to leave Ibarra.

The man, who introduced himself simply as Dionisio, owned a transportation company of one van and two employees, and only wished to arrive at an agreement with this señora Everton.

"I left Morelia on the midnight bus," he said, "and traveled while you slept."

Sara continued to inspect him. He believes I sleep through the night. And although his business is to help, I believe he is here to tear my world apart.

Together they moved slowly from room to room, pausing often, like visitors at an archeological museum. In the *sala,* Dionisio halted his circling. "A mirror like that one in the elaborate frame is hard to pack," he said.

Staring into the oval glass, wreathed around with brass flowers and vines, Sara scarcely recognized her face. This is how the mover sees me, a thin woman who should comb her hair more carefully, get more rest, learn to focus her attention.

"Señora," he said. "What about the kitchen table and the carved pine *cómoda*?" He looked into the glass for an answer.

"Are your men careful packers," she asked, "and your van reliable?"

Dionisio said his enterprise was of the highest confidence. Then he asked about Richard's desk and the bed with the altar-screen headboard.

"Those things are to go," she said into the mirror where she and the proprietor of Transportes Dionisio seemed permanently framed side by side, bound together by metal tendrils and metal buds.

Facing her own image, she watched her mouth move in speech. "How much will all this cost?"

Addressing the woman in the glass, Dionisio mentioned a sum. After she nodded, his hatted reflection announced that he would return with his van in six days. She nodded again. He kissed her hand.

At four o'clock that afternoon Padre Juanito, the new cura's new assistant, found Sara in front of her rock garden, uprooting and replanting succulents. He stood, dark-skinned as his

Indian forebears and gallant as his Spanish ones, between her and the sun.

"There will be a memorial mass for your husband," he said.

Padre Juanito, recently ordained, had brought a new clerical style to Ibarra. Today he wore green pants and a scarlet shirt. "Five nights from now at vespers," he went on. "The señor cura is out of town and I will preside."

He is like a macaw among ravens, Sara thought. She was accustomed to priests who wore habits in Ibarra. The others had walked the village on their rounds, driven the pickup to the ranchos, exhorted, absolved, and perhaps wept, all while wearing their black cassocks.

"You hesitate because you are not a Catholic," said the young priest.

"No, not that." But his words reminded her that the purpose of this mass, and of the one that had preceded it, was to lessen Richard's travail in purgatory. Sara tried to imagine her husband in that place, and failed.

The six days until Dionisio returned rushed by and at the end of each one everything still remained to be done. Sara wrote instructions for Paco, who had come back to Ibarra after half a year in the California vineyards. Nitrogen, phosphorus, manure, she wrote. She bought two brooms and a hose for Luis. She left a note for Lourdes under the stove polish. It was the manager of the Malagueña mine who would enjoy the results of her lists when he moved into the house the day after her departure. It was he who would walk through the mulched and weeded garden, notice the greaseless oven.

Sara continued to remake flower beds, a February habit she was unable to break. She pulled apart violet clumps and, deluded by custom, seemed to expect to witness their blooming.

One afternoon Sara found a white religious habit among the sheets in the laundry basket.

"What is this?" she said to Lourdes.

"Padre Juanito's habit."

"Why is it in our laundry?"

"Because your sink is more ample than his and your iron has steam."

Sara allowed the garment to fall back into the basket.

All morning, on the day of the mass, Sara packed books and records. Surrounded by boxes, she looked up from the floor at the sea-green blown-glass lamp, at the mirror entwined in brass, at the Virgin of Mercy observing her with a confounded expression from a painting on the wall.

Through the window she noticed a green haze of new leaves in the ash tree. "Watch for the cenzontle bird in the *fresno*," she would tell the mine manager. "It's earth colored and sings a backward scale."

In the afternoon Sara walked to the school where the nuns once taught. Crossing the hall that still echoed children's voices, she pushed open the warped door of the *sala*. In this room she had sat once a week for most of a year to learn Spanish from Madre Petra. Now she stood among leaves drifting in from the patio and listened. The nun's ghost addressed her.

"Conjugate the radical-changing reflexive verb, to recollect."

"*Me acuerdo*," Sara said out loud, and stopped. In the courtyard two cows grazed under a peach tree. Hens had discovered an open classroom door and were roosting on the first-grade desks.

On Sara's return to the house, her glance fell on a pile of stones at the edge of the road opposite her gate. Stopping to count them, she found there were eleven gathered into an orderly heap in the dust. Children playing, she supposed, building pyramids. But she recalled the cement cross set at a curve of the mountain road above the Malagueña hoist. Around it were dozens of stones like these.

"What is that cross on the road beyond the mine?" she had once asked Paco.

"The cross marks the place where a fatal accident occurred," he told her.

"Is someone buried there?"

"No, the victim of the accident is in the *panteón.* The cross is only to remind passersby of what happened."

"Why are those stones piled around it?"

"When people pass and remember, they bring stones."

Today, twenty-four hours before her spoons and sofas would be taken off in Dionisio's van, she stood in front of her gate and considered the heap across the road. When Luis, pushing a wheelbarrow, came up behind her, she said, "I suppose children have been collecting these stones."

"God knows," said Luis.

"Or someone is trying to mark this place for a bus stop."

"God knows," said Luis.

That evening Sara attended the memorial mass. She sat at the front of the church with Lourdes and copied what her cook did. In unison the two women rose, knelt, and resumed their seats side by side. Simultaneously the congregation behind them knelt and rose, with the sound of air moving in summer trees.

Padre Juanito appeared to have grown even younger since Sara saw him last. He looked no more than twenty as he spoke of Richard, whom he knew only by hearsay that was already turning to legend. "Don Ricardo Everton," said the priest, "has left footprints in this soil that neither rain nor wind can sweep away."

Cast under a blue spell by the fresh paint on the walls of the nave, Sara saw these footprints tracking the ruts of the road from the house to the plaza, from the house to the mine. She tried to place Richard in these tracks and bring him back to Ibarra in time to prevent the arrival of Dionisio's truck and the probable tears of Lourdes.

Padre Juanito was nearing the end of his remarks. "Nationality and language do not separate friends," he said. He paused for a length of time, then, fearless, stated his conclusion.

"It makes no difference what a man believes," he clearly said, "if he is a good person."

Sara stared in astonishment at the assistant priest as he stood before the altar in his freshly laundered white habit. The moment she heard his words, she foresaw his future and knew with terrible certainty that, as soon as the cura returned, Padre Juanito would be transferred. To a smaller parish, in a wilder landscape, without Americans.

Dionisio and his crew arrived at seven o'clock in the morning and maneuvered the truck through the wooden gates with less than an inch of clearance on each side. When the van was stationed behind the house, the proprietor entered the *sala,* kissed Sara's hand, and introduced the driver.

"Where is your other employee?" she asked.

"He is ill. He ate bad pork at a sidewalk barbecue." Dionisio took out his list. "Therefore we must depend on your men to help us."

Paco and Luis were called in from the garden and all day lifted chests, benches, and rugs. During this time the sick man lay with his head against the trunk of a eucalyptus tree and sipped Coca-Cola.

Dionisio spent much of the afternoon on the porch, spooning sugar into the coffee Sara brought him. He sat in the leather chair that had the finest view of Ibarra and checked the hands of his watch against the items left on his list.

"Three hours more," he said. Then, "An hour and a half." And finally, "Only thirty minutes." Now his eyes were doubly shaded, by his hat and the coming on of dark.

The sun had set when he returned from an inspection and announced departure. Sara walked out to the truck. She waved to the driver and nodded to the man, still half poisoned, who slumped beside him on the seat

Dionisio, neglecting to kiss her hand, was climbing to the cab when she spoke to him for the last time. "The gates are two hundred years old," she said. "For them to be harmed is beyond my endurance."

Moments later she stood with Paco and Luis at the unharmed gates and watched the van sway as it climbed the grade. Long after it was out of sight she heard its motor laboring in low gear.

Across the road the outline of the stones dissolved into the gathering night. Sara believed more had accumulated since yesterday.

"This pile of stones is getting bigger," she said to Paco and Luis, but they were already turning toward the village.

They glanced over their shoulders in the other direction. One of them said, "From here the house looks the same." And the other, "As if the movers had never come."

Looking up the driveway, Sara saw that Lourdes had lit the remaining lamps and that, indeed, the exterior of the house revealed no evidence of the inner pillage.

Through the gates she watched trees lose their green and the tile pattern of the driveway disappear. As she stood next to the heap of stones a miner passed her on his bicycle, then two others coasted by. She raised her hand and the riders waved back. But her intention had been to stop them.

Stop, she wanted to call out. Stop for a minute. Look through these gates and see the lighted house. An accident has happened here. Remember the place. Bring stones.